The FREEDOM CHASER

This story is inspired by true events and most are true names.

JOAN M KOP

For Don Kopczynski, my brother,
who shared his love of genealogy with me

And, for Larry and Dawne Drake,
who inspired me to write this book.

*"Hit the Poles so hard that they despair of their life;
I have full sympathy for their condition, but if we
want to survive we can only exterminate them."*

—GERMAN PRIME MINISTER OTTO VON BISMARCK
IN A LETTER TO HIS SISTER IN 1861[1]

Chapter 1

March 1867, Eastern Prussia

August wiped the sweat from his brow, dusted off his heavy leather, apron and kicked the anvil. His father, Martin, as well as the owner of the blacksmith shop were out sick, so August worked alone that day. *I'll never be more than a peasant. Not in this dead-end job. Damn Bismarck! Made slaves of all of us. Can't own a business or the land I farm. And why? Because I'm Polish, that's why.*

He had a heavy workload this morning and one more horse to shoe before breaking for lunch. The Arabian whinnied as August cleaned and shaped its tough, nerveless hoof with a knife and a rasp. He paused to inspect his handiwork, then selected a horseshoe and heated the U-shaped iron red hot. The smell of manure lingered in the air.

August stopped what he was doing and looked up when a visitor walked in. *Bitteschön?"* he asked in German, recognizing the uniform of a Prussian officer: stiff, high-jacked boots, and a large two-cornered hat with national cockade and regimental button.

The officer came a little closer and whacked August across the face with the force of his large hand. "You Polish swine!" the officer said. "We've heard you've been speaking ill of Prussia."

August lurched from the shock. Blood gushed from his nose.

He wanted to gouge this officer's eyes out, but before he could act upon his anger, he remembered his father bragging how compassionate and kind his son was. He would not let him down. Besides, the Bible taught him to "turn the other cheek." He didn't want the officer to arrest him, so he calmly wiped the blood from his face with his handkerchief.

"We don't want any more excuses for not agreeing to go to war against the French." The officer glared at August. His eyes grew hostile. August tried to back away, but the anvil was in his way.

"You foolish son of a bitch. Do you have any idea what you're doing, what you're giving up?" He looked at August. "Forget your stupid pride! Admit it. You're a traitor!"

August froze. His face reddened. He vowed not to give in to the officer's desire for a fight, vowed not to let the officer have power over him. He spoke calmly and quietly, trying to diffuse the situation. "What makes you think I am a traitor? I don't recall ever talking to you before."

"We have our sources."

Touching his sore nose and jaw, in a kaleidoscope of rapid recall, his conversation with Alexander, a gray bearded, elderly Russian who some weeks ago stood at the bar at a Prussian tavern near the red brick *Schneidemühl* train station, returned to him. *That man was a Prussian spy? Shouldn't have told him I'd never fight in another of Bismarck's wars. Clearly drank too much.*

The shop was pitch dark except for the two lanterns located near the anvil. August turned and faced the Prussian officer. "Did your spies also tell you that when I was only seventeen, I helped *your* Prussia fight the Danish for two years when

Denmark lost Schleswig-Holstein and then the Austrians for seven weeks in 1866?"

"We are well aware of your background."

August glanced down at the hay, avoiding the officer's eyes. "I was damn lucky to survive, but I lost many friends in those battles. I remember the bitter cold at the Eider River in Holstein—the stench of men soaked in blood, dying on the battlefield."

"All wars have costs," the officer said, flatly.

He struck a nerve. August stood there seething. "I helped Prussians fight your wars for nothing. I am still considered a peasant farmer who, in your eyes, doesn't deserve freedom."

August spat on the dirt floor of the dark, hot blacksmith shop. *The manure and the horseshoes aren't the only things that smell.* He had enough sense not to express these thoughts out loud. "There's never an end to Bismarck's wars. I'm tired of being called for military service when we don't get anything in return for the sacrifices we've made. Why should we fight another war for a country that isn't ours? We're Polish, not German."

"You're a damned fool, Kopczynski! There is no Poland anymore. It's been wiped off the map. We're all Prussian citizens now and we *must* continue to fight for Germany."

August moved in front of the anvil, nearer to the officer and held out his hand, palm up. "Listen to reason, my friend! Prime Minister Bismarck is mad. Let him go after France but without the help of the Poles. He thinks Poland only exists to provide able bodies to fight his Prussian wars. He may be able to change the names of our villages and cities and force us to speak and write a language that is not our own, but he'll never own us completely!"

August shook his head as if that would bring him clarity. His body tensed and he glared at the officer. "Bismarck will never possess our minds or our Polish souls. We owe our allegiance to God, not him!"

After the words were out of his mouth, August immediately regretted them. *His eyes are filled with hate. This poor bastard is not capable of conceiving an almighty God.*

"We have ways of dealing with anarchists like you." The officer punched August in the stomach with both fists and watched with hostile eyes as August doubled over, writhing in pain on the dirt floor.

August's breath tightened, his temperature rose and his pulse raced but he kept his anger in check. He hated the officer. He hated all that Prussia represented. He hated that he was forced to speak and write German. He hated the way Prussia favored Lutheran Prussians and treated Polish Catholics like dogs. He hated the German colonists who invaded his homeland. He hated that many Polish cities and counties had been given German names.

But, arguing with this Prussian officer was useless. It could only get him into further trouble which he feared would escalate the tension. He didn't want that. So, August stood up and said nothing, averting his eyes at first, then facing the intruder.

"You can expect more of the same if you continue to defy almighty Prussia." The officer walked toward the door, paused before retreating, and turned. "I'll see to it that you will be shot or hanged for treason if you don't show up for service."

August returned his icy stare.

Chapter 2

August came home from work that night and told his father and stepmother what had happened.

"Papa, what should I do?" August said, his fearful eyes searching his father's face for answers. The elder Kopczynski was lying in bed with a throbbing headache and sore throat.

August's stepmother put a cold cloth on his father's forehead. "Your father is very sick," she said. "He needs his rest."

"I don't want you fighting another war, but I don't see how you can avoid it," the elder Kopczynski said, his voice weak. "You need to report this to the priest. He'll know what to do."

Like most of the homes in Grabionna, as well as in other areas of East Prussia and Poland, the Kopczynski house had a kitchen and two bedrooms but no living room. His father and stepmother slept in one bedroom. August's sister, Henrietta, and his five half-sisters, who ranged from fourteen years down to two years, slept in the second bedroom. August and his seventeen-year-old brother, Wilhelm, and his five-year-old half-brother, Albert, slept in the barn loft.

That night, August lay in his bed of hay in the barn unable to sleep.

How did the officer know I had talked ill of Prussia? August figured they must have spies, but who? *Friends, neighbors or relatives? Bosses or workers? Strangers or customers? Men or women? Who should I trust?*

He snuffed out the lantern, promised himself to report the incident with the Prussian officer to the priest the next time they spoke, and tried to get some sleep.

A few minutes later, the barn door creaked open. The intruder made her way up to the loft.

"August, are you awake?" Henrietta's laced leather boots shuffled across the hay.

"Yes, what do you want?"

"I need to talk to you."

"At this hour? Can't it wait?"

"I can't sleep. I was hoping you could give me some advice, little brother."

He had his own problems to deal with, but nevertheless, he knew that sometimes listening to others' problems was a way of lessening his own. He lit the lantern again and she sat beside him on his bed.

"Keep your voice down," he said as he looked at her long sandy locks that were braided and tied on her head. *She's so pretty.* "You might wake up Wilhelm or Albert. So, what is keeping you awake?"

"You've always been kind to me."

Not always.

He couldn't help but think about the many times he had taken money from her; the money she'd made from cleaning the church. First he only took a few coins, then he came back for more over time. She never seemed to miss it until she wanted to buy a new dress for their sister's wedding. He'd often been close to telling her the truth, but in the end he never did. Only God knew what he had done.

"Remember when I fell and skinned my knee when I was ten?" Henrietta continued. "You were by my side comforting me?"

"Yes, I remember," he said. "You cried a lot."

"Well, I can't stop crying. I need some comfort now."

"Why? What happened?"

"We've always told each other our secrets since we were little, right?"

"Yes, that's right."

"I have a secret now. I think I'm in a family way and I don't know how to tell Rosalia." Because both August and Henrietta were in their twenties, they sometimes referred to their stepmother as Rosalia. "She would kill me if she knew."

His eyes almost popped out of his head. *"Ach du lieber Gott! Are you certain?"*

"No, I'm not sure yet, but Emil and I...well, you know...we didn't plan it or anything...it just sort of happened."

"Have you had your time of the month?"

"Not yet, but I'm scared. I can't sleep at night worrying about it. I'll be humiliated. Might as well be dead. I'll have to go to a convent. I'll be shunned the rest of my life."

"Easy, Henrietta. God is a God of Mercy. Don't be so hard on yourself. Have you spoken to Emil about it? Maybe he'll marry you."

"I don't want it to be like that. You should marry someone because you love them, not because you have to." She started sobbing. August put his arm around her.

"There, there," he said. "God gives us darkness so we can appreciate the sunlight. Wait until you actually find out if it's true. I'll help you handle Rosalia then. No sense worrying if it isn't true."

"But..."

"You should definitely talk to Emil. He will do the right thing because he loves you. Also, put your faith in God. Ask Him to calm your fears. Trust Him and your problem will be solved. God is with you. If you are lucky this time, promise God you won't do it again until you're married."

Henrietta wiped her eyes and smiled. She caressed August's face and gave him a kiss on the cheek. "You're so wise," she said. "Thank you."

Once he knew she had left the barn, August snuffed out the lantern and prayed a rosary before falling asleep.

Chapter 3

Alone once again in the blacksmith shop two days later, August looked up when a man in a wagon pulled up to the shop. Tall and lean with reddish brown hair and a thin mustache, the stranger jumped off the wagon. The blue shirt he wore brought out the blue in his eyes.

"*Guten Morgen. Kőnen Sie mir helfen? Mein Wagenrad ist kaput.*" He pointed to the left front wheel, which was clearly in need of repair.

August, adjusting his blacksmith apron, detected a slight French accent. "*Guten Morgen, mein Herr.* Let me have a look."

August wiped the dust off the wheel before he loosened it from the wagon. He found a slight crack around the hole where the wheel was fastened to the wagon. "Yes, it looks like the wheel is broken. I can fix that." He stood and gave the man an estimate of several Prussian Taler to fix it. The man pulled some money out of his pocket and gave it to August.

August tipped his head. "Do I know you? Your face looks familiar. Are you from around here?"

The man stiffened and handed August a piece of paper with a note written on it. August took it to the lantern near the anvil so he could see it better. The note, written in German, read:

*Monsieur, I was at the tavern in Schneidemühl and over-
heard your conversation with the Russian. I can assist you
in avoiding the war and escaping to America.*

Puzzled, August felt his knees going weak as he raised his eyebrows and stared at the Frenchman without blinking. "You're suggesting I avoid the draft and become a Prussian traitor?" he whispered. "Most ships embark from Germany. I'll be apprehended as soon as I board."

"Promise me your utter silence in this matter," the Frenchman whispered back, as his eyes darted around the shop as if to make sure that the horses didn't listen. "It would be very dangerous if the authorities found out."

"You have my word, my friend. I won't even tell my father."

"We can help you find passage," the Frenchman continued as he leaned closer to August so he could hear. "There are various methods to get out of the country such as wearing women's clothing, posing as wives, leaving without a passport or using a false passport. I've heard youths over seventeen have gotten a pass to leave for six months if they promise to return for later induction into the army but, of course, many leave with no thought of returning."

August stepped back. "I don't have the money. How would I pay for the voyage?"

"Don't worry. A sponsor will pay your way. America has just been through a civil war and the country needs workers. The newspapers are full of advertisements. It's relatively easy to get a sponsor, especially in your line of work. You should have no difficulty."

August eyed him suspiciously. "So, why are *you* trying to help *me*? What's in it for you?"

The Frenchman's eyes twinkled. "We're not fully organized yet—the French military intelligence against the Prussians[2] — but some Frenchmen, are patriots like me, who care deeply about our country and what happens to it. It would be a shame if Bismarck were to win the war. My friend and I were at the tavern spying on the Russian. It is clear to us he is led by the Prussians. You came along as a bonus. We need every man we can get. With you, we're hoping Bismarck will lose one of his better marksman."

August paused for a minute. His heart seemed to freeze, then pound. *America? What an adventure that would be.* But then he thought of his family. *I can't go, not without my family. Besides, I like it here.* He liked the countryside—the rolling hills, the yellow fields surrounded by green forests, the dirt, wagon-rutted roads lined with linden trees, the walnut tree in the open field across the street; the smell of plum and cherry trees as well as dirt from the field and wheat or rye, and old needles in the forest—even horse poop, cow dung, or chicken and bird droppings in the barn. *This is home, I don't want to leave it. And I shouldn't have to.*

"Tempting, but no," he said, shaking his head. "I need to stay here. I need to fight for Poland's freedom."

"If Napoleon wins, the Polish people also win."

"You're sure? Sounds like an empty promise."[3]

"As sure as I can be," the Frenchman said, and smiled.

"I trust you, my friend, but I must stay here to see that it happens."

"Don't be a fool! You might go to war and die. Or, you could refuse and be shot or hanged. Either way you lose."

August's eyes widened and his mouth dropped open. *Ach du lieber Gott!* His facial expression did not go unnoticed by the Frenchman.

"You're not the only one in this predicament. Think it over. Let me know if you change your mind. It's too dangerous for us to meet again, so here is how to contact me if you're interested in a way out." He handed him another slip of paper, the note again written in German.

August folded the paper and put it in his pocket. "I'll let you know. Now, let's fix that wagon wheel of yours, my friend."

Chapter 4

On Saturday, in late afternoon when the bright sun was setting in the west, August saddled up his dark brown, Arabian horse and rode to the church in nearby *Miasteczko Krajeñskie.* He passed through empty green fields on flat, wagon-rutted, dirt roads lined with linden trees. At the bottom of a small hill in *Miasteczko* stood a small, wood-framed Catholic Church, built in 1726, called *Parafia Podwyzszenia Krzyza Swietego.*[4]

The Roman Catholic Church in Poland felt threatened by the predominately Lutheran population in Prussia, but offered a safe haven to Polish Catholics, giving parishioners hope for independence from Prussian, Russian and Austrian domination,[5] who had sliced up Poland. Because of the power the Catholic priests had over their congregations, every boy dreamed of becoming a priest, but only the smartest and most charismatic were chosen. The Catholic Church was a place where Poles could speak their native language and preserve their Polish heritage and customs, despite the fact that German was being taught in schools and demanded in business, becoming the predominant language in this new Prussian territory.

August loved the stability and the structure the church offered. His faith defined him. His faith came first in his life, then his family and friends, then his church, and finally his occupation. He attended mass daily before he rode to work at the blacksmith shop or out in the fields to farm. It was peaceful in church. His mind wandered to a higher place and his heart rose to the heavens whenever he heard the Choir sing or the Gregorian chants from visiting monks.

Today he waited in line for confession. The ten-foot-tall open confessional,[6] like most of them throughout Poland, was located in the back of the church and looked like a huge piece of intricately designed furniture made of polished wood with a seat and a waist-high door in the front which opened for the priest. He sat inside in the middle of the confessional on a red velvet seat cushion. A parishioner knelt on a triangular wooden kneeler outside on either side of the priest.

The confessional meant more to August than a piece of furniture. It was a place where his sins would be redeemed, taking a load off his heavy chest, offering forgiveness from God for his misdeeds. Confession gave him a feeling of light-headedness and reassured him of God's love.

When it was August's turn, he fell prostrate on the kneeler and whispered first the sign of the cross in Latin, *"In nómine Patris, et Fĭlii, et Spĭritus Sancti, Amen."* Then he continued in Polish asking for the priest's blessing and letting him know it had been a week since his last confession. *"Pobłogosław mnie Ojcze, ponieważ zgrzeszyłem. Ostatni raz u spowiedzi swiêtej byłem tydzień temu."*

Leading a very prayerful Catholic life, he had few sins to confess. Yet, he felt obliged to go each week not only because of the absolution and grace he received but also for the priest's guidance. A priest would be able to help him reach his goal of getting to heaven or even becoming a Saint. Intelligent and charismatic, priests were the epitome of power in Poland, since Catholics often heeded the Pope's or priest's advice more than that of a government official. Not only was the priest more educated or learned, Catholics believed the priest represented God on earth—a priest's counsel was God's counsel. August remembered what his father had once told him: *Never trust anyone except your priest and your doctor.*

The smell of frankincense permeated the air. The priest, sitting inside the confessional, reciprocated the sign of the cross. They each continued to whisper. "Yes, my son..."

"Father, I got in a fight with the German authorities over something I said."

The priest leaned closer and said, concern in his voice: "What happened? What did you say, my son?"

August told him about this altercation with the Prussian officer in the blacksmith shop.

"I told the officer that Bismarck thinks Poland only exists to provide able bodies to fight his Prussian wars. He may be able to change the names of our villages and cities and force us to speak and write a language that is not our own but he'll never own us completely. He will never possess our minds or our Polish soul. We owe our allegiance to God, not him."

"Well spoken, lad."

"This isn't the first time I had a confrontation with the Prussian authorities. Last time they wanted our family to give up what they called our show horses, saying we had more beautiful Arabians than the Kaiser. I am galled at the lack of freedom of speech in this country. You can't say anything. It all gets back to the Prussians and causes an uproar."

"Yes, Poland has jealous enemies on every side, my son. It is our duty to defend against them."

"I'm tired of it. When will we Poles ever get our freedom?"

"It's not the Prussians who will protect your freedom. Salvation comes only from the Catholic Church. You need to ask the Black Madonna, the Blessed Virgin of *Czestochowa*, to protect your liberties, my son."

"I will, Father. But, now they are making it difficult for me. If I refuse to go to war for them, I could be shot or hanged."

The priest paused, then a mischievous look flitted across his face. "Perhaps there is another way."

"Well," August hesitated. "Someone suggested that I escape to America." He paused, waiting for a reaction from the priest. When none came, he sighed deeply as he continued. "I just don't know if leaving here is the right thing to do. I'd miss my family and I'm worried about Poland's future."

Up went the priest's eyebrows. "Worry about your own future, my son. You can't stay here. If you die in war or are shot or hanged if you refuse to go, you won't be able to do anything about Poland's future. We are each in control of our own destiny. I suspect you want what all men want—freedom and a chance for a better future with more economic opportunities to increase your wealth as well as sons to carry on the family name."

"Yes, that's exactly right, Father."

"I know it's a lot to ask—that you leave your family—but I've heard America is full of opportunities. You could own your own land, be your own boss, maybe even own your own blacksmith shop. You'd have a better future! That will never happen if you stay here. We both know that. You would be destined to a life of poverty in *Grabionna.* If I were you, I'd escape to America. I assume you're Martin's son, aren't you?"

"Yes, I'm August. August Kopczynski."

"He is a good man, your father. One day you, too, shall be blessed with sons to carry on your family name and Polish heritage." He paused and gave a dismissive wave of his hand. "Very well, August. Meet me again here in a few weeks for your next confession. Keep holy your Catholic faith. Be strong. Never forget your Polish heritage. Now, say your contrition and recite the Hail Mary and Our Father ten times in reparation for your sins. Go with peace, my son."

"And you, Father. I promise I'll always remain faithful to the Catholic Church and to Poland."

Chapter 5

A week later, as August finished brushing his Arabian horse in the red brick barn near the house, he caught a glimpse of a man wearing dark clothing lurking in the shadows near the walnut tree in the unkempt field across the road. *Ach du lieber Gott, this man won't leave me alone.*

Every day this past week August had noticed him stalking him a short distance from the blacksmith shop, in the morning, at noon, and also at closing time on his way home, riding his horse past the houses which, facing west, lined the left side of the street where he lived. August suspected he was a member of the *Preußische Geheimpolizei,* the Prussian Secret Police, watching him to see if he showed up for service and to make sure he didn't have contact with members of the Polish resistance. Why he was so important to the Prussians he didn't know.

Ha, he'll never get me. I'm too smart for that sorry bastard. But I won't be part of that Prussian troop contingent they're planning. I hope to be long gone before they even realize I'm missing.

August was a deep thinker. He often ruminated about a problem for hours at a time, trying to come up with a solution. And he had found a solution for his current predicament. He dug in his pocket for the note the Frenchman had given him.

Before he took it out, he looked around to make sure no one was watching.

Put a piece of red tape on the sign at the entrance to Kaiserswalde. When a piece of yellow tape replaces it, go to the nearby shrine of the Blessed Mother. On the right-hand-side of the steps near the first bush will be a brown packet with instructions. Be careful!

In the middle of the night, when his Prussian shadow was not around, August rode his horse out to the entrance of the village. As he neared the blue *Kaiserswalde* sign, he heard the clomping of another horse. His heart beat faster and his breath quickened as the horse and its owner rode past him in the opposite direction. So as not to draw attention, he continued on the road, riding past the sign. A few minutes later, he turned the horse around. Once sure he wasn't followed, he dismounted near the sign and quickly put a piece of red tape on it.

Each successive day, he rode his horse out to the small lake nearby, looking for a yellow tape on the entrance sign. The Prussian Secret Police member tailed him every time, but August used his creative instincts and managed to foil his plans both days.

On the third day, coming back into town, he spotted the yellow tape. He rode past the sign and stopped at the Blessed Virgin shrine. Knowing full well he was being followed, he stopped his horse near the shrine which was about eighteen feet off the main road. He climbed off his horse, walked up the cement steps and knelt down to pray. Looking out of the corner of his eye, he saw the brown package near the first bush. *How can I retrieve it without being noticed?*

August rose from his knees and then acted as if he suddenly lost his balance, falling off the shrine steps to the right, landing near the first bush. He quickly snatched the package, and secretly put it in his pocket. Then, regaining his balance, he stood up and climbed back on his saddle. He rode his horse a few feet until he was back on the main road.

He turned around and smiled at the man following him to let him know he was aware of his presence, to give him the idea he wouldn't do anything foolish while he was being watched. When August was alone in the blacksmith shop, he took the package from his pocket and unwrapped it. Inside was a false passport with a new birthdate and birth place and a note.

You are to enlist as an Assistant Cook on board a ship leaving from Hamburg. If you do not know how to cook, you must learn to make a meal. Do not tell your family you are leaving.

A cook? I can't even boil an egg! How can I get my stepmother or my sister to give me cooking lessons without telling them why I need them? Men don't cook! They'll surely think I am crazy for wanting lessons.

Tired after a long, hard day at work, he sighed. He patted down his horse in the barn, bedding him down for the night, when Henrietta suddenly appeared at the doorway.

"I thought I might find you here," she said. "I waited for you."

"So, any good news?"

"Yes, I got my monthly visitor."

"That is good news. Did you ever tell Emil about it?"

"Yes, he knows. We agreed to be more careful...to wait until we're married."

"So, he said he'd marry you? Did he propose?"

"Not officially, but we talked about marriage."

"Are you sure about him? That he's the one you want to marry?"

"I think so. As sure as I can be. I love him. I'll wait for him...when the time's right."

"Most women your age are already married."

"Don't rub it in. What about you? Anything happen at work today?"

He avoided eye contact. "The usual. We'd better go eat. I don't want to keep Rosalia waiting."

Shuffling down the stone walkway between the barn and the house, they entered through the kitchen door. He took off his hat, and hung it on the nearby rack.

"All done with your chores, August?" Rosalia said, smiling. She hugged him hello. Her dark hair had streaks of gray and was fashioned in a bun at the top of her head. Five months pregnant, she wore a long, black dress showing a slight bump. Rosalia and August's twenty-seven-year-old sister, Mary, were busy cooking *bigos*,[7] a hearty, hunter's stew. The smell permeated the air in the steamy kitchen. Mary, her husband, Anton Otto, and their son, Theodore, lived nearby and often rode their horses to the Kopczynski house for a family meal.

"Yes, I'm done with my chores," August answered, thinking that perhaps this might be the last time he'd share a meal with the woman who had raised him since the day his mother had died when he was six. Glancing at Rosalia and Mary, his oldest sister, he felt a tug at his heart when he thought of leaving his family behind, knowing he might never see them again.

As the house had only a kitchen but no living room, the family gathered in the kitchen. August's chair scraped the floor as he sat down at the wooden table and glanced at the flowered tablecloth and table settings—bowls, soup spoons and knives, water glasses, salt and pepper shakers, a basket containing hard crust rye bread and a butter dish.

"And how was your day, Mama?" August asked as he winked at the two youngest kids, ages four and seven, seated across from him. "Did the children behave themselves?" The kids both shot back a frown at him.

"A lot of confusion and noise around here, like always," Rosalia said. "Martha fought with Albert over a ball. Be glad you go to the blacksmith shop every day where it's quiet."

"You need to mind Mama," he said to Albert and young Martha, who was nineteen years younger than August. "She's a good mama and she loves you."

August's father entered the kitchen and hugged Rosalia. His hands were dirty from working in the field. He brought an unannounced guest with him.

"Rosalia," the elder Kopczynski said. "I'd like you to meet Frederick Horstmann. Frederick has been helping me in the field today and is interested in purchasing one of our Arabians. He will be joining us for supper."

"Please," Rosalia said, as she turned to her husband. "Go wash up before you sit down to eat."

"Whiskey?" August's father said to Frederick as they returned a few minutes later.

"Yes, please."

"Have you seen to the horses?" his father asked August, pouring himself and his guest a glass of whiskey.

"Even though it's warm out, the Arabian chomped the hay as if it was cold outside and he hadn't eaten in weeks. And he whinnied when I petted his nose. He's highly intelligent for a horse. I managed to calm him down and put him to bed for the night." *Who will take care of my horse when I leave?* August had trouble concealing his sadness.

His father nodded at Frederick in approval. "It's true what I told you about our Arabians." He offered Frederick a cigar and lit it for him. Turning to August, he said, "Anything new at work?"

August shrugged. "Not many customers. It was a slow day."

"Have you heard anything more about when you'll have to leave for service?"

August slunk down in his chair. He tented his fingers in a prayer position and took a deep breath before he spoke. "Not yet, but I think it's soon."

"Nothing you can prevent," Frederick said. He raised his whiskey glass in a toast, catching August's eye. "To war!"

"No," August said, frowning, raising his own glass. "To freedom, my friend!"

Frederick blew a smoke ring towards August. "Freedom is for fools," he said. "Only the feeble of heart prefer it over war."

August almost dropped the glass he was holding. "I disagree, my friend. A person always hungers for freedom unless they can taste it. I've heard from my friends who live in Chicago, Wisconsin and Minnesota that there is more freedom and opportunities in America."

"Don't get any crazy ideas like those fellows," his father said. "Haven't you heard the Latin proverb: *'Fertilior seges est alieno emper in arvo'*?"

"No, what does it mean?"

"The corn in another man's ground seems more fertile and plentiful than does your own. Our landlord lets us farm and we have our blacksmith jobs. What more could you want? Be grateful! Your friends omitted the problems they encounter and I'm sure there are plenty. America has been fighting its own civil war. If you were older, you'd know better."

August shot him a venomous look. "I'm not naïve, Father. I know the cost of war. One never forgets the stench of war or the blood of soldiers left dying on the battlefield soiling your uniform. Some were my friends. What shook me to the core is when I got called to fight in the war against Austria. Shooting and killing former allies? It wasn't for me."

"But, that war only lasted seven weeks. That's not so long." Frederick took another swig of whiskey.

August bit his lip, then took a sip of his drink. *Seven weeks was like seven years of bloody hell.* "The fact that we claimed total victory, even though we were outnumbered, boiled down to Prussia's excessive training and drilling. I hated it, but most Germans are in love with organization."

"It was necessary." Frederick drained his glass. "Like your father said, you're too young to understand."

"But apparently not too young to die on the battlefield?"

"That's enough talk," Rosalia said to stop the tension from boiling over. "The *bigos* is ready. Please, let's eat." The blue candle on the table flickered. The table was noisy with the children jostling for seats and attention. Martin quieted them. "We'll pray the rosary later to the Blessed Virgin of *Częstochowa*. Now, let's say grace together."

They all made the sign of the cross in Latin."*In nómine Patris, et Fĭlii, et Spĭritus Sancti, Amen.* Then continued in Polish, asking God to bless their food: "*Pobłogosław Panie Boże te dary, które teraz spożwać mamy. Amen.*"

After they finished the meal prayer, Rosalia dished up their plates, and August took a bite, savoring a chunk of stew. "Mama, this is delicious," he said. "You're a great cook!"

Rosalia smiled at the compliment.

August winked at her. "I'd like to know how you made this. I'd like to learn how to cook."

Martin and Frederick both stared hard at August, their brows furrowed in strong disapproval.

"*You?*" Rosalia said. "Cooking is women's work."

"Well, I might be a bachelor my whole life," August said. "After all, who would ever want me as a husband?" He laughed.

"He may have a point," Henrietta chimed in. "I say we teach him."

"A *man* learning to cook?" Rosalia said as a deep frown crossed her brow. "I've never heard of such a thing." Then she stared at August. "Cooking is a lot harder than you think."

"It can't be any more difficult than learning my blacksmith trade, can it?" He took another bite of stew meat and smiled as if he had won her over with his reasoning.

August became good at his blacksmith trade in part because Rosalia had encouraged him to solve puzzles in his youth. He grew to love puzzles. Fixing a wagon to him was like solving a puzzle. Cooking also seemed like a puzzle. With help from Rosalia, he felt he could master that, too.

Rosalia put her fork down and shook her head. "It takes years to learn how to cook. Just ask your sisters."

"I just need to know the basics. Besides, I'm a quick learner."

"Could you pass me the rye bread?" Henrietta said. "We could at least teach him how to boil an egg. That way he won't starve to death."

August passed her the bread. "Henrietta, my dear sister. You're always looking out for me!" *If you only knew how much I will miss you, how much I will miss all of you.* He looked down at his plate and quickly wiped a tear away from his eye.

"You'd do the same for me," Henrietta said, nodding.

He winked. "*Ja cie kocham,*" he said, although his words would never be able to express how much he loved her.

They said another meal prayer in Polish after they finished eating. "*Dziekujemy Ci Panie za Wszystkie dobrodziejstwa Twoje, który żyjesz I królujesz no wieki wieków.*"

"Okay, August and Henrietta," Rosalia said, standing up to clear the plates. "I know when I've been overruled. You win. We'll teach you the basics after we finish with the dishes."

The Otto family got up and everyone gathered round to say their goodbyes before they left. August embraced his sister Mary with a hug so tight she gasped for air.

"Pray for me," he said as he kissed her cheek.

"I always pray for you my dear brother."

In a minute they were gone. Then his father and Frederick went to the barn with Albert and Wilhelm while Henrietta and Rosalia washed and dried the dishes by lantern light.

August sat upright. "I'll need a cook's uniform, an apron. Do you have an extra one that's not too feminine that I could use?"

Henrietta opened a kitchen drawer, rummaged through the aprons and pulled out a simple, black one. "This should do." She helped him tie it in back.

"I'm ready," he said. He stood near the stove.

Henrietta started the lesson while Rosalia stood by watching. Henrietta could not believe how ignorant men were about cooking. She had to teach him such simple things like which pot and pan to use, how to season food, the difference between flour and sugar, how to cook eggs and vegetables and other basics like making soup.

"In order to make soup, you must first boil the water." Henrietta poured water into the pot and set the kettle on the stove.

"Why do you have to boil the water?"

Henrietta started cutting up vegetables at the sink. "The recipe calls for it. I assume the soup cooks faster that way."

August scratched his head. "What is a recipe?"

Her tone of voice rose. "You don't know what a recipe is?"

"No, what is it?"

She had always sought out her younger brother's advice because, as she often said to him, she thought he was more intelligent. After all, he was a man and men were the breadwinners in the family. Now, however, she was the expert, she was the one giving advice. It made her smile that the tables were turned.

"A recipe is cooking directions. It tells you step-by-step how to make it. Being a man, I doubt you will follow directions." She giggled, covering her mouth with her hand.

"Who needs a recipe?" August said, irritated, as Rosalia hovered nearby. "Is it possible to burn water?"

Henrietta winced. She couldn't believe his ridiculous questions, yet she didn't want to demean August by not answering them. After all, he was her brother and she loved him.

"No, not unless all the water evaporates. Then the pan will burn. Watch." The temperature in the kitchen rose as steam poured out from the kettle. "When the water boils, bubbles spring up from the bottom of the kettle. That's how you know when to add vegetables or meat."

When Henrietta finished answering all his exhausting questions, she said, "It's late. Let's have another cooking lesson tomorrow."

"But, I want to know how to make *bigos.*"

"It might be too advanced for you, August." Rosalia said, wrinkling her nose.

"Nonsense, Mama. I can do it. I just need to know how."

"We'll continue our lessons tomorrow," Rosalia said, hugging him goodnight and sending him to sleep in the barn.

<h1 style="text-align:center">Chapter 6</h1>

The cool air made August shiver as he watched the bright sun go down in the orange sky as he rode his Arabian horse home from work the next day. He spied four-year-old Martha playing in the yard, hopping up and down.

He hollered at her. "Martha! You're like a bunny rabbit!"

She looked his way and squealed in delight. "*Raebyt?*"

"Yes," he said. "My favorite *little* sister. You remind me of a bunny."

She ran over to him, smiling. He got down from his horse, gave her a tight squeeze and patted her head.

"Don't do that," she said, pulling away from him. "You're messing up my hair."

"Both you and I could benefit from a good washing and maybe even a haircut. What do you think about that?" He winked.

She rolled her eyes. "I think I'd better ask Mama."

When they reached the barn, seven-year-old Albert was waiting near the stable.

"Did you hear something in the barn last night?" Albert said, his eyes wide.

"No," August said. "What did you hear?"

"I think someone was lurking around there in the hay loft near where I was sleeping."

"And, you're afraid he was going to kidnap you and carry you off in a sack to chomp up and eat for dinner?"

"Quit teasing me. I know I heard something."

August wondered if it was the man shadowing him. He feared there might be danger for his family, but didn't want to scare the children.

"Albert, I guarantee there was no monster or boogeyman there."

"I heard it, August."

"All right, you win. I won't let anyone get you though. If you hear it again, wake me up. Now, come help me bed down my horse for the night."

He took a deep breath. *What will Albert and Martha do when they find out I've gone?*

"Please sit," Rosalia said as they entered the house through the kitchen door. His father was already seated at the table, smoking a cigar and sipping a glass of whiskey. "We're having leftover *bigos*. It's always better the next day."

"I started seeding the wheat today," his father said, taking a swig of whiskey. "We need your help in the field tomorrow, August."

"I don't think we ever started seeding this early before. Are you sure it's time? Isn't the ground still frozen?"

"The soil is soft already," his father said. "Besides, the landlord expects us to get all the spring planting done before the rains come."

August knew he wouldn't be around to help the next day, but didn't intend for any of his family members to know about his plans so they could reply honestly if any Prussian authorities questioned them.

"The owner will be in the shop tomorrow," August said. "I'll get up early and meet you in the field."

"If you're exhausted, August, maybe you don't want a cooking lesson tonight," Rosalia said.

"Nonsense, Mama. Cooking is relaxing."

"*Relaxing*?" Rosalia said, raising her eyebrows. "Did you hear that, Henrietta?"

"He's only learned a few basics," Henrietta said. "Tonight is the big test. We'll teach him something harder, like *bigos*." She smiled at August.

When they were through with dinner, Rosalia cleared the plates and she and Henrietta washed the dishes by lantern. Martin left with Wilhelm and Albert to head to the barn.

August went to the apron drawer, retrieved the black apron and Henrietta helped him tie the strings in the back.

Rosalia dried her hands with a towel and she and Henrietta took several minutes to gather the ingredients, as well as the necessary pots and pans. Then Rosalia began explaining how to make *bigos*.

"Okay, first, you rinse the mushrooms and soak them in water for two or more hours and then drain them and cut them into slices. Then you put them aside. Then you stew the meat—pork, beef and game—for one hour in three cups of water with the onions, peppercorns and other spices like..."

When she finished, there was a pile of dirty dishes, utensils and pots and pans to clean. August was amazed at how long and how much trouble it took to cook *bigos*. "Mama, I'm afraid I haven't been appreciative enough of your good cooking till now. I had no idea how hard it was. I'm sorry."

Rosalia smiled. "Apology accepted. Henrietta, let's you and I tackle these dirty pots and pans before we call it a night. August, I know you're exhausted and it's getting late. You need to get to bed if you're going to get up early tomorrow to plant." She put her arms around his neck. "One last hug for me and your sister and then we'll finish the dishes and snuff out the lanterns."

He hugged them till it hurt. "Pray for me," he said.

Chapter 7

At three o'clock in the morning, while Wilhelm and Albert slept, August woke up with a start and looked at his watch. *If I'm going to leave, I'd better get going.* With the help of a lantern and a mirror, he shaved off his beard and mustache and closely cropped his hair so that he wouldn't be recognized by any Prussian official who might be after him trying to make sure he showed up for service.

He filled a rucksack with a jug of water, clean underwear, two sets of clean homespun clothes, socks, his prayer book, the amber rosary his father had made for him, a toothbrush, hairbrush, and his razor. He left a note for Wilhelm to pick up his horse at the train station. Then he silently crept into the house, and creaked open the kitchen drawer to retrieve the black apron.

Hearing a noise in the kitchen, his father woke up and called from the bedroom. "Who's there?" he said.

After a moment of panic, August replied. "It's just me," he said. "I came in to get a drink of water. Go back to sleep."

He poured water into a glass and drank it, then took the apron, put it in his rucksack and left the house.

August knew the man who was usually lurking in the shadows around the house would not be there at this hour. He mounted his horse under a full moon, carrying his rucksack, and headed out on the wagon-rutted, dirt road toward the *Weisse Hohe*[8] train station, or *Bialosliwie* as Grandpa Jacob called it, for the two-and-a-half mile trip.

His stomach felt queasy and his heart ached when he thought about leaving behind his beloved *Grabionna*, the only home he had ever known. He wondered what his life would be like in America, letting his imagination run wild. Would he like big cities like New York or Chicago and would he realize his dream of farming his own land or owning his own business? *Surely, I'll miss the smell of the barn when I go to sleep each night. The linden trees that line the streets in the bright sunlight. Yellow fields surrounded by green forests. The smell of Mama's cooking. Yeah, definitely the cooking.*

There were few houses on this wagon-rutted road. Most were made of brick and located several feet off the road. It was still dark outside and these homes looked as isolated as he felt.

The horse seemed to stumble so he yanked the reins. Once the horse calmed down, his thoughts ricocheted back to his family. *What will they do or say when they find out I'm missing? Will they ever forgive me?*

He finally arrived at the *Weisse Hohe* train station. The sun was beginning to come up and light bounced off the tall, pane-glass windows that were trimmed with white. He hitched his horse to a post, then went inside to purchase a ticket to *Schneideműhl.* He didn't speak to anyone besides the attendant and as far as he knew, he wasn't being followed.

Back outside with his horse, he saw that there were only a few people waiting for the early morning train. As *Grabionna* and *Bialosliwie* were small towns, August recognized most of the people waiting, but kept out of sight and to himself until the train came. He felt like a poor farmer in his shabby, home-spun clothes while most of the other men wore elegant top hats and black, homespun business suits. The women were dressed in bonnets with plumes, perched high on their heads, satin gloves and their finest dresses—pink satin hooped skirts with tiny rosebuds around the scooped neckline, emerald green gathered skirts with cream colored lace around the collar and cuffs, and baby blue taffeta hooped skirts. August, like some of the other passengers, despised these dresses because they took up so much room in already crowded train cars.

While he waited, he worried whether his disguise was good enough, worried whether he would be caught and arrested by the Prussians who were after him, but tried to block this out of his mind, tried to think positive thoughts about the new journey he was taking, tried to be hopeful that he had made a wise decision to escape. After all, his friends in America, living in Chicago, Wisconsin and Minnesota, had written him, telling him of their successful journeys and boasted of their new life and the opportunities to be had.

When he heard the train screech to a halt, he kissed his horse's forehead. "Be a good boy," he said, tying the reins to a post. "I left a note for Wilhelm to come to get you."

He walked around the building towards the train. It had a steam engine on the front with a lantern hanging on each side in order to light the tracks at night. White puffs of smoke bellowed from the steam engine. August stifled his desire to speak with fellow passengers, keeping mostly to himself out of fear of being detected by the Prussians, and hopped on board. He breathed a sigh of relief.

In *Schneidemühl*, he purchased a ticket to *Berlin* where he would spend the night. Since he had to wait a couple hours for the train to arrive, he went to the nearby tavern, drank a pint of ale and smoked a cigar but didn't speak to anyone besides the bartender. At three o'clock he boarded the train bound for *Berlin*. A man traveling from *Schneidemühl* to *Berlin* wouldn't arouse any suspicions, yet he remained careful not to say more than two words to anyone the whole trip.

In *Berlin,* he found a room at a nearby boarding house. Sitting alone in his room, eating a sandwich and drinking a beer he had bought at the station, he wondered what was happening back home, wondered about the people he left behind. *Are they worried that I'd had an accident? Is Father angry or sad? Did Mama and my sisters cry when they found out?*

He remembered how worried Rosalia had been when he fell from the walnut tree in his youth. Certainly, she would be worried about his safety now. *Did they realize I stole an apron? Did Wilhelm get my horse?*

He wondered what the *Preußische Geheimpolizei* would do to his family when they found out he was missing. Would they make it difficult for them?

The beer helped to calm his nerves. August tried not to think of the consequences his actions had on the people he loved, tried to think instead of the journey that lay ahead. *Two months on a ship! Ach du lieber Gott!* He wondered if he would be able to pull off this lie and avoid detection during that time.

Please God, help me be strong! Help me make it safely to America.

He never valued his freedom much, until he'd lost it to the Prussians. In America, he'd be able to say what he wanted without repercussion. Life would be better. No more scraping by. More opportunities. More chances. No more worries. Yes, he'd be happier in America.

When he awoke the next morning, he washed his face and hands in the basin and then knelt down by his bed and said his morning prayers.

Then he left for the *Berlin* train station. There were conductors shouting directions to passengers who were coming and going, women with children who filled the air with their noisy chatter or screaming babies they held in their arms, and men buying cigars or a newspaper from one of the vendors. The air was thick with cigar smoke and urine from wet diapers.

Relieved to get away from the noise, he boarded the train to *Hamburg* with apprehension. He worried about keeping up his identity. He found a seat and a few minutes later Prussian train officials boarded and checked the tickets of its passengers. August held his breath while a big burly Prussian official inspected his.

"Where are you headed?" the Prussian official said.

"To Hamburg." *Be calm. Don't volunteer any information. Our Father, who art in Heaven...*

"May I see your ticket?"

The official glanced at the ticket and then back at August, eyeing him suspiciously. After all, he wasn't dressed like the other men in top hats and black suits.

"Why are you traveling to Hamburg?"

Unprepared, he answered honestly. "My ship embarks from there."

"Then I assume you have a passport. Let me see it."

August, regretting his honest answer, complied with the official's request, holding his breath, his palms sweaty and hands shaking. He cursed his hands and worried that the tremor would give him away.

"And where is your ship headed?"

"To New York."

The official looked surprised. "In those clothes? Can you afford the fare?"

August felt his pulse rise with each question and a drop of sweat fell from his brow. He hoped the official didn't notice. He silently prayed. *Please help me get through this, dear Father.*

"I'm a cook."

"A cook?" the official said, unbelieving. "Your hands look rough and dirty. They don't look like a cook's hands to me." Then he looked August flat in the eye. "You're a fraud. Get off the train. NOW!" He blew a whistle.

The words stung. August's mind raced. *Is this the end? Have I been found out?* He wondered if he would be turned over to the Prussian authorities. He wondered if this would be his last breath before he was hung for treason. He wondered if he would ever see his family again.

"I'm an Assistant Cook." August pulled the black apron from his knapsack. "See, here is my apron."

Another Prussian official showed up and the two conferred with one another. Still not convinced, the first official glanced again at August's passport and then looked at August. "So, what's your specialty, Herr Katzenmeier?"

"*Eintopf.*" He knew if he had said the Polish name, *bigos,* he would have betrayed his secret that he was Polish.

"And how do you make it?"

August remembered his cooking lessons. "First, you rinse the mushrooms and soak them in water for two or more hours and then drain them and cut them into slices. Meanwhile, you stew the meat—pork, beef and game—for one hour in three cups of water with the onions, peppercorns and other spices... *He wished now that he would have listened closer to his stepmother when she rattled off the spices.* Then you put the cabbage in boiling water to soften it and continue to boil until half tender, about fifteen minutes..."

"I've heard enough. I remember my mother cooking something like it the same way. Here is your passport." Satisfied, the officials moved on to another passenger. August breathed a sigh of relief, looked at the ceiling of the train car and silently whispered *thank you.*

The train arrived safely in sunny Hamburg and August made his way to Vedders Island[9] on the Elbe River in Hamburg's tangy, salty-air harbor, where he'd board the ship that would take him to America.

After waiting what seemed like hours to register, August finally stepped up to the counter where an attendant asked him questions and entered his responses into a large book, the ship's Passenger List.

"Last name?"

"Katzenmeier," he answered, quickly.

"First name?"

"August," he replied.

"Male or female?"

"Male."

"Age?"

"Twenty-three." He gave the attendant the age which corresponded to his new birthdate on the false passport.

"Where are you from?"

"Berlin." He had rehearsed the answer in his mind a hundred times. No further explanation was needed because any Prussian, like the attendant, knew Berlin was the capital of Prussia.

"Where did you live before?"[10]

"*Immer Berlin.*" This was a lie, but since Berlin was heavily populated and had a mix of cultures, it was plausible that a German with a slight Polish accent might have come from there. Because August responded fast, the attendant rapidly went on to the next question.

"Married or single?

"Single."

"What is your job or profession?"

"Assistant Cook."

"Final destination?"

"New York." *Actually, Chicago, but I don't want him to know that.*

After the attendant was through with his questions, he checked August's passport, and then told him he would need to undergo a medical examination in order to detect highly contagious diseases. Each morning at 10:30 a trumpet sounded to signal the beginning of the medical examination which took only two minutes—a quick look at his appearance, and a check of his pulse and tongue. He was also given an eye examination in which his eyelid was flipped over to detect trachoma, a highly infectious eye disease. He passed both exams.[11] After the examination, they required him to bathe and get his luggage disinfected.

Then they herded him through the line, among the 600 other passengers, to board the ship. August sighed, feeling a great sense of relief. Now if he could just hide his true identity from anyone on board for two long months, he'd reach New York and be fine.

The three-masted, wooden sailing vessel had four tiers of white sails on each mast. The voyage was scheduled to take sixty-four days to cross the Atlantic Ocean with a final stop in New York, albeit with immense risk.

The sleeping quarters in the ship were over-crowded with long lines of bunkbeds. Almost five-hundred people slept in the same room as August. Unmarried men and women were separated from the families. Beds were assigned at random, based on when they boarded the ship.

August figured he could deal with the exhaustion since he, like a majority of emigrants on the ship, was used to living in poor conditions at home, such as sleeping with a large number of people in a single room, having to use a chamber pot for so many people and not having running water. He considered this experience on the ship to be just one last hurdle to overcome. Certainly a better future awaited him in the new world.

The cost for August's passage was forty Prussian Taler, equivalent to half of his annual blacksmith salary. Luckily, August had found a sponsor, Mr. August Weinrebe, of Cottage Hill,[12] Illinois, who paid for half his voyage. He paid the other half by working as an Assistant Cook aboard the ship.

They had mostly sunny weather during the first few days of the long journey which allowed voyagers to get well acquainted which August did when he was not working as a cook. Passengers contended with monotony, sea-sickness and home-sickness, but for amusement they played shuffleboard as well as other games or danced on deck or stood in groups relaxing in the fresh air, often engaging in heated discussions about politics or religion. August, a devout Catholic, became interested in a man on deck who professed to be an atheist.

"Christian people," the man said, "are superstitious. Believing in God is just a bunch of nonsense. Anyone in their right mind knows that God does not exist."

August eyed him with suspicion. "I disagree with you, my friend. Look around you. God is everywhere."

The man rolled his eyes. "Prove it," he said.

August cocked an eyebrow in surprise. He met the man's eyes. "Who do you think created you? Who created the ocean? The fish? The sun? The planets?" He smiled broadly as if he had won the contest.

"It's scientific, my dear man. They just evolved."

August scrunched his nose. "Nonsense, my friend. They didn't just evolve from nothing."

They stood staring at each other for a minute or two, then August looked up at the bright sunlight and turned around to go back to the dark galley. Before he walked a dozen steps, however, a young girl with a fair complexion, coal black hair and deep-set eyes came near him and stood a few feet away.

"I heard what you said to that man. I think you're right." Her black hair was in stark contrast to the baby blue taffeta dress she wore which had tiny rosebuds on the bodice and ruffles on the hoop skirt. She carried her bonnet.

August turned around to face her and smiled. He was astonished at her beauty and he liked her spirit. "And who might you be?"

Her thin lips smiled back at him. "My name is Marie Kaczyozska."[13]

A Polish last name! He felt less alone in an instant. He took a closer look and was mesmerized by the blueness of her eyes. They complimented the blue in her dress. She looked about eleven or twelve, young for sure, but she seemed mature beyond her age. And, besides, it was not uncommon for a man his age to be interested in her. Girls often married young to make ends meet. "Are you here by yourself?" he said, noticing that he could wrap his arms twice around her tiny waist.

"No, I'm with my grandparents. My parents died when I was three years old," she said nonchalantly.

August felt an immediate connection to her, that he could trust her, as if he'd known her his whole life. "I'm sorry. I know how you feel. My mother, Rosalia, died at the age of thirty-five when I was five years old. I don't remember much about her. My baby brother was just seventeen months old."

She smiled, batting her eyelashes. *She likes me, too.* He walked over to where she stood, close enough so he could hear her breathe and looked intently into her blue eyes. "My parents had five children and then my father remarried another Rosalia after my mother's death. They had six more children." August rolled his eyes and laughed. "I guess you could say my father liked the name Rosalia."

"That was a very popular name."

"Yes. There were five Rosalia's in the family. It was my grandmother's name, my mother and stepmother's name.

One of my younger sisters, who died at birth, was also called Rosalia and it's my half-sister's name, too."

"Your father is still alive?" She batted her eyelashes again.

"Praise God, yes. He turned fifty-three in 1865 after the Danish-Prussian war."

"Did you fight in that war?"

August immediately regretted mentioning the war. He didn't like answering questions about his service. It made him nervous, especially since he was traveling under a false passport. He decided to change the subject. "Hey, do you like to dance? There's dancing on deck."

"I love to dance, but I think my grandparents would frown on it. They're very protective of me. I should be getting back to them. They'll wonder where I am."

He wanted to put his arms around her and give her a hug, but decided against it because, after all, they had just met. "Very nice to meet you. See you again I hope." He smiled at her and walked back to the galley.

Chapter 8

August showed up in the ship's kitchen, wearing his black apron as well as a white chef's hat, and, although he felt timid about cooking at first and like a turnip in a fruit salad, he did his best to help the head cook prepare the daily meal. Lunch was served regularly at noon and the passengers could pick items off the daily menu written on a slate near the counter. The menu included several different kinds of bread, six hot dishes including soup, eggs and vegetables, when available, cooked in a variety of ways and salted beef and pork called junk or salt junk, a staple on long sea voyages.

With the exception of the captain, crew and first-class passengers, the remaining passengers ate their meals in the ship's kitchen which contained the necessary cooking appliances and a multitude of wooden tables and chairs in the galley of the ship. The wine cellar held three hundred bottles of French and Spanish wines, which, of course, would be consumed by the end of the voyage.

On his first day, August stood by in the kitchen as the head cook issued orders to him.

"August, I need you to put that beef salt junk on a plate with rye bread and then make a *Mehlschwitze* for gravy."

August froze. This was the first time the head cook had asked him to make something. He knew *Mehlschwitze* meant roux but he had no idea of what it was or how to make it.

He hurried and arranged the salt junk and rye bread on a plate and handed it to the head cook. *Gravy. What is gravy made from? I can't let him find out I can't cook.* He wished Henrietta and Rosalia were here to help him. Although he knew a good Catholic should never lie, he asked God to help him get over this because sometimes a lie is necessary.

He tried faking it. He took a kettle and filled it with water.

The head cook looked at him, puzzled. "What are you doing? I said *Mehlschwitze*, not soup."

"And for that we use a different pan?"

"Of course, you idiot! Don't you know how to make a *Mehlschwitze*?"

August sighed, looked downward, blinked hard, then shook his head.

"Some Assistant Cook you are! Who let you on the boat? I'll do it myself. Do you know how to peel potatoes?"

"Yes, Sir."

"Good. You can find them in the wine cellar."

Several days later, while August was busy cooking, a passenger came up to the counter around noontime in front of others in a queue. Because there were only three cooks and no waiters on board, the cooks were also responsible for waiting on customers. The head cook motioned for August to help this passenger.

He turned to face him. "*Bitteschőn?*"

"Hrrmph. You don't have anything good to eat here," the man grumbled. "Most of my other meals have been unsatisfactory. The soups had no flavor and were tepid." Then the man yawned as if he hadn't slept in three nights.

The sun shone brightly and August's face reddened, not because the weather was hot today, but because he thought about his own cooking efforts. Taken aback by the man's complaints, August wondered if he was just tired. *Papa used to say that every man has his own story to tell, his own challenges in life, his own suffering. People will tell you if you listen.* August looked into the man's tired eyes. "Did you get a goodnight's sleep last night, my friend?"

"I'm afraid not. I could hear a baby crying half the night in the family section. Kept me awake."

"I heard it, too, but the same thing happened in my family's home. We didn't have 500 people sleeping in the same room like we do on the boat, but our house was overcrowded. So, I learned to fall asleep even with noise." He smiled at the stranger.

The man nodded as if he understood. Then in a low tone he said, "I kept thinking about my wife who died in childbirth."

"I'm so sorry," August said, locking eyes with the passenger. "I'm sure you miss her."

Tears welled up in the man's eyes. "Everyone is sorry. It doesn't bring her back."

During the awkward silence where they could hear the boat creaking, a few more passengers queued up behind this man, so August changed the subject, cutting the conversation short.

"What would you like to eat, my friend?" *It's hard enough to cook, but harder to please everyone.* "I'm sorry we disappointed you with our soups. I assure you today's meal will be better."

"You're the cook. What do you recommend?"

"The beef salt junk with rye bread is our special today."

"I'll take it, and thank you."

"For what?"

"For your sympathy. I'm sorry I was so grumpy to you."

August winked and smiled. "Don't give it a second thought."

After the man left, a woman with a fussing baby in her arms and a young boy at her side with a sad look on his face stepped up to the front counter. *She reminds me of my stepmother.*

"Looks like you've got your hands full," August said. "*Bitteschőn?*"

"Some soup, please."

"Coming right up. Can I hold the young one?"

The woman nodded. "Here, take her." She handed the squirming baby to August. "She had a terrible night last night. Wouldn't stop crying."

"So, it was your baby I heard."

"Yes, I'm sorry. I couldn't get her quieted."

"No apology necessary. I have youngsters like her in my family. Maybe she's teething. Let's get her something cold to suck on."

Carrying the baby on his hip, August traipsed to the wine cellar and came back holding a carrot. He washed it off and let the baby chew on it. The baby stopped fussing, so he handed her back to the woman. Then he dished up the soup and turned to the little boy.

"Why the sad face, young man?" August said, lifting up the boy's chin.

"He's homesick," the mother said.

"Ahhh," August said, nodding. He smiled and bent down next to the little boy. "Cheer up, my good man. I have something for you. I have two of these so you can have one." He took off his chef's hat and plopped it on the little boy's head.

The boy's mouth curved into a smile and his face lit up.

"What do you say?" the woman said to her son.

"Thank you," he whispered.

"How can we ever repay your kindness?" the woman said.

"It's nothing," August said. "Glad to help. Enjoy your soup!"

While the waters were calm, the passengers avoided the monotony by talking to each other about the stars or the moon or politics or religion. They also played shuffleboard or danced polkas on deck.

One day, a month later, a sudden violent storm hit the sailing vessel. It started with a few raindrops, then progressed until rain came down in torrents. August, smelling the salty, damp air, stood on deck in a crowd of fellow passengers as well as the gray-haired captain and crew members. He heard a swooshing sound, which he had never heard before, and then saw white, angry waves as high as 100 feet bounce off the deck with the boat thrashing about, first one way and then the other. August stood by, holding his stomach, while another passenger near the railing vomited over the side of the boat.

Powerful seventy-mile-per-hour wind gusts and freezing rain whipped the boat and the sound grew louder, more intense. Water fell from the sky as if God had opened the floodgates from heaven. Passengers with freezing fingers tried in a desperate attempt to hold on to hats and scarves, but lost the struggle with the high winds.

Booms of thunder reverberated in August's ears, making him and the other passengers recoil. Then he watched the darkened sky as cracks of lightning bolts darted across. The rain pelted down and his clothes were so soaked his body felt like a wet dishrag, but, like other passengers, his curiosity got the better of him, so he remained on deck.

He heard women scream and babies cry. All of a sudden, he noticed the woman with the baby and the little boy standing near the railing on the side of the deck. *Ach du lieber Gott, what is she doing here?* The frigid rain slapped their bodies hitting them with the force of medium-sized hail and almost knocked them over on the slippery deck. Their faces grew pale and looked as if they feared death by drowning or being washed overboard.

"Madame, it's not safe for you and your children to be out here on deck," August said. "Please, come with me. I'll take you back to the galley." Putting his arms around the woman and her children, he tugged against the ferocious wind and rain, and managed to guide them to safety below deck to the galley.

August returned to the deck, but had trouble standing because of the fierce winds and high waves. Crowds of inquisitive onlookers stood on deck watching the storm, albeit naïvely not fearing for their lives. When many started to slide off the deck because of the high winds and rain, August heard their gut-wrenching screams.

August knew one wrong move and he and his fellow passengers could die. *Please, God, have mercy on us. Save us. I'll do anything you ask me to do. I'll give Henrietta back the money*

I stole from her. Just help me get through this. He took out his amber rosary and made the sign of the cross.

The captain tried to control the crowd, but no one was listening to him, until he finally ordered everyone to get off the deck. August and the head cook inched their way to the galley where they found that even in the midst of this ferocious storm, passengers, their clothes dripping wet, still demanded to be fed. *Unglaublich.*

The moment August put on his apron and chef's hat, a couple in their 50s walked up to him at the counter asking to be served. August smiled.

"We want today's soup for lunch," the man said.

He noticed Marie, the pretty young girl he became attracted to earlier in the week, standing next to them. She winked coyly at August, but didn't let the couple know that she had spoken with him. August didn't let on, either.

"It's pea soup today, but I wouldn't recommend soup in today's stormy weather," August said.

"We don't care what kind of weather it is, we want soup."

August was taken aback by their unfriendly manner and blunt response, but didn't say anything. After all, Marie was with them and he wanted to impress her.

"Okay," August said, raising an eyebrow, and obediently dished up the soup. "Pea soup it is."

Marie, her grandparents and the other passengers took their bowls of soup and sat down at a table. Soon, because of the brutal storm which rocked the boat first wildly to one side and then the other, her grandfather spilled his soup, and the table, chair and galley floor became green and slippery. Pretty soon everyone was spilling their soup. *Acht du lieber, what a mess!* Chairs slid around and customers found it impossible to remain seated or stand upright. Marie giggled at the chaos. August grinned at her. The amused head cook laughed, too. It was a welcome moment of relief from the horrific storm.

Marie and her grandparents got frustrated and left, and went up on deck to wash the spilled green soup off their hands and clothes. August and the other cooks scrubbed the galley floor and cleaned up the mess in the kitchen. Afterwards, the passengers let the cooks decide what they should eat at all future meals.

The violent storm continued for three endless days and each day the wind whipped the sails more intensely, the angry waves bounced higher, and crashing off the deck with more frequency and the thunder and lightning increased, terrifying the crew and passengers, as well as the captain, even though he wouldn't admit it and pretended to be brave. August and fellow passengers tried hard to maintain their equilibrium on deck but were deathly afraid of being washed away as the storm grew more intense.

The captain advised the passengers to tie themselves in bed with a rope for the duration of the storm, even though he had no idea of how long it would last. August and the other passengers on deck blindly followed his orders. Before they left the deck, however, the storm grew fiercer with heavy downpour and thunder and lightning illuminating the dark, gloomy sky overhead.

Meanwhile, the captain said, "All you passengers pray; if the Lord doesn't help you, I cannot."

August, standing near the atheist, almost fell over when he heard the atheist pray, "Dear God, please help us! Don't let us drown!"

"My friend, you had better admit that for you there is no God," August said, unable to hide his smile.

Chapter 9

After three sleepless nights and harrowing days, the violent storm ended. For the rest of the journey, August and his fellow passengers enjoyed sunshine and good weather, until a scorching hot day at the end of June in 1867 when they caught sight of land. *We made it!* August took out his amber rosary, made the sign of the cross, got down on his knees, bowing to God, and wept.

As they reached New York City's harbor, with its breathtaking view of sailing vessels and ships alongside the skyline of Manhattan, August spotted Castle Garden, a red sandstone, octagonal building, which functioned as an immigration center and stood at the tip of Manhattan Island. The tangy, salty-air of New York City's harbor burned his nostrils. The passengers had not had a proper bath for months and the salt air combined with body odor made August wince.

August packed his bag, said goodbye to his fellow cooks and the people he had made casual friends with. He was looking for Marie but couldn't find her among the 600 passengers on board. He was disappointed, but, alas, it was not to happen. And yet, his heart thumped faster and faster, fluttering with excitement, as he stepped off the clipper sailing ship and made his way through the crowd to Castle Garden where he underwent another passport inspection. He felt giddy and light headed and couldn't stop smiling.

Even so, August's palms were sweaty when he handed his passport to the attendant, not only because of the hot, glaring sun but also because he was afraid the attendant might discover his true identity and ruin his dream of freedom. When he could already taste it.

He held his breath and silently prayed as the attendant briefly glanced at his passport and shortened his last name from *Katzenmeier* to *Mr. Katzen*. Although the name on his passport was false and he realized the attendant probably didn't mean any disrespect since he seemed to just be herding people quickly through the line. August was offended by his actions. His last name was very important to him, even if others couldn't pronounce it correctly. But August pressed on. He planned on revealing his true name later, so his heirs would be known by the full Polish surname *Kopczynski*. The attendant quickly ushered him through the line and went on to the next passenger.

August smiled and breathed deeply, knowing that his dangerous journey had ended and that he had managed to escape detection by the Prussian authorities. Ecstatic about his new found freedom, he wanted to kiss every person he met.

He stood in line for about an hour with the other passengers to inquire about hotels, train routes and fares, and to exchange currency. He noticed the atheist a few feet in front of him, being helped by an attendant. The wrinkle-faced, stout man, who was impeccably dressed in a black suit and top hat, had black hair and a gray mustache and beard. After he was through with the attendant, he turned around. August smiled at him.

The man returned the smile and walked over to where August stood. "Hmmn. I see that that bloody faith of yours is not working out. You're not at the head of the line, Herr Cook."

"No complaints, my friend," August said, laughing nervously, not liking being singled out in this way and hoping that the man would just move on.

The atheist remained standing where he was. "Where are you headed?"

"To Cottage Hill, near Chicago."

"I am going to Chicago, too. The best deal is the Special Chicago Express train which leaves tomorrow morning at eleven from the Hudson River Railroad on 30th Street. The train station is about four miles from here and the train gets there in twenty-nine hours and has elegant drawing room cars attached."

August appreciated the tip and unexpected gesture of friendship. "Sounds expensive. I'm afraid I'll have to travel the slower route. My sponsor is paying for my ride."

"Your sponsor? You have a cook sponsor?"

August momentarily forgot he had boarded the ship as an assistant cook and regretted his words, but now he felt he owed the man an explanation. "I'm actually a blacksmith."

"Oh?"

August shrugged. "It's a long story, my friend." He noticed the expensive gold watch the man was wearing and wondered why the man was friendly with him. After all, they were from two very different economic classes and had conflicting views about religion.

"Yes, well, I'm an architect by trade." The man winked at August and puffed on his cigar.

"I'm on my way to Chicago to present my drawings at the Chicago Institute of Architecture. Well, let me tell you this. The other train takes two or three days and stops at every town or village along the way."

"I have more time than money."

"Sure you do. But, you'll have to pay for food each day. I assure you the express train is the best deal. Do you speak any English?"

"*Nein.*"

"I know a little. Not everyone in America speaks German, you know. And, not everyone speaks *Hochdeutsch* like us. Are you alone or are you meeting friends here?"

"I'm alone in New York, but I'm meeting some friends in Chicago. And you?"

Standing near August, he leaned on his cane. "I don't know anyone here either. I've booked a room at the Broadway Hotel which is located at the corner of West 42nd Street. Perhaps you'd like to join me to get a bite to eat. I could use some friendly conversation and perhaps you could help me carry my trunk."

August moved ahead, keeping his place in line. "I'd be happy to help, my friend. Wait for me while I attend to business. I need to find a room and exchange some money."

"Here is the name of the hotel where I'm staying." The man moved to where August stood and handed him a slip of paper with the name and address of the hotel on it. "It's reasonably priced. Perhaps they still have a vacant room. We can drop off our bags first and then go to the train station, purchase our tickets and find a place to eat."

"You're too kind. Thank you, my friend."

"My pleasure. My name is Henry."

"Mine is August." They shook hands.

After August finished at the immigration center, he joined Henry and they shared a horse-drawn streetcar ride to the hotel, dropped off their bags and then took another trolley to the train station.

"*Das Wetter ist heute sehr schön.*" The man spoke Hochdeutsch. "You couldn't have asked for a more glorious day for landing—no wind, no rain, no fog, the air unbelievably fresh—not like those three miserable days during the storm we spent on the boat. I don't hope to repeat that voyage again anytime soon. How about you?"

August nodded. "I'm thankful for solid ground. Don't think I'll ever go back."

"I left a brother and sister in Holstein. What about you? Did you have to leave your family, too?"

"I'm not married. Met a nice girl on the ship, but she was probably too young for me. Anyway, I didn't get her address. I'll probably never see her again."

"Too bad. But, you'll probably meet a nice, young American girl to settle down with. Are your parents still alive?"

"My mother died when I was five, but my father is still alive. He turned fifty-three in 1865."

"That was about the time of the Danish Prussian war. Did you fight in that war?"

August silently agonized over whether to answer that question. He still felt uncomfortable about revealing anything about his prior service or his personal life in *Grabionna*. Even though he was now in the land of freedom he couldn't help but think the Prussians were looking over his shoulder. He remembered the Russian betraying him in *Schneidemühl.* But, on the other hand, he was in America now, and by the look on Henry's face August realized that Henry wasn't spying; he was just eager to share his experience. August, feeling brave to test the waters again, reciprocated.

"Yes, I almost froze to death at the Eider River."

"Me, too."

"Were you in the infantry or cavalry, Henry?"

"Infantry. It was the first time I had ever shot a needle gun." He paused, rolling his eyes. "Ah yes, the Dreyse Needle Gun. I found its use extraordinary. We swept the field."

August nodded. "It was the first time I ever fired a rifle like that as well. We used it again more heavily in the war with the Austrians."

Henry paused. "I didn't fight in that war. I hurt my leg in the Danish war. Never fully recovered. I still walk with a limp."

"I hadn't noticed."

"So, tell me your plans, August. Do you hope to make your fortune in the United States like everyone else that immigrates to America?"

"A fortune? Yes, I'd like that very much. But, how?"

"If you want to become wealthy," Henry said, "you'll need to become a landowner and own a farm. The money is in agriculture right now."

Henry seemed not only wealthy, but wise. August appreciated his "fatherly" advice as much as he appreciated the priest's advice in *Grabionna.* Nodding in agreement, he explained his dilemma to Henry. "First, I must work a couple of years as a blacksmith for my sponsor in Cottage Hill."

Henry puffed on his cigar and blew smoke rings. "Do that and then save your money and buy some land. There's plenty of opportunities here in this country. The newspapers are full of advertisements enticing you to settle here or there. Grow some crops on your land and you will become wealthy in no time. The soil is rich and fertile. I've heard staggering news of bountiful crops out West. There is no limit to the possibilities."

At the train station they purchased their tickets, then took a streetcar ride back to the hotel and dined at a nearby tavern where they could get wine, ale, cigars and the daily meal at a modest price and set hour. The tavern didn't feature a menu, just served one "home-cooked" dish much like a mother would provide dinner for her large family.

They sat down at the table. August sliced into the roast beef and then ate a spoonful of mashed potatoes and gravy. *So different from the duck we eat at home.* As he bit into the cob of corn and tasted the fresh green beans he thought of Rosalia's vegetable garden in *Grabionna.* He wondered if Rosalia was even now standing in the kitchen, filling a pot with water to boil the vegetables. There were new sights and smells here, different from home.

When the waiter served bread pudding for dessert, August thought about his family back home and how much he would like to share this delight with them. He poured a cup of the whiskey sauce and fresh cream over the pudding and savored every bite.

Afterwards they smoked another cigar, finished drinking a pint of ale and then hopped back on the trolley to return to the hotel on this warm, balmy night. August noticed the street was lined with trees much different from the linden or lime trees he was used to in *Grabionna*. While the streets in New York City were rank with horse dung, he missed the familiar smell of the barn back home—the cow dung, the horse poop, the chickens nesting in their coop. New York City streets were congested and dusty and its five story buildings, crowds of strangers, as well as the sound of bustling horse-drawn carriages and street traffic, made him uneasy. Big cities didn't suit him. His heart was still in the village of *Grabionna* where it was quieter, not only because there were less crowds, but also because in *Grabionna* people actually knew each other and the pace was slower. Sure, New York City's skyline and shoreline were breathtaking but they didn't remind him of home.

When they returned to the hotel that night, the German-speaking owner of the hotel met August and Henry at the front door with a kerosene lamp.

"*Mein Herren*. I'm sorry but something terrible has happened."

"What?" August said.

"We've been robbed! Or, you've been robbed, Henry. A thief broke into your room and ransacked it. We scuffled but I'm afraid he got away with one of your bags. Better have a look. See what's missing."

Henry put out his cigar before he entered the hotel and ran to check his room. He opened the door. Inside the room, a pillow was tossed carelessly on the floor, the bedclothes were disheveled and the contents of his trunk lay strewn out over the bed and floor—his two best suits, underwear and socks, and pajamas. He searched the room for his other bag. He couldn't find it.

"My drawings! I can't go to Chicago without my drawings. I've spent months on them."

"Calm down," the owner said. "The police left a couple of hours ago. They said they'd try to apprehend the thief. We won't know the outcome until tomorrow."

"But I have a train ticket to go to Chicago tomorrow," said Henry, pacing the room. "We'll have to leave here by 10:30."

"I'm sorry," the owner said.

"Damned thief!" Henry said, wringing his hands through his hair. "I won't be able to sleep tonight. Damn! Damn! Damn! It might take longer than a day to clear this up."

August laid his hand on Henry's shoulder. "You can probably get a refund on your ticket and book it at a later day," he said. "Things will work out, Henry. Put your trust in God. It works for me."

Chapter 10

August woke up early the next day, washed his face and hands in the basin in his room, and said his morning prayers, thanking God for another glorious day and for keeping him safe and out of trouble. And he said a special prayer for his friend, Henry. As he picked up his bag and closed the door to his room, he saw Henry down the hall.

"*Guten Morgen, Henry, wie geht's?*"

"*Guten Morgen,*" Henry grumbled. "I didn't sleep at all last night worrying about my bag."

"I'm feeling bad for your loss, my friend. I hope you recover your bag. I wonder whether you need anything, if maybe I could help you in some way."

"My God, you are a pauper and yet you're offering help? *Unglaublich!* Thanks, but I don't suppose you have any architectural drawings in that bag of yours."

He chuckled. "No, I'm afraid not."

"Well, then, we'd best be going to the train station so I can exchange my damn ticket and you can board."

At the train station, August said goodbye to Henry and hopped on board the train. He sat down by a man who looked to be in his 40s.

"*Sprechen Sie Deutsch?*" August said, smiling.

"*Ja*," the man said. "My name is Helmut and this is my wife, Frieda, and our young son, Matthias."

"Mine is August." He held out his hand.

Helmut gripped his hand. "Pleased to meet you."

They exchanged pleasantries as the train clanked its way, day and night, on the Lake Shore and Michigan Southern Railway along the south shore of Lake Erie through Buffalo, New York; Pennsylvania; Ohio; and across northern Indiana to Chicago and offered breathtaking views of the countryside.

August stared out the window, gazing at the small towns the train passed through, dotted by a house or shanty here or there along the railroad tracks, not unlike those he had seen back home in Poland. He caught his breath, however, as the train crossed many unpopulated areas where he saw herds of wild horses and cattle grazing lazily on green fields in the distance, something unfamiliar, something exciting. *So this is America! Sehr schőn! Sehr schőn!*

The steam-engine train arrived at New Depot, corner of Sherman and Van Buren,[14] in Chicago where several German-speaking immigrants, including his friend, August Stolz, who crowded on the platform to meet their long-time friend.

"You finally made it," Stolz said, slapping him on the back. "I hardly recognized you with all your hair cut off."

Stolz, a good-looking, tall man with broad shoulders, pale skin and light blue eyes, had moved to Chicago from *Miasteczko Krajeñskie,* his small hometown. His family was among the many German colonists who didn't speak any Polish.

"It's good to see you," Stolz said. "*Wie geht's dir?*"

August momentarily forgot all his troubles—the Prussian officer who threatened to hang him if he didn't show up for service, the Russian who betrayed him, embarking at Hamburg under a false passport, as well as surviving three harrowing days during the storm on the ship. None of that mattered now that he was back among men he called friends, men he had bonded with long ago during many meetings at church back in *Miasteczko*. His heart beat faster.

"I'm blessed and so excited to be here. God has been good to me, my friends."

The men wore black, homespun shirts and pants, and as they walked through the train station, August noticed men dressed in handsome suits with top hats buying a cigar from a vendor. The women who accompanied them wore satin hoop-skirted dresses with a plume bonnet. Other women wearing shawls held fussing babies in their arms or carried small children. In the center of the train station, he heard the usual cacophony of voices selling newspapers, coffee, croissants, candy, as well as assorted other wares. The aroma of coffee wafted in the air.

Stolz guided August to an exit where his horses were tied to a post. Stepping outside the train station, August braced himself against the strong wind that hit him in the face.

"This wind reminds me of the powerful seventy-mile gusts on the boat."

"You could say Chicago is a wind-filled city," said Stolz.

"It's like New York City," August said, stepping through the crowd of strangers.

"It's much smaller," Stolz said. "It's only about 100,000 people.[15] It's growing though because it's becoming a railroad center connecting the East and West." He pointed in the direction of the Stock Yards. "Over there are the Union Stock Yards, the meat packing district where they butcher hogs and cattle. The Yards are also helping Chicago's growth."

"I don't like big cities," August said as he mounted the horse waiting for him. "And I miss my family already." He sneezed as he breathed in the air full of dust particles.

"I expect they will follow your lead and come to America," Stolz said. "You'll soon earn enough money to help pay for their voyages. They would be fools to stay in Prussia. There are more opportunities here."

"This is one fine Arabian horse," August said as he pulled the reins. "You must be doing pretty well here in America—a house and two beautiful horses."

"Yes, indeed," Stolz said. "I bought both of these from a man at the factory who was moving out West to Kansas."

"How do you like working at the factory?"

"It's a job. It pays the bills. Say, are you hungry?"

"I didn't eat much on the train. I could eat an elephant if someone put it in front of me."

"I don't cook much since I'm by myself, but I do have some bread, ham and cheese if you're interested."

"Nothing better than a place to sleep and food to eat. I'm much obliged to you, my friend."

"You'd do the same for me."

They rode the rest of the way in silence. A few horse-drawn streetcar lines were operating which enabled some people to leave the most congested districts. But, most Chicagoans inhabited tiny wood-framed houses that lacked water or sewage facilities. Most walked to work along crowded, wagon-rutted, dirty, garbage-strewn streets. Finally they reached Stolz's small wood-frame house at 45 West Monroe, located several blocks away from Michigan Avenue in the heart of Chicago.

When they got to the one-bedroom house, August put his rucksack in the kitchen and went to the outhouse in the backyard to relieve himself. That night he slept in the same bedroom as Stolz and woke up early the next morning. They ate a breakfast of bread, eggs and sausage and then saddled their horses and rode a short distance to attend morning Mass at St. Francis of Assisi Church,[16] on West Roosevelt Road in the German section of Chicago.

Before Mass, August knelt down and said a prayer.

Thank you, dear Lord, for this glorious day, for keeping me safe on my journey, for my health and for my good friends who met me at the train station. Please bless my family in Grabionna and let them know I love and miss them. Help me earn enough money to help them come to America. Help me also to one day own my own property. Please give me strength and courage to meet my blacksmith sponsor today. In nómine Patris, et Fĭlii, et Spĭritus Sancti, Amen

After Mass, Stolz and August rode to the train depot at the corner of Canal and Kinzie where August boarded a train to Cottage Hill, Illinois, in nearby DuPage County, to meet his sponsor.

Walking in the scorching hot July air, he noticed the warmer shift in the temperature from when he got off the boat in New York City's harbor, and took off his black, homespun jacket. He also noticed that the elliptical leaves on the young elm trees in a nearby grove had budded in shades of bright green. Hearing the sound of his own footsteps scraping the rutted, dirt road, he walked from the train depot, heading east two blocks, till he reached #15 on Addison Street.

The sign on the door of the shop said:

Horseshoer—A. WEINREBE—Village Blacksmith

The small wood shop was attached to the house. Remnants of horseshoes were scattered on the wooden floor beneath the thigh-high anvil in the building.

August noticed that not much light came in from the windows; the shop was dark except for the light from kerosene lamps. He observed the familiar blacksmith tools like the anvil and hammer as well as a supply of various size horseshoes hung on horizontal poles covering one wall. He felt at home here, since the shop was almost the same as the blacksmith shop he had left in *Grabionna*.

August Weinrebe, his blacksmith sponsor, was fifty years old with blond hair turning gray, he wore a red plaid work shirt, a heavy blacksmith apron and blacksmith cap.

Moving a lantern over to the horseshoe bin, Weinrebe selected a horseshoe, heated the U-shaped iron flaming red-hot, placed the iron shoe on the horse's left hoof, shaped it to the hoof, and then dunked the iron in cold water. He pounded each square nail through the pre-cut hole in the horseshoe till he had all the nails in place when August appeared at the door.

August cleared his throat.

"Mr. Weinrebe?"

"Yes, that's me." Weinrebe looked up from his work. "And who might you be?"

"Katzenmeier."

Weinrebe rubbed the dust from his fingers and extended his calloused hand toward August. "Welcome. How was your voyage?"

"With God's help we made it."

"Glad you are here, Mr. Katzenmeier."

August hesitated. *How can I tell him that's not my real name?* "My friend, I have something important to tell you," he said. "Even though my passport says otherwise, well..." He paused, finding the words difficult. "My real name is August Kopczynski."

Weinrebe's eyes popped wide and he gulped as if he had swallowed a canary. "Why, you goddamn liar! How can I ever trust you? I suppose now you're going to tell me you're not going to work for me to pay off your debt."

"No, that's not how it will be. Listen. I can explain..."

Weinrebe frowned. "Go ahead."

August explained that he fought in the Danish-Prussian war and the war against the Austrians and then how a Prussian officer came to his blacksmith shop, roughed him up for speaking out against Prussia and threatened to shoot or hang him if he didn't show up for service in the Franco-Prussian war, so he left under a false passport.

August noticed Weinrebe's face softened. He looked curious. "What are you hoping to find here in America?" Weinrebe said.

"Like a lot of other immigrants, I want freedom. Freedom to say what I want without being betrayed to the authorities for something I criticized them for. Freedom to voice my own opinion without reprisals."

Weinrebe didn't respond, so August felt compelled to fill the silence. "And I hope I can practice my Catholic faith in peace."

"Oh, so you're Catholic?"

"Yes, and you?"

"Lutheran."

There was an awkward silence. When August was a young boy, the Lutherans in *Grabionna* bullied him. They used to call him names and throw rocks at him when he walked home from school. He had to learn how to defend himself and his faith.

"I might have guessed," August said finally. "In *Grabionna*, Lutherans outnumbered Catholics. We were a minority."

"How many people live in *Grabionna*?"

"There are 348. It has about 245 Lutherans, 95 Catholics and a tiny amount of Jews and Calvinists. And, how many people live in Cottage Hill?"

"It's almost the same size. There are 329 people living here, but the town is growing, and we expect Cottage Hill's name to be changed to Elmhurst[17] in a couple of years, even though the name change doesn't make sense to me. One of the great things about America is that all religions are welcome here. I assure you, you will find it pleasant here. What will you do if I tell you that you can't work here but you need to pay back the money I spent on your voyage?"

"I have friends here who will help me, but I suppose I'll starve until I find work elsewhere. I am reliable and a hard worker. I promise you won't be disappointed."

Weinrebe raised his eyebrows and his frown turned into a smile. "All right, as far as the job is concerned, it is yours if you still want it, but I don't want any nonsense. I expect you to work the full two years to pay off your debt."

August nodded in agreement.

"Ok, then, let's go inside."

August picked up his bag and they entered the wood-frame part of the house which was connected to the blacksmith shop. Weinrebe told August he was to have a room of his own in the house and eat his meals with their family.

"I want you to meet my wife, Christina, who is from Hanover, Germany, and my two daughters—Mary and Caroline. Come here, girls. Say hello to August."

Mary was fifteen with long dark curls and brown eyes. She curtsied as her father introduced her. "Please to meet you, Sir."

Caroline was eleven, had shiny blond hair, piercing blue eyes and looked as old as Marie whom August had met on the boat. She also curtsied.

"Hello, Mr. . . .What is your last name, Sir?"

"Kopczynski."

"Oh. Pleased to meet you."

Weinrebe interrupted. "I also want to introduce you to Henry Weinrebe, another blacksmith in our shop, who is not related to me but also comes from Holstein, like I did. He is Mary's age. You'll like him."

August held out his hand to Mr. Weinrebe. "Thank you again, my friend. I promise I'll do a good job for you. You have my word."

Chapter 11

August was hammering a shoe on the anvil two weeks later when Caroline Weinrebe strolled in. Eleven years to his twenty-one, he felt she was like a little sister. If only she was a little older, say sixteen, which would be more acceptable for a man his age to court, she would still be off limits because she was his boss's daughter and she wasn't Catholic. Yet he felt attracted to her. She had shiny blonde hair which reminded him of a sunny day and she had a sunny disposition to match. The flowery perfume she wore made him think of springtime in Poland.

"Guten Morgen, Herr..." She struggled to pronounce his last name. "Kopscrynthis... I mean Kopskinski...er Kopschinski. I can never pronounce your last name."

August smiled. *"Guten Morgan, Caroline. Bitte,* call me August. How can I help you, my young friend? *Du schaust heute sehr schön aus!"* He regretted his words complimenting her looks immediately, afraid she might misconstrue them as flirting.

She blushed. "Dad wanted to know if you'll be here this afternoon."

He stopped pounding the horseshoe on the anvil and smoothed his blacksmith apron. "You can tell your dad I had planned to go to church to confession but I can be here if he wants me to be."

Curious, she lingered, standing by the door. "Do you go to confession every Saturday? You seem like a good man. What kind of sins do you have to confess, August?" She arched a questioning eyebrow in his direction.

Her brazen question made him wince. "Yes, I try to go every Saturday. Confession is good for the soul. We are all sinners, after all. Even you." He winked at her.

Caroline's eyes popped wide and she glanced at August with a puzzled look on her face. "Why do you tell your sins to the priest?"

"We believe the priest represents God."

Caroline was too polite to respond negatively to his answer, but got braver with another question. "You pray to statues, too, don't you?"

He rolled his eyes. "We don't pray to statues. We pray to the people they represent."

"Oh," she said, in a matter-of-fact tone. She moved closer to where he was working and looked up at him. Her face glowed in the light from the kerosene lamp. His heart fluttered and he felt his breath become shallow. He sensed a danger in falling in love with a non-Catholic and someone who was definitely too young for him, but he was overcome with feelings for her. He pushed them out of his mind.

"Dad said Lutherans like us read our Bibles and believe in Jesus Christ but you believe in the Virgin Mary, don't you, August?"

He winced again. He remembered how he had to defend his faith to the Lutheran bullies who threw rocks at him in

Grabionna. Must I always defend my faith? Even here in America? To this young girl?

He locked eyes with Caroline. "The priest interprets the Bible for us. Catholics believe in Jesus Christ, too, but we also pray to Mary. It's like as a child you also ask favors from your Mom, not just your Dad."

"I noticed you carry a rosary in your pocket. You pray to Mary when you're fingering your rosary beads?"

"Yes, we pray the Hail Mary and the Our Father when we pray the rosary. Never underestimate the power of prayer, Caroline. When we are struggling, we pray to God for calmness and peace, peace in our hearts, peace in our souls. Polish people, like me, pray to the Black Madonna, Our Lady of *Częstochowa*. People travel far distances to see her at *the Jasna Góra* Monastery in *Częstochowa*, Poland. It's now pretty much a shrine."

The corners of his mouth turned into a smile. There was chemistry between them, although not the chemistry he had felt with Marie on the boat. He and Caroline could be more than just a brother and sister though. They could be pals.

He noticed Caroline suddenly looked away as if unconvinced, uninterested. He felt he wouldn't have listened when he was her age either. He tried to explain further.

"Praying to the Black Madonna for the past six-hundred years has given thousands of Polish people hope in overcoming their struggles against the German colonizers and other invaders. Poland has no natural barriers, so it has been and probably always will be invaded. You're too young, my friend, to know all about this, but one day you will understand."

Caroline smiled and batted her eyelashes. "Why is the Madonna black? Are there Negros in Poland?"

August returned her smile. *She seems to like me.* "No, most Polish people are white. It's still a mystery why the icon is black but it could be because the painting blackened with age over the years."

He wondered if he should pursue Caroline when she was a little older even though she was of a different faith. Would they have problems later on because of it? Would her father ever accept him? How would they raise their kids? Catholics or Lutherans? He definitely was thinking too far ahead.

Caroline turned to go back in the house. "I'll tell Dad that you need to go to church. Nice talking with you. See you later, August."

"Okay," August said. "Tell your Dad I'll be in for lunch as soon as I finish here.

Chapter 12

Days turned into months as August continued working from sun up till sun down in Weinrebe's blacksmith shop. On Christmas Eve 1867, August watched the sun set over the new fallen snow outside the shop. Although he got along well with the Weinrebe family, his heart ached for the family he left behind in Grabionna. He had written them a letter to let them know where he was and what had happened to him. The outpouring of love in their letters only made him miss them all the more. That night he wrote the following reply by candlelight:

My beloved sister, Henrietta:

I got your letter and card. How much I miss you. I'm sorry things are not good between you and Rosalia. I'm grateful for the care Rosalia gave me after Mother passed away but I always felt she was partial to her own children, not us, her stepchildren. I'm sure you feel the same way.

I make good money here. I am able to pay Weinrebe back for my passage and have more money left over each month. I am willing to pay for your passage if you want to come to America.

If you come, the best time to leave Hamburg is in early April so you'll arrive in New York City in early

June. You'll spend your 25th birthday on the ship. Perhaps Emil will come with you. From New York, take a train to Chicago and I'll meet you at the New Depot train station, which is at the corner of Sherman and Van Buren streets.

When you and Emil arrive, I'll treat you both to tickets to see a traveling circus[18]—P. T. Barnum's Grand Traveling Museum, Menagerie, Caravan & Hippodrome. I've heard about it but haven't been to it yet. It's billed as thrilling performances and curiosities, including albinos, the Feejee mermaid (a creature with the head of a monkey and the tail of a fish), the world-famous dwarf, "General Tom Thumb," fat boys, giants, midgets, American Indian dancers, magicians, jugglers, and exotic women.

Although I'm one who thinks it might be wrong to go to the circus, they say the menagerie of animals and the clowns are really something to see and the tents are so crowded every afternoon and evening, there's a chance of suffocation. I have to see it at least once.

Give my love to Mary and Wilhelm. I hope one day they will also come to America. I cannot tell you how much better life is here. I learn about new opportunities every day.

God bless you.
Love,
Your brother, August

He folded the letter, inserted it into an envelope, and affixed a stamp. He would drop it in the outgoing post tomorrow when he rode to Chicago for Mass. He figured Henrietta would receive it in late January, enough time to correspond and receive money for the voyage she would take in early April.

Henrietta left Hamburg April 1, 1868, on the John Bertram clipper ship with her boyfriend, Emil Bensbemink who was her age. Although it was unusual for a girl not to be married at twenty-five, Henrietta wasn't just like any girl. She knew how much work raising kids was—after all, she had helped Rosalia raise her step-brother and five step-sisters. She was in no hurry to marry and have kids of her own. Henrietta had a manly-looking face and wore her hair pulled back in a bun. She was also headstrong and domineering and needed a strong man to tame her. She hadn't found one until she met Emil.

Traveling with them were their friends, Ernest Reide and his wife, Matilda, who were also from *Grabionna*. They arrived in New York City in early June and took a train to the New Depot train station in Chicago where August was waiting.

"My dear sister," he said, squeezing her. "I'm blessed. I'm so happy you're here." He kissed her on the cheek. She hugged him back.

August thought Henrietta's face looked pale as if she were frightened he might not have shown up, yet he never mentioned it. He felt the ache in his heart, the loneliness, the longing to be reunited with his family, had all but disappeared. Henrietta's arrival had breathed new life into him.

"August," Henrietta said, with her arm around August's shoulder. "You do remember, Emil, don't you?"

Emil held out his hand, but August was so overcome with emotion, he hugged Emil, too. "Welcome to Chicago," he said.

"You'll like living here. How was your voyage? Did you celebrate Henrietta's birthday aboard the ship?"

"We did," Emil said, in an enthusiastic tone. "The voyage was long, of course, but rather uneventful. Her birthday was the highlight. We danced on deck until the wee hours of the morning and the cooks even made a birthday cake for her."

I like that boyfriend of hers—Emil. I've always liked him. He seems to be a man of good character. I hope it will work out between them.

"I'm glad to be in America on firm ground," Henrietta said, smiling. "The boat often rolled one way, then the other. Made me seasick."

"I know the feeling." August laughed, remembering green pea soup all over the floor. "Listen, I made reservations for you at a nearby boarding house. It's not elegant, but comfortable and the price was right. I can help Emil carry your trunk."

"You're too kind, dear brother," Henrietta said. "We have a lot to talk about."

"We do indeed. Tell me more about what happened after I left."

"Father and Wilhelm took your departure hard. And Rosalia couldn't stop crying."

"I'm sorry," August said, lowering his eyes, feeling remorse over what he had done. After a short pause, he raised his eyes. "Was Wilhelm able to retrieve my horse from the train station?"

"Yes," Henrietta said. "Your horse is doing fine. I wish I could say the same about Wilhelm. He is lost without you."

"I shall write him and invite him to America. Rosalia wrote me that she and father had a baby in November who they named Michteldis Rosalia."

"Yes," Henrietta said. "The house is getting more crowded each day and Rosalia is in a family way again. This will be her eighth child. Father expected me to do most of the work around the house. I just couldn't stand it anymore. It was time for me to leave and get on with my own life."

"I'm so excited and happy you've come. I can help you find work here. I know of a doctor and his wife who need help with housework."

Henrietta smiled as if he had just made her the happiest girl on earth. "That would be perfect."

"I would do anything for you, Henrietta. You mean that much to me."

By mid-June, August rode to the widely-advertised circus in a wagon with the Weinrebe family on a Saturday afternoon, amid laughter and excitement. He had hoped to only invite Caroline but it was clear to him that he couldn't do that. Her dad would never have allowed it. So, he invited the whole family and Mr. Weinrebe took him up on his offer. Emil and Henrietta were waiting for them at the entrance.

In the middle of Big Top was a forty-two-foot ring where stunning acrobats, tightrope walkers, trapeze artists, jugglers and clowns performed as well as a display of exotic animals in a menagerie. The audience sat in curved rows of seats surrounding the ring.

It was hot inside the tent and the smell of sawdust wafted in the air. They heard a circus band with brass instruments and drums warming up and took their seats inside the already-crowded big tent, seated next to each other: Emil, Henrietta, August, Mr. Weinrebe, Caroline, Mary and Mrs. Weinrebe.

Soon the lights were lowered and amidst the darkness a spotlight highlighted the center of the ring. Barnum, the ringmaster, appeared wearing a black velvet jacket, white linen shirt and tan pants and he introduced each act, the first of which was an acrobat dressed in an aqua sequined costume and plumed headdress.

The young woman in costume walked on tightened ropes about twenty feet off the ground high above the circus ring carrying an umbrella as a balancing tool. She had a very good sense of balance and body control, performing graceful, lithe maneuvers. At one point, however, as she tried to run across the rope, she tittered and almost fell as the audience gasped, but she managed to regain her composure. After her performance, the tent swelled with applause.

Clowns wearing oversized jackets and trousers, large shoes and tiny hats with their faces painted with white grease entertained the crowd in the pauses between acts with their clever wit and songs: "Old Zip Coon," "Billy Barlow," and "Sweet Kitty Clover, She Bothers Me So."

August's heart thumped so fast he was afraid it might pop out of his chest. The clowns were better than he had imagined. He noticed Caroline giggling and turned toward her. "I'm glad to see you smile, Caroline," he said. Weinrebe glanced at him with suspicion, but August ignored it and continued. "How do you like the show so far?"

"I love it. Thanks for inviting me, August. This circus is the greatest thing I've ever seen."

"I am thankful your dad allowed you to come." Weinrebe nodded. August turned to face Henrietta and Emil. "And, what do you two think of it so far?"

"It's unbelievable," Emil said. "How does this guy Barnum do it? I never imagined something like this."

Weinrebe smiled, scratched his head and interrupted, turning toward August. "You weren't here in 1850, but Barnum promoted Jenny Lind, the soprano known as the Swedish Nightingale. I was thirty-three years old at the time."

August relished his relationship with Weinrebe and was grateful for the tidbits of history and information to learn more about the country which was becoming his own.

"The newspaper said Barnum promised to pay her an unprecedented $1,000 a night (plus expenses) for up to 150 concerts in the U.S."

"That must've been a risky proposition," August said.

"It was a huge risk. They say he had to commit over $187,000. But, the risk paid off for him. He's become the greatest showman on earth."

"I'll say he has," said Emil.

The circus continued. Barnum introduced some of his freaks like the albinos, the fat boy and finally the dwarf, "General Tom Thumb."

Weinrebe leaned in to August and chortled, "Barnum said Tom Thumb is eleven but the newspaper reported he is only four years old. His real name is Commodore Nutt. The kid has natural talent—he can imitate both Hercules and Napoleon—but he has been heavily coached by Barnum. Look at that—a kid smoking a cigar!"

While the crowd roared with laughter, August cringed. *My father always told me to stand up for what I believe in, to fight for what's right.* "I'm not amused," he said, testing the waters, being unafraid to express his contrary views in an America which espoused freedom of speech. "These are human beings made by the same God who created you and me. I think Barnum's freak shows are disgusting. We are all God's creatures—even fat people, giants, midgets, dwarfs, albinos—everyone."

August noticed the horrified look on Caroline's face as she turned to her Dad to get his reaction.

"Why, it's all just for show!" Weinrebe said, shaking his head.

August's voice rose an octave. "It will affect future generations. Anyone a little different will be laughed at or thought of as a freak. It's a terrible thing. We shouldn't support someone who promotes this." He stood up to leave.

"Sit down. Be patient," Weinrebe commanded. "We haven't seen the menagerie of animals yet. Besides, Barnum doesn't mean any harm. It's just showmanship. Barnum started out as a showman when he exhibited a blind slave woman, named Joice Heth, who he claimed was George Washington's nurse, and to be over 160 years old. It was just one of his many hoaxes. Joice Heth died in 1836, at the age of eighty."

"What good is showmanship when it ruins the lives of human beings?" August said, as he sat back down. Weinrebe was his boss, after all, not the enemy. His views might be reasonable. Perhaps it was just a misunderstanding.

"Maybe so, but Barnum has done a lot of good for the slaves. He opposed the Kansas-Nebraska Act which supported slavery. It caused him to leave the Democratic Party. He became a member of the anti-slavery Republican Party."

August gritted his teeth for control. "Is that true?"

"Yes. Now he promotes and produces blackface minstrelsy. All minstrel performers,[19] are white men in blackfaces with white gloves. Many are educated musicians and comic actors. His minstrel shows often use satire to parody popular lectures today that try to "prove" the superiority of Whites. They refute it, using a Negro's dialect speech. I don't know about you, but I don't think the white race is necessarily superior."

August admired Weinrebe's intelligence and valued his opinion. After all, he had a successful blacksmith business and had been living in America longer. August looked up to him, regarded him as a father-figure, and felt Weinrebe could teach him ways to be successful.

August felt he was being challenged. "I've never met a Negro, so I don't really know how I would feel about them. However, I think all men, Negro or white, are created equal in the eyes of God."

"It was fugitive slaves or freedmen who established the first Negro community in Chicago," Weinrebe said. "I think it was around the 1840s." He put a hand on August's shoulder. "I see your view is based on your religion, which is not altogether bad. Just know, there are many, even in this tent, who would disagree with you. Emil, what is your opinion?"

Emil grimaced at being put on the spot. "It's hard to like someone who is different from you, who maybe has a different religion, maybe more or less money than you, or a different color of skin, but I agree with August that, like the Bible teaches, all men are created equal in the eyes of God."

"Henrietta, you're awfully quiet," said August. "Are you enjoying the show?"

"I'm speechless. This is better than I imagined. Thank you so much for inviting Emil and I. Oh, look, here come the cages with the big cats and bears. I don't want this night to end. I hope to remember it forever."

Ach du lieber Gott, look at them!" August said. The audience roared with applause and August clapped along with them. *"Sehr gut! Sehr gut!"*

"Now, aren't you glad you stayed?" Weinrebe said, smiling.

August returned the gesture. His smile grew wider until it reached his eyes.

<h1 style="text-align:center">Chapter 13</h1>

It was Saturday in late December 1869, there was a foot of snow on the ground and patches of ice on the wagon-rutted, dirt road. August felt chilled by a cold wind coming from the west as he rode his horse to a general merchandise store in Chicago to pick up a new saddle for himself and horseshoes and other supplies for Weinrebe. His thoughts were consumed by the news of his inheritance and he silently thanked God for his blessings.

August couldn't believe his good luck when he found out that he and Wilhelm were to receive an inheritance from their mother's property in the quiet village of *Grabionna*, then under Prussian rule.

Their mother, Rosalia Polej Kopczynski, died in 1851, when Wilhelm was only seventeen months old, and their father married Rosalia Lipinski in 1852. August and Wilhelm submitted a claim against Martin's property.

He drafted the following receipt for the inheritance:

Without further claim the undersigned persons shall receive a certain sum.

The following gentlemen are the recipients: August and Wilhelm Kopczynski, formerly of Grabionna, now of

Chicago. The mortgage book shows the following property at Grabionna: #12 Schnell Rubric III #2, for which they are to receive the following sum: 100.00 Thaler[20] as the inheritance from their mother's properties. This is dated June 11, 1853.

We have received 100.00 Thaler[21] either late 1869 or early 1870. We agree to nullify any further claims against the property of Martin Kopczynski of Grabionna, County of Bromberg. This said property is now up for sale. We ask you to stop any further court proceedings against Martin Kopczynski.

P.S. This receipt will have to be notarized here as well as by the Polish Consul.

The receipt was to be signed by both August and Wilhelm. Receiving this money came as a surprise to him. He wondered if he should save it to buy a house or land or to maybe own his own blacksmith shop. Or, should he give it to Henrietta in reparation for the money he stole from her in her youth? Or, should he buy a brand new Peter Schuttler wagon? Or, should he loan it to Mary to pay for her family's voyage to America? He said a prayer and asked God to help him decide.

August dismounted and went inside the store. As he stood inspecting a saddle, he was surprised to find Father Baak, the priest at St. Francis of Assisi church, a few feet away inspecting a different saddle.

"Father Baak, it's good to see you! What are you doing here?"

"Hello, August," he said, extending a hand. "Why, I heard about a sale on saddles, probably like you did. I needed a new one so here I am."

August shook his hand and then pointed to the saddle in front of him. "This leather one is a better deal, Father. It will last longer."

"A bit more than I was planning to spend. We priests need to be frugal."

"I'll help you pay, Father. I just received word that my brother and I are due to get an inheritance."

"Surely, you have other needs."

"I prayed to God earlier to help me make a good decision." August told the priest how he might otherwise use the money.

Father Baak put his arm on August's shoulder. "I am reminded of Psalm 112:5: "Well for the man who is gracious and lends." The priest paused, giving August a chance to think about those words. Then he continued: "In other words, good, meaning well-being and prosperity, will come to him who is generous and lends freely."

There was a comfortable silence. August stood dumbfounded, thinking about the priest's words. Maybe it was just a coincidence, but August felt he had the answer to his prayer. There was no question in his mind now of what he must do. He helped pay for Father Baak's saddle and would also help pay for Mary and her family's voyage to America.

Nineteen-year-old Wilhelm left *Grabionna* and embarked at *Hamburg* on the Friedeburg clipper sailing ship April 14, 1870

and arrived in New York's harbor in mid-June, just in time for Henrietta's wedding. From New York he took a train to the New Depot train station in Chicago where August was waiting to greet him. It had been three years since they had seen each other. Wilhelm had paid for his passage himself from his inheritance.

"Good to see you again," August said, slapping Wilhelm on the back.

"You've aged."

"So have you!"

"Where's Henrietta?" Wilhelm said.

"She couldn't get off from work. She's cleaning house for that rich doctor she lives with on Lake Shore Drive. She's their maid-servant like two thirds of female workers in this town. Henrietta said she'd see you tomorrow. She has Sundays off."

"I'm glad I arrived before her wedding."

"Yes, she and Emil planned it so that you could attend. They're getting married at St. Joseph's Church."

"Is that the church you attend?"

"No, I go to St. Francis of Assisi. St. Joseph's is located on South Heritage Avenue back of the Union Stockyards. It was built by Polish-German immigrants like us. The pastor speaks German. Henrietta and Emil like to go there."

"I like Emil a lot. He has always treated Henrietta well."

"I like him, too. He's a good man. So, tell me about your trip. Did you meet anyone interesting aboard the ship? Any girls, perhaps?"

"The ship was great," Wilhelm said. "A few storms, but not bad. The worst part was sleeping below deck with 500 people. The stench was unbelievable and the noise...babies crying...

homesick children. It's hard when you're not used to being around it all the time."

August nodded, remembering his own voyage.

"There were many eligible young girls on the ship. I got acquainted with some of them, even danced on deck with some, but at my age, I'm too young to settle down."

August smiled. "During my voyage I met a young girl named Marie. She was so pretty—fair complexion, coal black hair, tiny waist, lips that you'd want to kiss. It was love at first sight, although at the time I thought she was too young for me. I've never met anyone since who I like as much. I've never forgiven myself for not getting her address. I'd give anything to see her again."

Wilhelm's eyes lit up. "My brother who has an easy time falling in love with girls!"

"Hardly. Right now, I'm living in the same house as Caroline Weinrebe, my sponsor's daughter. She's about the same age as the girl I met on the boat, and I've got my eye on her, but she isn't Catholic. The Weinrebes are Lutherans."

"Ah, like those bullies we knew in *Grabionna*."

"No, these are nice folks, but they have some rather strange beliefs, like they're all about following Jesus Christ but they barely mention the Blessed Mother. So, how are Mama and Papa, Albert and the girls?"

Wilhelm smiled. "They're well. Mama is with child again. The baby is due in December. They're hoping for a boy this time. She asked me to give you her love."

"I miss her and the others." He sighed. "Are you ready to go to work? Stolz said he has a job for you at the factory."

"I can't believe I'll be making Peter Schuttler wagons. I'd give anything to own one."

"Me, too. They're pretty expensive. Save your money. There are a lot of things you'll want to buy in America. I'd like to own my own farmland someday. It's good to have dreams. It's different here than it was in Poland. Here your dreams might come true."

Emil and Henrietta were married in June 1870 in a small ceremony at St. Joseph's Church back of the Union Stockyards in Chicago. Henrietta wore a black wedding dress and white veil and August was best man at her wedding. Her matron of honor was a maidservant friend of hers. Wilhelm also attended as well as the doctor and his wife who employed Henrietta as a maidservant. They hosted a small reception for her at their residence.

"Look at them!" August said to Wilhelm at the reception. "Your sister has that star-struck, love-look in her eyes."

"Yes, I've never seen someone who looked more in love," Wilhelm said, nodding.

"I'm so happy for them," August said. He put the cake down that he was eating and wiped his mouth with a napkin. "Henrietta has wanted this for a long time. She risked everything by coming to America. She deserves a good man like Emil. She deserves happiness."

Henrietta moved in with Emil and nine months later, March 25, 1871, Henrietta bore a son, Edwin. August and Wilhelm rode their horses over to Emil's and Henrietta's to inspect the newborn.

"What a cute baby Edwin is!" August said. "You make us very proud uncles, Henrietta, and also a little bit jealous." He winked at her.

"You will have children one day, August," Henrietta said, smiling. "I'm sure of it."

"I'm not even married. I have no prospects, except Caroline." He rolled his eyes. "And she probably wouldn't want to raise her children as Catholics."

Henrietta kissed Edwin's cheek and changed the subject. "I was always close to Mary growing up and wish she could have been here for my wedding and the birth of my first child." Her eyes teared up as she said it and her voice cracked.

"She and Anton and the boys will be here soon enough," August said. "They're leaving *Grabionna* in April and will arrive in New York harbor in June. You can bring the baby and come with me to pick them up at the New Depot train station."

"Did you pay for Mary's passage?"

"I sent them some money, yes."

"All of us are deeply indebted to you, August."

You wouldn't think that if you knew I stole from you as a kid.

"I'm just happy our family will be reunited. It was painful to be alone here without family. We'll finally be together again. I think our mother would be proud and is smiling in heaven."

Chapter 14

August continued working hard for Weinrebe, putting in long, grueling hours at his blacksmith shop to try to get ahead. On a balmy Monday, on the 9th of October 1871, he noticed the sky at sunrise was a hazy orange and the air smelled foul, but the air in his shop always smelled foul so he didn't think anything more about it until a customer came into the shop. He was someone August didn't recognize, so he straightened up and his voice became more businesslike.

"The wheel is loose on my wagon and my horse needs a new shoe."

"I can fix that, my friend. Let me take a look." He lifted up the horse's hoof, took off the old horseshoe and eyeballed the size of it. Then he retrieved a new one made of wrought iron about the same size off the wall of horseshoes. "Are you from around here? Do you live in Elmhurst?"

"No, I'm from Chicago. You've heard about Sunday's fire, haven't you?"

August's mind raced. *A fire? In Chicago?* "No, what fire?" August put the new horseshoe into the furnace and heated it until the metal first glowed red, then turned a bright yellow-orange. With tongs, he carefully lifted the horseshoe out, fitted it on the horse's hoof, then laid it on the anvil and began hammering the shoe into the desired shape.

The customer watched him intently and waited until the noise subsided before he spoke. "My brother is a news reporter for the *Chicago Evening Journal*. He said they are running a story about the fire in today's Journal."

"What did he say?"

"He said the fire broke out on the corner of DeKoven and Twelfth streets, at about 9 o'clock last night."

August stopped what he was doing to listen.

"Apparently the blaze started in Patrick O'Leary's barn. Mrs. O'Leary lit a lantern in her shed and the cow kicked it over, starting the fire."

"*Ach, du lieber, Gott.* How big a fire was it?"

"My brother said the fire destroyed factories, offices, hotels, boardinghouses, homes, saloons, lumber and coal yards, and warehouses. It affected nearly all of the city east of the river from Fullerton on the north to Harrison on the south."

I need to get to my family as soon as possible to know what's going on. Henrietta, Mary and Wilhelm might be hurt! August motioned for the man to leave, but he didn't take the hint.

"There's more. I heard more than sixty insurance companies went bankrupt. Over 100,000 people were left homeless and three hundred died. I keep thinking why did it happen to them and not me? Why am I still alive?"

"I'm sorry, but I need to hurry." August finished pounding the nails into the horse's hoof and then began tightening up the loose wheel on the wagon. "I need to find out about my brother and two sisters who live in Chicago. I need to find out if they are safe."

"Before you go, I'm collecting money for those left homeless. I was wondering, could you spare a dime?"

Caught off guard, August paused a moment, thinking. He thought about what he would feel like if he or a relative or a friend had lost everything in the fire. He thought about his faith and the homily the priest gave last Sunday about a poor widow who put in two very small copper coins into the temple treasury and how she in her poverty had put in more than all the others. *How could I not help?*

"I can spare more than a dime, my friend. God has blessed me. I'm glad I live in Elmhurst and not Chicago. I've been very fortunate. I have no wife or kids to support. I don't mean to brag but just last year I received an inheritance from my mother's property in Poland. I used the money to help my sister and her family make their voyage to America."

He reached in his pocket for some coins. "I'm a Polish Catholic and we Kopczynskis believe in helping those in need, those less fortunate. You can count on my contribution. I'm glad to help. There is no charge for today and here is some extra money to help the homeless."

"That's mighty kind and generous of you."

"I feel it's the least I can do. It might be my relatives who are left homeless. I have enough money to help them, too. Now, if you'll excuse me, I must be going."

"Thank you."

"Stay in touch, my friend."

Chapter 15

Minutes later, Wilhelm, riding his Arabian, halted the horse outside Weinrebe's blacksmith shop and shouted at August.

"August, come quick!" he said at the top of his lungs. "There's been a fire in Chicago. The flames are still burning."

"I just heard about it." August came running out. "Is everyone okay?"

"Henrietta and baby Edwin are okay." He paused as he got off his horse and approached August. "But Emil. . . he didn't make it."

"Dead?" August asked.

Wilhelm nodded.

August cupped his hands over his mouth. *"Ach du lieber Gott!"*

"I'm so sorry, August."

"What about Mary, Anton and the boys?"

"They're okay. The fire didn't reach the west side. I took Henrietta and Edwin over to their house to stay with them. Henrietta is not doing so well, August." Wilhelm put his hands on August's shoulder. "She is distraught. She needs you."

August didn't hesitate. "Let's head over there. Let me saddle up my horse. You can tell me what happened as we ride over there."

Minutes later, they headed east to Mary and Anton's house at 127 Barber Street.

"The fire spread quickly in their neighborhood. No one had water to put it out. Henrietta and Edwin escaped by the grace of God, but Emil went back inside to get their wedding photos." He paused as he noticed August's gaze on him. "He never made it out."

"*Photos?* He went back in to get their *photos?*"

"Yes, August. Precious memories of their lives together."

"And now they are charred remains and so is he."

Wilhelm didn't say anything.

"Where were you when all of this was going on?" August's voice seemed to carry a tinge of reproach. He couldn't tell where his anger came from, except that he didn't understand God's plan if it included taking the life of his sister's husband at a time she most needed him.

"I rushed over there to help as soon as I'd heard that the fire spread to Henrietta's neighborhood. When I got there, Henrietta was outside the house holding onto Edwin, screaming. I couldn't calm her down. She kept yelling for Emil, but bystanders told me there was no way he'd still be alive. Apparently he'd been in that inferno for twenty minutes."

"So the house was still in flames when you got there?"

"Not really. I mean there were still some flames, harmless ones, you know, but the house was no longer there."

"All gone? She was sitting there in front of a heap of ashes?" August asked as he stopped his horse and looked at Wilhelm.

Wilhelm swallowed hard. "I didn't know what to do. Finally I persuaded her to go to Mary and Anton's house. She protested at first because the Ottos already had a houseful and

Mary was with child again, but Henrietta finally relented... There were no other options."

August and Wilhelm rode in silence the rest of the way.

"I'm so sorry," August said as Henrietta fell into his arms. Her eyes were swollen and red; tears rolled down her cheeks.

"I can't believe this happened to me." Her voice cracked. "What should I do now? Where will we live? How can I support Edwin on my own?"

"Don't worry about that now," August said embracing her tightly. "Put your trust in God. He will see to it that you are taken care of."

"Will he? Why did he let Emil die if he is concerned about my welfare?" Henrietta yelled as she pushed August away from her.

"Henrietta!"

"I am nothing without Emil!"

"I know you're grieving right now, but your brothers and sister love and care about you, care about what happens to you." August approached her calmly, took her face in his hands and gently wiped away her tears. "We will help you. I won't let you and Edwin starve."

August hugged Henrietta again. He and Wilhelm left. After they mounted their horses, Wilhelm broke the silence.

"What do you think will happen to Henrietta?"

"Henrietta's in a desperate situation. Most women in her predicament get married right away. She is a tough woman, but she can't support herself and Edwin on her salary alone. And neither you nor I have the money to support her. She needs a moment to grieve, but she also needs to get married again, and soon." He knit his eyebrows in concentration. "But, to who?"

"What about Stolz?" Wilhelm said.

"That's a great idea," August said. "But, it might take a miracle to persuade him, especially since Henrietta comes with a baby. But, it's worth a try. I'll talk to him."

The next Saturday August rode over to Stolz's house at 45 West Monroe and brought beer and cigars along with him. The house had miraculously escaped the fire. Stolz ushered him inside. They sat at the kitchen table, drinking a beer and smoking a cigar.

August took a sip of beer. "I see you survived the fire. How's life and work been treatin' you?"

"Can't complain," Stolz said, puffing on a cigar. "At least I'm still alive and have a job. What's new with you?"

"My sister, Mary's third child is due soon. She said if it was a boy, they're going to name it after me and call him Gus for short. Just what we need—another August! Don't think I'll ever name one of my kids August. But, I've always wanted a *Stammhalter*. How about you? Do you care if there are any Stolz boys left after you die?"

"I never really thought about having kids. I guess I should, maybe. Never found a woman to marry. I think I need to find one first."

Here's my chance. "I'm glad you brought that up. My sister, Henrietta, is available. She just lost her husband in the fire. It was such a tragedy. Henrietta's a strong woman and would make a nice pioneer wife. She's also an obedient, devout Catholic. Only problem is she has a six-month-old son. He's a good baby, doesn't cry much. A woman can't support a child on a maid's salary though. You won't be disappointed if you marry her. She cleans house real well and she's a great cook."

"I'll think about it." He leaned back in his chair, took another puff on his cigar and blew smoke rings.

"How old are you?"

"I'm thirty-one. I'll be thirty-two in January."

August took another drink of beer and drained half the bottle. "Henrietta is twenty-eight. Just perfect for you. It's time an old bachelor like you got married."

"I suppose you're right. But, I don't know if I'm ready to be a father. That's a lot of responsibility, plus he wasn't born of my blood. I don't know if I can accept that."

"If you do marry her, no one, except our families, will ever know she was married before. No one will ever know the baby isn't yours. People forget things like that over time. Besides, all the records were destroyed in the fire, including all the records at St. Joseph's Church since it burned down."

Stolz gulped down his beer. "But *I* will know. But, of course, he might accept me as his father. He's young enough not to know any different. Will it be too soon to call on your sister next week?"

"Praise God, no. I'm sure she'd be delighted and grateful. She's staying with Mary and Anton on Barber Street in West Chicago. I'll tell her to expect you."

August knew he had some fast talking to do to convince Henrietta that she needed to marry Stolz. He thought about the objections she might have like it was too soon after Emil's death or that Stolz was nowhere near the man Emil was or that maybe the family could help share the burden or cost of raising Edwin. *This is not going to be easy. Dear God, please help me say the right words to her.*

He rushed over to Mary's house and found Henrietta alone in the kitchen nursing Edwin. She covered her breast and the baby's head with a soft blanket.

He took off his hat and sat down at the table. "I am on my way back home from visiting Stolz and I thought I'd stop by and see how you are doing."

"As well as can be expected." Her eyes teared up. "I'm doing the best I can."

"Stolz also asked how you were doing. He was glad you and Edwin survived the fire. He cares about you, Henrietta, cares about your welfare."

"Don't tell me this now. It's too soon." She pushed him away. "I can't think about anything now except for Emil." She started sobbing.

August put his arm around her shoulder. "There, there, Henrietta. I know this is a hard time for you right now, but you've got to think of Edwin's welfare. You can't raise him on your own and God knows your family doesn't have the wherewithal to help you."

By the look on her face, August could tell she didn't like the choices she was faced with. "But Stolz isn't anything like Emil. I hardly know him."

"He's a devout Catholic and one of the hardest working men I have ever met. Plus he owns a house and two horses. You'd be better off with him."

"His ears stick out and his clothes looked unkempt in church last Sunday. He had on a shirt that was torn at the sleeves and no buttons."

Her honesty astonished August. "His looks will grow on you. Besides, you can't be picky at your age. Listen to me, Henrietta. You need to do this—for Edwin, if not yourself. Just tell me you'll agree to a visit from him."

Henrietta hesitated.

"You know I only have your best interests at heart. You won't regret it, I promise."

She shrugged. "Oh, all right, if I must. I'll do it for Edwin." She caressed the baby's cheek and rumpled his hair.

"Give me a hug. I've got to get going. Stolz will call on you next week. Life is never easy but it will get better I promise you."

Henrietta and August Stolz were married three months later on his birthday, January 6, in 1872 at St. Francis of Assisi Church.

Chapter 16

August continued working for Weinrebe after he had fulfilled his obligation, partly out of loyalty but also because he made good money, liked the small town of Elmhurst, and had few other prospects for work.

By April 1872, he had finally worked up the courage to invite Caroline Weinrebe to attend Mass at St. Francis of Assisi Church with him in downtown Chicago.

August felt a cold chill as he approached Weinrebe in the front room of the house to ask his permission. He swallowed hard. "Sir, I promise I'll take good care of your daughter if you let her go with me to church today."

Weinrebe's brow furrowed. "I hope you're not trying to convert her."

"That thought never crossed my mind," August said, a drop of sweat falling from his forehead.

"So, why do you want her to go to church with you?"

"Caroline has a high sense of curiosity. She's asked me several questions about my religion and I thought I'd take her to church to see for herself my peculiar faith."

"You wouldn't be planning to marry her, would you?" Weinrebe said. "She's too young."

"No, no, no. I couldn't agree more with you. You don't have to worry about me. Your daughter is safe. I'm only asking your permission for her to accompany me this one time to Mass."

Weinrebe hesitated. "Well, I guess it couldn't hurt. I expect you to take good care of her and return her here soon after the service is over."

"You have my word, Sir."

The sun peeked out and started to warm the surrounding area, but August and Caroline felt a cool breeze on their backs as they rode horses together early Sunday morning from Elmhurst down Roosevelt Road to Newberry Avenue in the German section of Chicago.

When they got to the church, Caroline's eyes perked up. She politely remarked how lovely it was and what a tall steeple it would have when it was finished with construction.

"It is the same as the church in Poland," August said. Upon entering the church, he took off his hat, dipped his hand in the holy water font in the back, and made the sign of the cross, whispering the words in Latin. *"In nómine Patris, et Fĭlii, et Spĭritus Sancti, Amen."*

He and Caroline gazed at the main altar, above which stood an oversized picture of the Virgin Mary, Our Lady of Guadalupe, standing in front of Juan Diego with his arms and hands outstretched. August whispered to Caroline as they stood in the back of the church. He told her that Juan Diego saw an apparition of the Virgin Mary on December 9, 1531 at the Hill of Tepeyac, near Mexico City. Juan had asked the lady, who wanted a shrine built in her honor, for a miraculous sign to prove she was truly the Virgin Mary.

Rather than describe the lengthy process it takes for the Roman Catholic Church to document a miracle, August just told Caroline the first sign was Juan's uncle's healing and the second was Castilian roses, normally not found in Mexico, inside Juan's cloak, with an impression of Mary on the fabric.

Caroline arched an eyebrow but politely nodded as if she understood.

August also pointed out that to the left of Our Lady of Guadalupe on the main altar, stood a statue of St. Patrick, and to her right a statue of St. Joseph. Below, in the middle, a golden tabernacle rested where consecrated hosts were kept, which Catholics believed symbolized the Body of Christ.

August strode quietly and confidently up to the front of the church, genuflected as a sign of respect and knelt down in the fifth pew from the front. Out of habit, he always sat in this same pew every Sunday. Caroline followed, although she sat down instead of kneeling.

The pew had uncomfortable wooden benches with no padding on the kneelers, but that didn't discourage August. He fingered his amber rosary beads, and took out his prayer book to pray before mass started.

He prayed that Poland would be a country again one day and that it would be free from its oppressors. He prayed for his brother Wilhelm and his sisters Mary and Henrietta who lived in Chicago, and the rest of the family left behind in what was once Poland. He thanked God for the Weinrebe family even though they were Lutherans. He even prayed for the Prussian officer who had caused him harm back in *Grabionna.*

He smelled incense and heard the soft rustle of other people gathering in church pews as they genuflected and knelt down. The soft sounds evoked a sense of quiet and stillness echoing within the walls of the church.

"Why doesn't the priest turn around and face us?" Caroline was puzzled when the priest said the Mass in Latin with his back to the congregation.

"We Catholics believe that God is present in the Tabernacle, therefore, the priest prays to Him," August whispered. "He faces the congregation during his sermon."

The Latin Mass and hymns were familiar to August from Mass in Poland. Even though he didn't understand Latin, he could read the words along with the priest in his missal.

Besides, reciting the same prayers over and over felt as healthy as if he were reciting a mantra. It also felt comforting, like he had never left home, like he had returned to his youth. Life changed but his Catholic faith and the Catholic services he attended remained the one constant in his life.

The church could seat 150 parishioners comfortably; each pew allowing for ten people. He knelt down several times throughout the service as a sign of respect, especially when the Host was raised.

Caroline whispered, "August, are these ups and downs in the service so that people won't fall asleep?"

August smiled and shook his head. "No," he whispered, "We stand while the gospel is read, sit down when the Epistle is read, sit down when the priest preaches the homily, and kneel at other times."

"It doesn't make any sense to me," Caroline said, rolling her eyes and shrugging her shoulders.

August phrased it another way. "We sit when we are learning, stand when we are praying, and kneel to show reverence. Shhhh, now," he whispered. "We're not allowed to talk in church. If you still don't understand, I'll explain later."

At communion, the first row stood up and got in line to receive the Host. A tall man with a toddler in his arms, handed the little girl, dressed in a pale yellow dress, to one of his youngest daughters, and took his place in line, and eventually knelt down at the communion rail to receive the Host.

The dark-haired, two-year-old girl, the tall man had left behind, yelled at the top of her foghorn voice, "I...WANT...MY...DADDY," her arms outstretched and her voice echoing within the vast walls of the church.

Soon, all eyes were on her. August watched as she fought with her sibling, and moved to the right side of the pew where the line of parishioners were coming back from communion, so she could be reunited with her daddy.

August cautioned Caroline to remain seated, since only Catholics were allowed to receive communion, while he stood up to get in line. As he observed the reunion of the toddler and her daddy, he spied a girl directly behind the man, with black hair wearing a blue bonnet with striking blue eyes.

Ach du lieber Gott, it's Marie! It can't be. Or, is it? Yes, it is. It's her. He suddenly wished he had not brought Caroline with him to church today. It felt awkward. He had feelings for Caroline but seeing Marie made his heart skip a beat, although he hadn't seen her since his passage to America two years ago.

"Marie!" he yelled, as she turned to go in the pew. Even he was surprised at his outburst, but he felt overpowered by a fear of losing Marie again.

Marie looked in his direction and for a brief moment she stared at him, then waved at August and smiled so sweetly it reminded him of his first taste of chocolate as a child. He continued his gaze and saw her sit down next to an elderly couple. *Probably her grandparents.*

After the service was over, he and Caroline piled out of the bench and joined the congregation outside.

"Who is this Marie who you yelled for at church?" Caroline asked in a quiet voice.

August felt uneasy, but he knew he owed Caroline an explanation. He stood there poker-faced and mumbled a reply. "Marie is the girl I met on the ship."

Caroline's eyes teared up. "But, I thought we…"

"That we are a couple?" he said. "It's no use, Caroline. It could never work between us. I had to promise your father that I would never marry you before he would give his permission to let you go with me today."

"I don't care what my father thinks," she shouted. "This is my life, not his."

"Caroline, we have different belief systems," August said. "If I had children, I would want to raise them as Catholics, not Protestants. Surely, it would put stress on you, and create tension between you and your parents. I know how much you love your parents. It could never work. I still care about you and want us to remain friends."

Caroline stood there, her face ashen, as Marie approached. August hugged Marie hello, and then put her cheeks in the palms of his hands. Without thinking, he spoke to her in Polish, telling her she was beautiful and had always hoped he'd see her again.

"Me, too," she said, blushing.

He smiled, his heart swimming, his mind racing. He almost forgot his manners.

"Let me introduce you to Caroline Weinrebe. Her Dad is a blacksmith, too, and my sponsor. Since his first name is also August, I call him by his last name. Caroline, this is my long lost friend, Marie. We met on the ship. Marie, this is Caroline Weinrebe."

They eyed each other with suspicion for a moment or two, then Marie held out her hand. "Pleased to meet you."

"Likewise, I'm sure," Caroline replied, politely, looking uncomfortable.

"The Weinrebes are Lutherans, but Caroline decided to go to church with me this morning to see for herself this peculiar faith I belong to." Caroline hesitated, then nodded.

August turned toward Marie and spoke to her in Polish. "Where do you live, Marie? May I call on you?"

Marie's eyes beamed. "Please do." She wrote the address down on a piece of paper which she had in her purse and handed it to him.

Chapter 17

August called on Marie the next day and from the end of April till early July in 1872 he spent time getting to know her better. He found out she was a good dancer, loved parties and concerts, as well as picnicking in parks, and attending Sunday Mass. Caroline, clearly unhappy at first, grew to accept Marie, and treated her almost like a sister.

August and Marie were constantly around people—the crowd at church, her grandparents when he went over to her house, the Weinrebes when she came over to his, their friends when they were at parties or concerts or picnics. He wondered when they would ever be alone. Just the two of them. He longed for it.

He savored every small detail about her—the sweet scent of her flowery perfume, the glow on her face when she looked at him, her irresistible toothy smile, her tiny waist that made him want to squeeze her, breasts like full grown apples, and the feel of her thin, velvety soft hands when she touched him. And, while he noticed that she always dressed in the latest fashions, he rarely complimented her, because he felt a stimulating conversation was more important than good looks.

After they attended Sunday Mass at St. Francis, he rode with her taking her back to her grandparent's house. He was enamored with her insatiable curiosity and her ability to converse about a wide range of topics—the moon, the stars, Jenny Lind polka music, new dance steps for waltzes, growing flowers, weeding a vegetable garden, as well as keeping up to date on the latest fashion. What appealed to him even more was her genuine concern for him.

"Why do you have that bandage on your finger?" Marie said.

"I burned my hand in Weinrebe's blacksmith shop," August said. "I heated the horseshoe red hot and put it on the horse's hoof and the tongues slipped and I burned myself."

"I'm sorry. There's a new product called Vaseline petroleum jelly that is supposed to heal wounds or burnt skin. I could get some for you if you'd like."

"Thank you," August said. His horse stomped, its ears flattened at the tight hold on the reins. "I'd like that. No one besides my mother has ever tried to take care of me. I feel like I'm six years old."

"You need someone to take care of you," Marie said. She smiled and gave him a look that said she was eager to help. "That's women's work. That's why a man needs a woman." It made his heart flutter.

"Speaking of new things," he said, "I read German-language newspapers. Sometimes they have information about farming. I'm curious about that. I want to learn. Do you want to learn although you no longer go to school?"

"I guess so," Marie said, batting her eyelashes, "although not everyone is thrilled with new ideas. My girlfriend who came from Kentucky said her family owned slaves and she feels people have a right to own them. She said her parents referred to them by numbers instead of names."

"You know it's wrong to think like that, don't you?" he said, straightening his posture, sitting up higher in his saddle. His heart seemed to freeze, then pound. "Why would one human being would treat another human being this way? After all, we're all God's children."

He saw her give a nervous nod, then she offered a rebuttal. "But, you can't deny the wisdom passed on by the elders. Maybe her family knew better."

"Have you ever met a Negro?"

"No, but I've heard stories about them."

He was astonished at her reply. It seemed far too naïve for her. "Don't believe everything you hear. Just because a man's skin is a different color, it doesn't mean they are a bad person or that they will harm you. There are plenty of white people who are crooks. Besides, the face of the Madonna of Our Lady of *Częstochowa* is black."

He could see she had a sudden change of heart. There was a comfortable silence, then she said, "President Lincoln was against slavery, wasn't he?"

"Yes, he was a progressive and a Republican, like me. Jefferson Davis was a Democrat."

"Didn't I read where Pope Pius IX called Davis "the illustrious and honorable President of the Confederate States of America?'"

His jaw slackened. "Did he really say that?"

Marie nodded. "Yes, I think he did. Do you think the Pope is infallible? I mean, if he is, his opinion about Jefferson Davis must be right."

August felt uncomfortable in answering that question. He believed that no human was infallible yet Pope Pius IX had decreed papal infallibility at the First Vatican Council in late 1869.

"I disagree with the Pope," August said. His horse stumbled, but August pulled on the reins to guide the horse back onto the wagon-rutted, dirt road. Marie's grandparent's house was within sight.

"Isn't it a mortal sin to disagree with the Pope? You're not Catholic if you disagree with him."

August immediately regretted telling Marie his true feelings. He backpedaled.

"I guess since we're Catholics we should believe it. He's eighty years old, old enough to be wise, my father would say. And like my father always said, 'Never trust anyone except the priest and the doctor.'"

Marie didn't say anything. She just smiled. "Well, here we are at Grandma's house," she said, pulling the reins to stop her horse. "Would you like to come in?"

"I'd better not," August said. "The Weinrebes are expecting me for dinner. Maybe another time." They both dismounted and August put his arm around Marie and squeezed her tight. She kissed his cheek.

"Will I see you again next week?" she said, her voice hopeful.

"I wouldn't miss it for the world. You're the light of my life." He gave her a longer hug than usual and then left.

Chapter 18

It was Saturday and was unseasonably warm in mid-July in Elmhurst. August finished shoeing a horse in Weinrebe's blacksmith shop when he felt a cool breeze of fresh air, which contrasted with the smell of horse manure and iron from the horseshoes. Weinrebe and his family had unexpectedly gone to Chicago to visit some friends and attend a church function.

Almost noon, August expected to see Marie any minute as she was bringing lunch to share, like she had done many times before. They would finally get a chance to be alone. August smiled when he heard the plop of horse hooves on the soft dirt outside.

Marie carried a picnic basket she had packed with a bottle of August's favorite red wine, thin slices of ham and Swiss cheese, a loaf of fresh homemade bread, pickles and olives, and strawberries as well as chocolate bars for dessert. She dismounted from her horse and hugged August hello as if he were a long lost friend. Then they went into the house, August washed his hands while Marie spread the food out on the linen tablecloth covering the dark-wooden kitchen table.

Before they ate, they said a meal prayer, then perched themselves on the wooden chairs and August politely waited for Marie to pour him a glass of wine and fix him lunch. Although he portrayed himself as a manly man with gritty blacksmith hands who was rough around the edges, August became a perfect gentleman around Marie—polite and respectful.

It never occurred to him to be more romantic, perhaps by sweeping her off her feet with an occasional gift of flowers or chocolates, or for him to serenade her. Usually her efforts to change him were in vain, although she was able to coax him into taking ballroom dance lessons at a local dance hall, even though he had two left feet. He was in love and there was nothing he wouldn't do for her.

Marie handed August a slice of homemade bread, two slices of ham and Swiss cheese and poured him a glass of red wine. Although she had mentioned it to him before, she reiterated again her love for gardening. "I'd rather do gardening than housework," she said. "Growing things, especially flowers, excites me. I love budding roses, blooming petunias, yellow daffodils and sweet-smelling lilacs. There's nothing like watching a tiny seed grow into a plant. It only takes water and a lot of patience." She brushed her hair from her face.

August took a bite of his sandwich and nodded in approval. *Marie would definitely make a good wife.* He picked at the nail on his right thumb.

"I plan on raising crops one day, like my father and I did in *Grabionna*," he said. "There's more freedom in farming."

Marie said nothing, but responded with a smile.

He felt close to her, closer than he had ever experienced with any other girl. Yet he felt there was an air of mystery about her because she left him wondering how she felt about something more important to him, like Poland's subjugation to Prussian domination. Even though she was Polish, she never talked about it.

After they finished eating their sandwiches, they continued to sip wine. The effects of the wine made him feel brave and he asked her outright. "What do you think about Poland's dilemma? Do you think it should be ruled by Prussia?" His eyes locked with hers.

Taken aback by his abruptness, she straightened her posture and smiled. She obviously didn't like being put on the spot.

Realizing he was serious, she knit her eyebrows and said, "I think it's complicated. There is no easy answer. On the one hand, if the Polish people fail to revolt, Poland will never gain its freedom and independence, and it will always cease to exist. On the other hand, I wouldn't wish war on the Polish people."

August bristled at her indecisiveness, but he loved how she always weighed both sides to an argument, loved that war made her heartsick, that she hated bloodshed.

But it's so important to fight for freedom! He paused a moment to gather his thoughts.

"While I hate war, too, I think freedom is worth dying for. A life without freedom is like living with a noose around your neck. In Poland I felt anxious a lot, like someone was cupping my mouth shut every time I spoke."

He shrugged his shoulders, looked out the window at the bright sunshine, then looked back at Marie. "Here, it's different. Better. The anxiety is gone. I can say what I want. I give thanks to God and the Blessed Virgin every day for the freedom I now enjoy."

Marie listened intently. August took a drink of wine and then continued. "Most of the men I know are Republicans who, like Weinrebe and I, support President Grant and his efforts to end slavery in the South. Recently a man named Jim came into our blacksmith shop who said he was a conservative white Democrat who disagreed with Grant. He said, 'Five hundred fifty thousand Americans died fighting the Civil War, most of them Grant's men. President Grant is a drunkard who failed to root out federal corruption and bribery and mismanaged the economy by implementing a gold standard. It only causes deflation. It helps banks but hurts farmers. I think Grant should be impeached!'"

Marie's eyes widened. "He actually said that?"

"Yes, I couldn't believe his outburst. I remembered my own conversation with the Russian stranger at the tavern in *Schneidemühl* and the Prussian Officer who came into my blacksmith shop, called me a traitor and punched me in the stomach. I wondered if Jim would face repercussions for his negative comments about the President. Surely I wasn't the only one he made those remarks to."

"So, did you ever find out what happened to him?" Marie said, her eyes searching August's face.

The warm kitchen caused a bead of perspiration to roll down August's forehead. He took another sip of the tangy, red wine. "As far as I know, nothing became of it. Several weeks went by and no one ever threatened Jim and he never lost his job. We are all free to voice our opinions publicly. This is a great country."

"That's good news for you, my dear," said Marie. "You who always enjoys defying public opinion." She ran her fingers through her hair. Her eyes met his. "Maybe you should think about becoming a U.S. citizen. You could vote in the elections, choose your own leaders, and own property—if you do."

August smiled. "That's what I like about you, Marie. You see both sides to everything. I'm thinking about it. Henrietta's husband told me how to go about getting a Letter of Intent to declare my citizenship. I'd have to sign a document renouncing my allegiance to the Emperor of Germany. That would not be difficult. I know I should. Anyway, I just don't have the time right now to deal with it."

"You will know when the time is right." She nodded. "You'll make time then."

"Yes, well, I know I can never go back to Poland, but I'm feeling homesick. I miss Polish food. What I wouldn't give to taste *bigos* or *kielbasa* again. You don't realize what you miss until you don't have it anymore."

"Yes, I suppose that's true."

"Nothing here is ever like home. These elm trees here have hardly any leaves on them yet. They're not like the linden trees in *Grabionna*. And the pace was slower in *Grabionna* than it is here in Elmhurst or Chicago. Here people rush around to get things done or go somewhere. Life was less complicated in *Grabionna* and I knew all the people there, even the people who attended the church in *Miasteczko Krajeňskie*. I grew up with them. Here there are just strangers. I'll never know all the parishioners at St. Francis of Assisi parish in Chicago because it's so huge."

Marie took a bite of the chocolate bar, then wiped her mouth with a napkin. "I like it better here," she said. "You'll get over being homesick."

"I'm not so sure." August munched on a couple strawberries. "I miss my father and my stepmother and young Albert, and the rest of the girls. I wonder what their lives are like now. I wonder if there are still so many people living in that house on Grabionna Way. I wonder if they miss me as much as I miss them."

"But, you get letters from Rosalia." Marie took another sip of wine and poured what was left in the bottle in August's glass. He gulped it down.

"It's not the same as sitting down and talking with her."

"It's natural that you'd have feelings for the area where you were raised or grew up, but you have a new life now." She reached across the table and touched his hands. "Don't look back, August. Look ahead."

August looked up, a sad smile playing around his lips.

"I consider Poland my home." He sighed and his voice quivered. "Poland doesn't exist anymore but I continue to pray that Poland will one day be a country again. It could happen. Maybe in my lifetime. I *know* it will happen."

"Spoken like a true Pole. I love that in you." She stood, went over to where he was sitting, leaned in to him, smiled, and kissed him tenderly on the cheek.

He arose from his chair, grabbed her, squeezed her tight and kissed her on the lips. "*Ja cie kocham,*" he whispered.

"I love you, too, August," she whispered back, breathing hard.

August glanced at the empty wine bottle. He took Marie in his arms and danced around the kitchen with her. He never felt so uninhibited or so attracted to someone. He felt she was the best friend he could ever find or hope for, felt swept away by passion, like he had to have her right now, at this very moment.

"You're beautiful, you know," he said, caressing her breasts and kissing her neck.

"We shouldn't be doing this," she said.

"I can't help it," he said, the passion of the moment overtaking him.

Her face touched his and she moaned softly, kissing him from his chin to his ears. "I'm so glad I met you. I hope it will always be like this."

"Upstairs," he whispered, breathing hard.

She nodded. He took her hand and led her up the stairs to his bedroom. The bright sun shone through his bedroom window. He pulled the shade down and then threw back the sheets and blanket on his bed and they laid upon it, sharing his pillow.

Too excited to be nervous, he rolled on top of her, fondling her. It felt so right, holding her, whispers of conscience vanishing in the sounds of her expectant breath. Although initially awkward and fumbling, with her help, he opened a few buttons on the front of her emerald dress. The sight of her pale skin sent sparks through him. She moaned softly and caught her breath, the motion stirring her lustrous hair that cascaded down on one side of his pillow. He wanted to bury his face in it and smell its fragrance.

At first timid and ignorant, she began caressing his ears, shoulders and neck. He found her small hand and put it on the button of his pants. The surge of feeling almost overwhelmed him as she slid the button through, all while catching quick glimpses of her eyes—dear God, those eyes that looked at him as though he contained no flaw at all.

After he had her dress and petticoat off, he cupped her face with his hands and kissed her hard with a passion so fierce it seemed to frighten her. Marie gasped for breath and winced as she gave in to him. Her eyes were wide. She had a blank look on her face and he couldn't tell if she was enjoying the experience. Then in a moment or two their lovemaking was over. He never felt so satisfied, so utterly spent. They continued to hold each other, not moving, realizing the gravity of what had just transpired between them, feeling a pang of conscience for what had just happened.

Suddenly, he heard a sound, like distant footsteps crunching underbrush outside.

"Someone's coming. Quick, Marie, get dressed!"

They hurriedly threw on their clothes, but not before the Weinrebes had entered the house. August could hear their chatter when they discovered the remnants of August and Marie's lunch still on the kitchen table.

Weinrebe, whose smile had turned to a frown and his face crimson, opened the upstairs door. His voice sounded loud and suspicious. "August, are you up there? What is going on?"

August went sheepishly down the stairs in bare feet, his clothes disheveled, and Marie followed red-faced. Feeling an adrenaline rush, they found it difficult to physically breathe. Guilt shone on their faces.

"Christina," Weinrebe said, speaking slowly to his wife, "take the girls into the other room. I need to speak with August alone."

Marie stood erect. "You can speak to me, too," she said, defiantly, smoothing her dress. "I'm not going anywhere."

Weinrebe, highly irritated, could barely speak. He wrinkled his forehead and spoke in an angry tone. "It's obvious from the looks on your faces that there's been fornicating going on here. Maybe your religion allows it, but mine doesn't!" He pointed at Marie. "And you, my dear, are a whore!"

"Sir, I beg you not to talk to Marie like that." August moved his fingers through his hair, straightening it. "She's a lady, after all!"

Weinrebe shouted at August. "She's no lady, and you're fired! I can't believe you would act like this after all I've done for you. You shamed my family. I want you out of this house *immediately*!"

Chapter 19

In the middle of July in 1872, the hot, glaring sun beat down on the wagon-rutted streets of Chicago. The city was bustling with new rows of wood-framed houses, new hotels, rebuilt boardinghouses, new saloons, refurbished factories, new offices, lumber and coal yards, and reconstructed warehouses. Although August didn't like big cities, after Weinrebe fired him, he had no other choice except to relocate there from Elmhurst.

His sister Henrietta offered him a place to stay so he moved in with her and Stolz, and their one-year-old baby, Edwin. They lived in a one-room, wood-framed house, with an outhouse out back at 45 West Monroe Street near Michigan Avenue in downtown Chicago. Like many other Polish and German immigrants in Chicago, they lived with relatives under the same roof in order to cut down on expenses and save money.

Since it was Sunday, August and Marie attended Mass together at nearby St. Francis of Assisi Church, as usual. After Mass was over, the couple lingered near the entrance with other members of the congregation. Although they greeted other parishioners, they huddled together in the midst of the crowd in deep conversation.

"How is living with Henrietta's family?" Marie said, as she gave August a hug.

"Good," he said, "but Henrietta definitely has her hands full. Little Edwin has started crawling and gets into everything—the garbage, the pots and pans. He plays with the dishes and his food. And Stolz is no help to her. I don't think he even likes Edwin."

"Really?" Marie said, shaking her head, her eyes wide.

"Yes," August said, taking Marie's hand in his. "I think it's odd. I never see him holding Edwin or playing with him. I remember clearly my father playing with my younger brother Wilhelm when he was that age."

"Maybe because he isn't his real son," Marie said, squeezing August's hand. "It's too bad Emil died before Edwin was born."

"You've got to admit, Stolz did a noble thing by marrying her," August said. "Can't blame Stolz for not accepting Edwin, but I worry for Henrietta."

"She's a strong woman," Marie said, smiling. "If anyone can handle it, Henrietta can. What does Stolz do for work? He's a carpenter, isn't he?"

"He *is* a carpenter," August said, nodding. "He used to build houses but now he's got a job at the Peter Schuttler Wagon Factory, one of the leading wagon makers in the U.S. I'd love to own one of those wagons. Who wouldn't?"

"What would you use it for?" Marie said, puzzled.

"Most people use them to move out West or on a farm or ranch, or haul gold or freight across the country."

"What do they cost?" Marie said, a quizzical look on her face.

"About seventy-five dollars," August said, his mouth curved into a smile. "That's a *lot* of money and it's not in my budget."

"That's too bad," Marie said.

"Stolz wants me to work at the factory. He said they also make horseshoes for horse-operated street cars, and I could probably get a job doing that. He offered to help me."

"What did you say?" Marie said, her expectant voice full of hope.

"*Danke, aber nein danke.* I want to be my own boss and work independently, not in a factory."

Marie seemed disappointed. "You might regret not taking him up on his offer," she said.

"Every night at supper he asks me the same question with suspicion in his voice: 'What did you do all day today?' It's as if Stolz thinks I'm lazy and sit on my butt all day while he works to put food on the table. That isn't the truth but how would he know that?"

"Have you found any other work?" Marie worried

August frowned. "I've been looking for blacksmith work in Chicago, but I'm not getting anywhere because I can't count on Weinrebe to put in a good word for me and no one will hire me without it."

"What a pity!"

August nodded. "Stolz said I need to swallow my pride and come to work at the factory. He says it's high time for me to start pulling my own weight. I feel terrible."

"You'd better plan on moving out soon," Marie said. "I'll pray that you make the right choice."

August locked eyes with Marie. "The Bible says, 'It is hard for a rich man to enter the kingdom of Heaven. It's easier for a camel to go through the eye of a needle than for a rich man to enter the kingdom of God.' I want to go to Heaven, so I don't need to be rich, yet I don't want to be poor either.

I want to make a good living, but I also want to be free and independent. If I take this job at the factory, I'm afraid I might get stuck there forever."

"No, you won't," Marie said. "You can always go back to your blacksmith trade again. There will be other opportunities. Besides, you might learn something at the factory that will help you in your blacksmith work."

"Okay," he said. "You win. I'll take the job at the factory." He pointed near the entrance. "Father Baak has come out of Church. Let's say hello."

$$Chapter\ 20$$

Two months later, in September 1872, August and Marie attended a Saturday night dance contest at a local ballroom dance hall that housed seventy-five people. The hall was decorated in gold and glitter and, as usual on such a prominent night like this, everyone, in full regal attire, was on their best behavior. The sweet smell of French perfume and aftershave wafted in the air. August and Marie danced the waltz, along with fifty other guests, to the latest classical music by the Viennese composer Josef Strauss.

Before the contest, Marie and the other ladies were offered punch and dainty lace cookies which they ate at surrounding tables while August and the men ordered whiskey or beer from the bar, which helped to lower their inhibitions.

August and Marie made an elegant pair on the dance floor. Marie was in her new, deep blue dress with a bodice trimmed with lace along the neckline and a skirt of multiple layers of ruffles and flounces with extra material gathered in the back into a high bustle, offset by her coal black, curly hair. August wore his black, homespun suit and bow tie. Energized by being around people, he felt at ease in the crowd; she relished the one-on-one relationship.

The couples on the dance floor practiced first before the contest began. August took Marie in his arms.

Marie's face was pale. "I'm sorry, but the fish from dinner is still making me gag." She looked as if she was about to faint.

"Did it go bad?" August said, embracing her tightly. "When did you buy it?"

Marie spoke in a whisper. "I bought it from the market this morning. I don't know what's wrong with me lately." She smiled, confusing August a little. Why would she smile if she was about to get sick? "I wake up in the morning and feel like I have to throw up even though I haven't eaten anything."

"How long has this been going on?"

"For the past month." She batted her eyes at him, her smile growing even bigger.

"Why didn't you say something before?"

"I didn't want to worry you. Besides," she paused looking up at him, "Grandma said it happened to my mother when she was pregnant with me."

He stopped dancing and stared at her. "You don't mean…"

"Yes…. you're going to be a father." She smiled, with the naïveté of a sixteen year-old girl hopelessly in love.

He paused a moment, processing what she just said. His speech was slow and quiet. "I guess…. I need to marry you."

She hung her head in disappointment. Fighting back tears, her voice cracked. "I never thought it would be like this. I had always expected a proper proposal."

"I'm sorry," he said, embracing her while continuing dancing. "Please forgive me. Would you like to marry me?" he whispered, holding her close.

"I'm thinking," she said, smiling, teasing him.

"I promise that I will always be faithful." His eyes pleaded with her, then he playfully added, "I'm known to be unpredictable at times."

"You can say that again," she said. "However, unpredictable is good. Then life will never be boring. On the other hand..."

"Uh, uh, uh," he said, shaking his head and putting his thumb and forefinger on her chin. "You're being indecisive again. What you mean to say is yes, don't you?"

"I'm not indecisive," she said, blushing. "Yes, I'll marry you." She smiled, nodding. "Yes. Yes. Yes."

"Let's go see Father Baak at St. Francis tomorrow and ask him to hear our confessions. He won't be happy about you being in a family way, of course, but I hope he will still marry us and give us his blessing."

"We need to plan a small wedding.[22] I'll wear a black wedding dress maybe trimmed with white lace around the collar and sleeves, and a white veil. I'll go shopping for it tomorrow."

"And, I'll wear my suit and a bow tie. Who should we invite?"

"I think we should ask Maria Lapnoroski and Tahat Uslzaipa to be our wedding attendants, and invite my grandparents, your sisters and their husbands, Henrietta and Stolz, Anton and Mary Otto, of course your brother Wilhelm, and maybe some of your friends from work."

"By the way, I'm happy about the baby, Marie. That's really good news!" His mind raced with excitement. "*Ach du lieber Gott*, what shall we name him?"

"*Him?*"

He grinned. "Ok, maybe *her*. What shall we name *her*?"

"If it's a *her*, we could always call her Rosalia."

He laughed. "No. No more Rosalias and no more Augusts."

"I like the name Leo, do you?"

His eyes brightened. "Leo is a great name. He will be a leader, a King or the next President. For a girl, I like the name Mary."

"Hmmm, Mary is too close to Marie. Maybe Malinda instead."

"Yes, I like Malinda. Do you think the baby will have your dark hair and curls?"

"I don't care who he or she resembles, only that the baby is born healthy," she said.

He smiled and touched his face to hers. She reached up to rearrange her hair as it cascaded over his shoulder as she leaned into him. He felt a tingling sensation as his eyes met hers.

"I wish this moment would last forever," she whispered. "I've dreamt about this for some time."

"I know," he said, squeezing her. "You've made me the happiest man in the world. We are going to have a wonderful life together. I promise I'll take good care of you."

They strode off the dance floor and waited at the sidelines for the next dance number to begin which would start the contest. Oblivious to others in the crowd, Marie lowered her eyes and looked at August through her lashes. "Where will we live? What kind of home will we have?"

"I'll build you a new house when we can afford it. Our home will always be warm and welcoming to others."

"I'd like that," she said, quickly changing the subject. "How was work today? Anything unusual happen?"

"Stolz's doctor told him today he is suffering from fume exhaustion at the factory."

"*Fume exhaustion?*" Marie said. She knit her eyebrows. "What about you, August? Aren't you worried for yourself? I am."

"Don't you worry your pretty head! I work in a different section. There's no chance of me suffering from fume exhaustion."

"What's Stolz planning to do about it?" Marie said.

"His doctor told him to move out west for fresher air."

"That sounds like a great idea, but, what will he do to support himself and his family?"

"The railroads are being built to connect Chicago with western frontiers like Kansas. It's easier to travel now and move out west. Stolz saw an ad in the newspaper by the Atchison, Topeka and Santa Fe Railroad that offered lands in Southwest Kansas. It advertised temperate climate; excellent health; pure and abundant water; good soil for wheat, corn and fruit; and the best stock country in the world."

August intended on joining Stolz but felt he needed to build up to that before he sprang it on Marie.

"Sounds maybe too good to be true."

The announcer interrupted their conversation, saying, "The judges are ready. The contest is about to begin. Please have your number pinned on the back of the man's jacket. My associate will tap you on the shoulder if you are asked to leave the dance floor. Based on your dancing skills, the judges will select only those left dancing. The winning couple will receive a prize valued at ten dollars."

Marie pinned their number on August's jacket. She beamed. What more could any girl her age want besides a husband and a baby? Now, if they could just win the contest, all her dreams would come true.

They sauntered over to the middle of the dance floor. Soon the Viennese music started and they began waltzing. Although he enjoyed it, August felt he wasn't cut out for dancing, wasn't good at it, but felt compelled to try his hardest out of his love for Marie. In order to keep his mind off the anxiety of trying to win the contest, however, he continued his sales pitch to Marie.

"There's also the Homestead Act, my dear. I could lay claim to 160 acres[23] if I lived on the land for five years, but I'd also need to build a dwelling on it and cultivate the land."

"Sounds like a lot of work," Marie said, mopping her brow because it was hot inside the ballroom. "Is that all you'd need?"

"No. I'd also need to be a U.S. citizen or at least have a Letter of Intent but that's not a problem. Just think of it, Marie. The weather, soil and water are good and the opportunities are endless. Stolz can own his own land and all the profits from raising crops will be his. He'll be his own boss. I'd like that freedom myself."

Marie looked him squarely in the eye. "August, my love, please concentrate on dancing. We want to win this contest. Besides," she said, patting him on his cheek, "you are always chasing freedom."

He held her close and kissed her on her forehead. "And, I will until my dying breath, my dear."

The announcer's associate tapped a man on the shoulder who was dancing near them. There were only six couples left dancing on the floor. Marie smiled and nodded at August as if to say she was pleased they were still in the contest.

"You're doing fine, my dear. Remember, step 1, step 2, slide…"

August didn't care about the dance contest. It would be forgotten in a day or two. He was more concerned about their marriage and the practical things in his life like his work and how they would survive financially.

"Stolz will also do fine," August said. "I'm sure of it."

"Didn't you say Stolz is a carpenter?"

August nodded.

"Well, my guess is that most carpenters don't know anything about farming. You've got to know when to plant the crops, how much water to give them, how to hoe and weed and when to use manure to increase their growth. It isn't an easy task if you don't know what you're doing."

"Nonsense. He can learn. Farming your own land is way better than working for a tyrant boss you don't like or getting only a portion of the profits."

"Moving to Kansas will be expensive. Will Henrietta and Baby Edwin move, too?"

"He said eventually they will, but he wants to build a home for them first and try his hand at farming, and, of course, see if his health improves. If he fails, he can always ride the train back to Chicago and hope to get his old job back at the wagon factory. If he succeeds, I hope to try it myself."

August noticed a sudden look of alarm in Marie's eyes. Her tone of voice rose. "You expect that the baby and I will go with you?"

"Of course. Won't you?"

She didn't say anything.

"We need to start saving money. I recently inquired about a job at the McCormick Machine Company.[24] It's better pay than the wagon factory and I can learn something. I think I'll take the job."

"August, this is so sudden," Marie said. "There are so many things to consider."

August stumbled on the dance floor. He immediately apologized. "I'm sorry, dear. I wasn't paying attention."

The associate tapped August on the shoulder.

Marie frowned. "You made us lose! I am *sooo* disappointed!"

"I'll make it up to you, I promise." August ushered her to the sidelines.

"What kind of machines does McCormick make?" Marie finally said after an uncomfortable silence.

"Reapers."

"What are reapers?"

"Farming machines. Cyrus P. McCormick invented the reaper in 1831. Heard that he had help with the final version though from a slave named Jo Anderson. Anyway, with the invention of the reaper, farming can now be done by machine instead of by hand using a sickle or scythe. McCormick mass produces the machine at his Chicago plant using an assembly line. I'm not crazy about working in an assembly line, but I can learn how the machines work and be able to fix them for farmers later."

"How many people do you suppose work there?"

"About a thousand and about a half dozen foremen to supervise them."

She locked eyes with him. "Are you sure you want to work there?"

Only one couple was left on the dance floor and the announcer proclaimed them the winner of the dance contest.

Marie shrugged. "I still can't get over we lost."

August, glad the contest was over, smiled at Marie, his mind focused on getting a job with McCormick. "It would be more money and we need to start saving more money so we can afford to move to Kansas and homestead a place. Just think of it, Marie. We're going to be rich one day."

"I hope to God you're right."

Chapter 21

Black clouds were in the sky the next day when August and Marie went to see Fr. Baak at St. Francis of Assisi church. They waited until after Mass when all of the parishioners had gone. The priest was alone in the sacristy in the back of the church, putting away his vestments.

August held Marie's hand as they approached the priest.

"What brings you both here?" the priest said.

August found his lips lightly trembling. "Marie and I are in trouble, Father."

The priest held his gaze. "Oh?"

August glanced at Marie, then at the priest. "She thinks she is with child." Even though he felt a tinge of guilt when he said the words, he hoped they didn't sound too rushed or anxious. Marie twisted her handkerchief.

The priest's eyes perked up and he arched an eyebrow. "By no means does the church condone fornication; however, this isn't the first time or last I've heard this happening to one of my parishioners. Do you love Marie and wish to marry her?"

"I do love her. I would marry her anyway even if she wasn't with child."

"I love him, too," Marie said, looking up at August.

"Marriage is a lifelong commitment. It shouldn't be entered into lightly. But, it sounds like you both want to be married.

Very well, then, we can't waste time. I need to marry you immediately, maybe next Thursday or Friday, perhaps in the sacristy. We'll dispense with the banns announcing the wedding to the parishioners."

"Friday would be good. I can take a day off from work. It will give us enough time to prepare and invite our friends and relatives."

"That's settled, then. Do either one of you want to make an individual confession?"

They both nodded.

"Let me finish up here and I'll meet you at the confessional."

By now the church was empty. August and Marie knelt in a back pew in front of the confessional and said a prayer to the Holy Spirit that they might make a good confession and be given the gift of true repentance and contrition. They also asked the Blessed Virgin Mary to intercede for them.

The enclosed confessional booth or dark box was located near the entrance of St. Francis but was not a stand-alone piece of wooden furniture like those in the churches in Poland. In the Chicago church, it was built into the wall and had one door for the priest and another for the penitent. The parishioner knelt on a wooden kneeler inside the box, facing sideways toward the middle of the confessional, and folded his hands in prayer on the ledge in front of a grille and curtain used to separate the priest from the penitent. The priest sat facing forward toward the front of the confessional. They spoke in whispers in the dark, the penitent's voice and breath up close to the priest's or confessor's ear.

August knelt down in the confessional and whispered in German: "Bless me Father, for I have sinned. It has been a month since my last confession... I have a sin of impurity to confess. It only happened once and I am truly sorry. I am sorry for this sin and all the sins of my whole life, including those that I cannot remember. I humbly repent and ask for absolution, and penance."

"My dear Son, although I'm sure God does not condone your sin, He is a God of Mercy and He is a forgiving God. From now on, you must make a change and start a new life in Christ. For your penance, say a decade of the Rosary. Now please make an Act of Contrition."

After he was finished, August got up from the kneeler inside the confessional and went to tell Marie it was her turn now.

Chapter 22

After the wedding, August went to work for McCormick in Chicago with the thousand factory workers employed there. August complained to Marie that unlike his blacksmith trade where he felt challenged to diagnose a problem, which to him represented a puzzle, this job entailed making only a part of a machine which he felt was repetitive, boring and sweat-inducing factory work. Although he got paid more for his work on the assembly line than as a blacksmith, his wages depended on the size of the piece. For example, a sickle-guard cost five cents apiece, bigger pieces cost more. And, because of this assembly-line construction, six foremen were adequate to supervise the men.

On Friday that first week, August's foreman Gunther told him that he needed to pick up his paycheck Sunday at one of the saloons owned by McCormick. August reserved Sundays for prayer and attending morning Mass at St. Francis. So, after attending Mass, he rode his horse over to the saloon. He felt he had no choice. The saloon was wide open on Sunday, like every Sunday, with a crowd of men smoking cigars, drinking Kentucky whiskey and discussing politics.

When August appeared at the door, Gunther walked over to where he was standing and slapped him on the back. "Good to see you!"

"I came to pick up my paycheck," August said, smiling.

The foreman turned around facing the crowd of men. "Boys, August is here to pick up his paycheck!" They smiled, hooted and whistled. Gunther and the other foremen knew what good workers these German-speaking immigrants like August were, but they also took advantage of how "green" and naïve they were.

Gunther turned to the bartender, "Louie, another round of drinks for these fine fellows." He put his arm around August's shoulder. "Men, this is August's treat since he gets paid today, isn't that right, August?" Gunther glanced at him expectantly.

Taken by surprise, August felt uneasy. His jaw tightened. Hesitating, he scratched his head.

"You want to get paid, don't you?" Gunther said, smirking.

August's mind raced. *He's my boss, my foreman. If I refuse, will I lose my job? Is this how that other German immigrant I heard rumors about found himself suddenly out of work?*

Squirming, he shifted his weight from one leg to the other, put his hands in his pockets and raised his eyebrows. *God knows, I took this job to save money. A slim chance now.*

He shrugged. "Ok, I'll buy this time," August said, joining the others drinking Kentucky whiskey and beer.

The men cheered. "That's the spirit," said Gunther, as he patted August on the back.

Several months later, on May 1, 1873, Marie, whose baby was due any day now, said she felt fine, so she accompanied August to early morning Sunday Mass at St. Francis. They both watched the morning sun glisten off the church's stained glass windows, warming the surrounding air. Feeling a cool breeze from the south, Marie put a shawl around her shoulders. August gave her a quick hug.

He worried about Marie because she had learned a few months ago that her best friend, who was helped in childbirth by a midwife, died from complications. She bled to death. The baby also died. Marie cried and fretted over it for weeks and was unable to sleep for days, fearing that it might happen to her, too. August tried his best to calm her.

She'd had her good and bad days, but that day she seemed stronger and better able to cope. Marie smiled, yet complained about August going to the saloon after church to pick up his paycheck. Although he wanted to stay home, too, he kissed her on the cheek, told her he loved her, and said goodbye.

Marie's grandmother and Henrietta, Marie's sister-in-law, came over to the house after church. They acted as midwives to Marie and planned to stay till she delivered her baby. Marie was lucky. Her grandmother had many years of experience helping women give birth. Although Grandma had witnessed a few tragedies, most of the time the births were successful, yet sometimes there were complications.

August rode his horse over to the saloon and, after picking up his weekly paycheck, Gunther, his foreman, expected him to buy drinks again for the men. August complained but it fell on deaf ears, so he complied with the now weekly request. He was about to gulp down a whiskey and chase it with a beer when a neighbor stopped by on a horse and said Marie needed him home immediately in case there was a complication. August quickly excused himself and was out the door in a minute while the men hooted and hollered after him.

Henrietta and Grandma were in the bedroom with Marie when August arrived home. August didn't go into the bedroom to see Marie, but rather waited in the kitchen because, like other men, he believed it to be indecent for a man to be in the same room while his wife was having a baby. He was afraid that if he saw his wife giving birth it might disgust him.

Henrietta came out to the kitchen with some bad news. "Grandma thinks the baby is breech."

"What does that mean?"

"It means its buttocks will come out first instead of the head, and will likely die because of it."

August felt his muscles tense, his jaw tighten and a pit in his stomach. His heart sunk to the floor. He knew that the odds were against him, that his baby and Marie might not survive. He didn't understand God's plan for him. He wondered why God seemed to be punishing him. He thought maybe it was for not staying in Poland and fighting for freedom.

Henrietta told him she and Grandma were trying to help turn the baby. They were applying pressure to her abdomen and trying to gently massage the baby down. She turned and hurried back into the bedroom.

August felt despondent but tried to be strong and hopeful for Marie. He got down on his knees and prayed a rosary to the Black Madonna, Our Lady of *Częstochowa*, Poland. If anyone could help, it would be her because she was a mother herself. He prayed like he had never prayed before. He prayed for a miracle.

While waiting three hours for any news, he puffed on a cigar, read the newspaper, puffed some more on his cigar, took out the garbage which he had neglected to do earlier, lit another cigar, and went outside and chopped wood for the fireplace. Then he came back inside, got something to eat, and tensely waited another two hours till finally he heard Henrietta's excited voice in the next room. "Good!" he heard her say. "The baby's head is down." *My prayers must have been answered,* he thought. *Thank God!*

Then he heard Marie's loud scream. It seemed to him each burst of pain was followed by an excruciating scream and then a minute or two of silence while she rested until the next one.

The sun went down, it was now almost midnight and the night air turned chilly. Finally, after ten hours of labor, August heard Henrietta shout, "Now, push!"

At 11:55 p.m., the baby entered the world and started to cry. A few minutes later, which to August seemed like hours, Henrietta ran to the kitchen to tell August he had a son and that it was okay for him to come in now. He smiled like a proud papa. With tears in his eyes, he embraced Marie. He gazed at the tiny, helpless babe and promised: *No matter what the future holds, I will love and care for you forever.*

Chapter 23

By December, August was fed up with McCormick's factory in Chicago and the foremen's racket. It cost him almost ten dollars a treat each time he had to treat the crowd of men to drinks at the saloon. *Every week!* That was a considerable amount! After seven or eight weeks he could have purchased a brand new Peter Schuttler wagon with that amount of money. At this rate, he told Marie, they wouldn't be able to realize their goal of moving out west. Just thinking about it, his jaw tightened and his knuckles turned white as he balled up his hand into a fist.

August felt the time had come for him to make a decision about moving to Kansas. He had recently read an alluring brochure, printed in German, about the town of Ellinwood,[25] which was produced and distributed to German-speaking communities across the United States by C. B. Schmidt, an immigration agent in Kansas who worked for the Atchison, Topeka and Santa Fe Railroad Company. Schmidt, also known as Smith, designated Ellinwood as a German colony, enticing German immigrants to purchase railroad property or homestead government land in the hope that these German-speaking settlers would raise crops and livestock which would be shipped via the railroad, thereby profiting the railroad companies. August only cared about being able to homestead 160 acres of farmland.

His brother-in-law, Stolz, who had already moved to Ellinwood without Henrietta, had told him that in order to homestead a property you had to be a U.S. citizen or at least sign a Letter of Intent to become one. So, on Christmas Eve, 1873, when Leo was just eight months old, he went to the Cook County Courthouse, rebuilt after the Chicago fire in 1871, and signed a Letter of Intent.

The document he signed read:

I, August Kopczinski, (the clerk had misspelled his name), do solemnly declare oath before Austin J. Doyle, Clerk of the Criminal Court of Cook County, in the state of Illinois, that it is BONA FIDE my intention to become a Citizen of the United States, and to renounce FOREVER all allegiance which I may in anywise owe to any foreign prince, potentate, state or sovereignty whatever, and in particularly the allegiance which I may in anywise owe to the Emperor of Germany whereof I was heretofore a citizen or subject.

Signed December 24, 1873—August Kopczynski.[26]

August loved puzzles. He loved his work as a blacksmith and the challenge of fixing equipment by solving puzzles with iron. So, on Christmas Eve, he couldn't help but wrap up a puzzle for Marie to solve. Even though their house was small, they managed to put up a small Christmas tree in the front room and decorated it with lighted candles, with a bucket of water nearby to douse any flames. They opened their gifts early on Christmas Day.

The card on August's present to Marie read: "What's something I should have done a long time ago?"

"Take out the garbage?" Marie smiled as if she had just won the contest.

"Wrong," he said, smiling back, tweaking his beard. "This is definitely not garbage."

She paused. Her eyes lit up. "Okay, then it's something to shave off your beard."

"Wrong again," he said, shaking his head. "You think I should shave off my beard?" he asked, incredulous, as if she had entered hallowed ground. He had grown a beard as a sign of his manhood. He thought it made him look more like a farmer or blacksmith, not to mention that he didn't have to waste time shaving every morning.

Marie smiled.

"If it were a razor, the package would rattle. Try again."

Marie fingered the present and shook it. "I give up. What's in it?"

"I'll give you a hint. It's something that affects our future."

She was silent for a few minutes, thinking it over. "More money for our trip out west?"

"You're close. What do we need first besides money to homestead a piece of land?"

"A document to claim U.S. citizenship?"

"Exactly," he said, smiling, his voice excited and passionate. "I went to the courthouse yesterday and signed a Letter of Intent. I wanted to surprise you."

"What a great surprise!" She opened the gift. "How long will it be before we leave? Next year?"

"Stolz said planting season for corn is the month of April so we need to leave soon. I've had it with the factory and the foremen at McCormick! I'm tired of the racket they have going, tired of buying drinks for the crowd of men at the saloon on Sundays, and tired of working there. Assembling the same sickle guard day after day makes me want to scream. *Ach du lieber Gott,* it's so boring and repetitive! And, Gunther is always breathing down my neck, asking me to hurry up. I can't stand it anymore so I'm quitting!"

Marie looked stunned like she hadn't realized leaving would be so soon and voiced her concern. "How will we survive?"

Although there were several presents left under the tree, they stopped opening gifts. "We're moving to Kansas. It's now or never. We can stay with Stolz in his dugout till I get our own house built. Just think of it, Marie, we'll be pioneers! It may be rough at first, but the opportunity is there for a better future for us." He put his finger on her chin and then stroked her hair. "We'll be free from the foremen's racket, free from tyrant bosses, free to farm our own land. All the profits will be ours. We're going to be rich some day!"

Marie sat upright underneath the tree, her eyes reflecting the light from the candles. "It sounds too good to be true. What about my grandparents and your sisters? When will we ever see them again? I can't leave Grandma now. I can't bear to break her heart. This is her only great-grandchild. I can't do this to her. She's been like a mother to me."

"Marie, you need to start your own life. You have your own family now. You can't live your life for your grandparents. They won't be around forever. I'm asking you to come with me. It will be a new start for us."

"But, won't you miss them?" Her voice rose. "I know I will."

August put his arm around her. "This is our chance for happiness, for prosperity. When you have an opportunity, you have to take it."

Marie shook her head. "Life might not be as rosy as the picture you paint of our future life. I've heard stories of pioneer life. It sounds like people go through hardships."

August frowned at her. "Try looking at the positives instead of focusing on the negatives."

Marie ignored his response and glanced away. "What about the Indians?"

"What about them?" he said. Although August never revealed it to Marie, Stolz had warned him of Indian raids along the Santa Fe Trail, and that neither the Comanche tribe nor the Apaches of the southern high plains tolerated who they considered trespassers on the Trail. Stolz said the Comanche tribe took scalps of their enemies as trophies, attacked on nights with a full moon, and were known as expert horsemen with highly-developed fighting skills.

Stolz told him the Comanche Indians wore breechcloths made from soft, tanned buckskin, their black hair tied in two long braids. They also wore war bonnets decorated with eagle feathers and beadwork. Sweat glistened on their chests under the moonlight. *Better to not tell Marie this. It'll just scare her.*

"Well, weren't they there first?" Marie said. "Won't they fight us for the land? It doesn't seem fair to run them off."

August stared at Marie. "You know, my dear, I make friends with everyone, even Indians. Besides, it's God's land, not theirs. They'll just have to make room for us."

"Like the Polish people had to make room for the German colonists?"

The words stung. He hadn't thought about his Polish roots in a while. He still harbored hope that Poland would be a country again, free from its oppressors. He shrugged. "Marie, it's exasperating sometimes that you always see both sides of an argument."

She raised an eyebrow. "It's good that I do. You always think things will be rosy. Stolz said there was a problem with the Indians stealing horses. What if they try to steal our horses? What if they try to steal Leo?"

August winced. "Nonsense. Stolz also said after the military campaign against the Plains tribe in the winter of 1868, the worst battle was over. He said the settlers have been relatively free from Indian raids since. So, don't worry your pretty head, my dear."

Two months later at the end of February 1874, August quit his job, and they took a train bound from Chicago to Ellinwood, a small town located just north of the Arkansas River on the plains in Central Kansas. August's twenty-two year old brother, Wilhelm, went with them.

August and Marie sold most of their possessions, taking with them only the necessities, figuring they could later order items such as clothing and even saddles and tools from Montgomery Ward's[27] mail-order house.

Passing through the states of Illinois, Missouri and then Kansas, the train ride was cold, the seats uncomfortable and the air inside the train car smelled of body odor. August gazed out the train window while Marie unpacked the food she had brought with them to eat—bread, cheese, thin slices of ham and pickles, as well as an apple for dessert for her, August and Wilhelm.

August noticed the land he saw from the train was flat, sparsely populated, and appeared desolate almost except for a sprinkling here or there of large herds of buffalo, antelope or wild horses—very different from what he saw or experienced in Chicago. Although amazed at these brand new sights, they did not scare or deter him as he felt they were headed for better territory in Kansas. After all, the Promised Land and their dreams awaited them.

Pregnant again, Marie was suffering from morning sickness, but nonetheless took care of the baby, ten-month-old Leo, during the long train ride. August and Wilhelm had negotiated the suitcase and the trunk. The suitcase was full of cloth diapers; the trunk contained August and Marie's homespun clothes.

"I think I will miss the shopping in Chicago," Marie said, as she was nursing Leo.

August took a bite of the apple. "Nonsense. Ellinwood has a general merchandise store as well as a post office, a hotel, a schoolhouse and a train depot. The town has a lot of German-speaking people like us. What more could you want?"

"What about living in a sod house? Walls made of dirt don't sound sturdy or clean."

August wiped his lips with a napkin and took a drink of water. "The requirements for homesteading are that you have to build a dwelling on the land. Since there are no trees there, the only way to build a house is using the earth itself—sod. Progress takes time. We won't live in a sod house forever. Think of the first couple years as an adventure."

"I worry about Leo and the baby I'm expecting."

"Leo will be fine. And, you've had experience in childbirth. The second one is always easier."

"Says who? That's easy for you to say! Grandma and Henrietta won't be there this time to help."

"Trust me, my dear." he said, nonchalantly, looking out the window again, ignoring Marie's frown. He noticed there were no mountains or hills in Central Kansas and unlike the fields back in *Grabionna*, hardly any trees. The plains were flatter than he had imagined, stretching out to the horizon, filled with large numbers of ducks and geese, and some wild turkeys. He couldn't wait to have one of them on his plate for dinner.

They arrived in Ellinwood at dusk in the chilly air. Stolz met them at the train depot with a team of horses. It had been a long journey and yet, they felt their adventure was just beginning.

"How many people live in Ellinwood?" August asked.

"Less than 300 people,[28] Stolz said, "and most of them are German-speaking like us. You'll like living here."

"Yes, I think I'll like it here," August said. "I didn't like living in Chicago. I'm looking forward to living near a small town again, away from the crowds."

August and Wilhelm got up early the next day and after breakfast immediately went to work choosing land to homestead. Because the railroads and land speculators already owned most of the choice land in Kansas, which they sold to prospective buyers, August selected an abandoned farm to homestead by driving stakes in at the borders, laying claim to 160 acres northwest of Ellinwood in Buffalo Township not far from Great Bend. Then August rode his horse to Ellsworth, thirty miles away, so that he could catch the Kansas Pacific train in order to visit the nearest government land office in Junction City to register the claim and pay a ten dollar filing fee. After the filing process was completed, he and Wilhelm immediately started to make improvements to the land. First they needed a dwelling, and so they began to build their sod house while they continued to live at Stolz's dugout.

Even though the temperature was cool, they were sweating and their backs ached as they plowed the tough grassland using oxen and a breaker plow to turn over the sod. They got up early in the morning and worked twelve hour days until dusk six days a week cutting the turf into foot-long blocks which they laid like giant bricks, piling one on top of the other, placing the grass on the bottom, the sod on top, till the structure reached 12- by -14 feet long. They rested for an hour at noon each day while they ate a lunch of duck meat and potatoes which Marie cooked on an open pit. Vegetables and fruit were scarce. They filled up a water jug from the nearby creek; the water tasted clear and refreshing.

They used a shovel to even out the brick-like sod, filled the cracks with loose soil, and even mail-ordered a stove pipe for 30 cents to be used as a chimney. They left space for an 8- by 10-foot glass window which they purchased for $1.25 at a general merchandise store in Ellinwood along with 18 feet of door lumber for 54 cents, a door latch and hanging for 50 cents, and three pounds of nails for 20 cents, as well as wood for the rafters to support the 16-inch weighty sod roof.

When the door and window were installed, they wall-papered the inside with newspaper which made it virtually windproof, the walls able to survive tornadoes. It was cheap to build, cool in the summer months, warm in the winter, and took them about a week to finish.

Marie found the sod house dark, damp, and dirty. August and Wilhelm laid an old carpet over the dirt floor to help keep the dust down. On occasion, a glob of mud would drop from the sod roof into a kettle of stew, but what really panicked Marie was seeing a bug or a snake inside the soddie.

A week later, the Kopczynski brothers, with help from Stolz, began turning the rest of the grassland acreage, which was overrun with roots and rocks, into farmland. Since part of the 160 acres had already been filed on and abandoned, it had some sod broken out which was ready for planting.

By working twelve hour days and using a team of oxen and a John Deere foot burner, they plowed almost an additional acre a day, for a total of fifteen acres in three weeks' time, into soil that they could plant. August had plenty of grassland left for pasture for summer grazing to feed his four farm animals—two oxen and two cows—which he had purchased. Both man and beast were tortured by the John Deere plow, and at the end of six weeks their muscles ached, but the soil was ready for a crop. On March 17th, they planted an acre of potatoes.

With April came the back-breaking job of planting all the rest of the crops by hand—regular sweet corn, a crop which he could sell, Kaffir corn,[29] or sorghum, which he would feed to his draft animals through the winter, and soft wheat which was good for making cookies and pastries, but not bread. He planted fourteen acres of regular corn, two of soft wheat, and four acres of the Kaffir corn. He planned to store the Kaffir corn in a hole in the ground for the draft animals in the winter.

Physically exhausted, one night August lay in bed in his soddie, wondering whether he had made the right decision to move to Kansas. *Mother of God, he prayed, why did I ever attempt to do this? What was I thinking? I never imagined the work would be this hard. Every bone and muscle in my body aches. It hurts just to move. If it's your will, dear Lord, please ease my pain.*

Marie stirred. He looked at her and smiled. She had not only survived the hardship of the first few weeks—the lack of privacy while staying with Stolz, the discomforts in the new sod house, having to cook with scarce food, traipsing to the river to bring back buckets of water—but August was amazed that she never once complained or expressed regret over their decision to leave Chicago. He couldn't have asked for a better partner or mother of his child. He knew without her, he would never have been able to pursue his dream of more freedom, more prosperity.

August continued praying. *Thank you, God, for my faith. I will always be true to you and Catholicism. It gives me the inner strength to persevere through these tough times and not lose hope for a better life. Please watch over my family and my farm and bless us. May we continue to prosper!*

Then, while reciting the rosary to himself, he fell asleep.

Chapter 24

At the end of March, shortly after they arrived in Ellinwood, August and Wilhelm scoured the rolling plains for food. They found scores of ducks, geese and other fowl amid the tufts of prairie grass, as well as brown trout and catfish in the clear and cold Arkansas River, but the real prize was buffalo meat.

The buffalo with its 1,500-pound carcass stood larger than a cow and, like a cow, was considered a dumb animal, though it did have good instincts. Thick, dark brown hair covered its body in the spring, but later in the summer, the animal would shed its hair behind the shoulders, by wallowing in the earth or rubbing against trees, and would look like a lion from a distance. Their meek calves were tawny-colored.

The Kopczynski brothers learned thick buffalo herds travelled north in early spring and returned south in the fall. Covering hundreds of square miles, these herds were most plentiful on the Plains in June and July, and could be found grazing within a mile south of the Arkansas River. Although the herds were not as large in March, they spotted several near the sand hills by the river.

The sun peaked over the Plains when they spied an Indian riding a pony following alongside running buffalos. The Indian had a shaved head, with only the scalp lock left uncut. Vermilion, a brilliant red pigment made from the mineral cinnabar, colored the edge of the lock. He was bare-chested, and yellow paint covered the Indian's face on the middle of his forehead, nose, mouth and chin. Red paint camouflaged his cheeks and eyes. He wore strings of small silver beads around his neck from which hung a silver medallion the size of a baby's palm.

They had heard stories of nomadic renegade bands such as Sioux, Kiowas, Kaws,[30] Cheyennes, and Arapahos who migrated to the Plains and became expert buffalo hunters. What tribe did he belong to? Stolz had told them about the federal act passed in May 1872 which provided removal of the Kaws, the largest tribe in central Kansas, to northern Oklahoma. Was this Indian a holdout from the Kaw tribe?

Although aware of men who wanted to get rid of all Plains Indian tribes,[31] August and Wilhelm didn't share their opinion. The Kopczynski's, followers of the Ten Commandments, believed "thou shalt not kill," and tried to make friends with the Indians, even though they had heard stories of massacres, attacks on ranchers and wagon trains, horse and mule stealings, as well as scalpings. Although it made them cautious, they believed it would never happen to them because they were willing to befriend the Indians.

The pony cut a buffalo out from along the edge, which permitted the Indian, riding bareback, to use his bow and arrow, to bring down the buffalo. His rapid actions were too quick for the brothers to notice that the animal was struck along the backbone about midway down the body, which did not cause the beast's immediate death. The Indian then shot another flint arrow immediately behind the shoulder. The buffalo dropped to the ground.

They watched from behind a sand hill with curiosity as the Indian skinned the buffalo. He prepared the hide for curing by staking it, hair side down, flat upon the ground. Later, he folded and creased the hide from nose to tail and walked on top of the fold.

He loaded the hide, hams and loins, as well as the tongue, the choice parts, onto his pony and trekked back to where he had come from. They followed him at a distance.

When they arrived at the Indian camp, they were puzzled by the teepee poles laying on the ground. They watched as another Indian, who began coughing, tried to hoist up a pole. August looked at Wilhelm as if to say, "Let's help." Wilhelm nodded in agreement. They dismounted and walked over to the Indian. August smiled and held up his right hand in a greeting.

The startled Indian hesitated, eyeing August with suspicion.

August wondered if the Indian understood, wondered if he would turn on them, wondered if they were in danger. His heart raced. Instead of reaching for his gun, he froze.

There was a long tense silence.

August smiled again. A drop of sweat fell from his brow. He began reciting The Lord's Prayer in his head.

He locked eyes with the Indian and used sign language to communicate. August pointed to the poles, then at his chest as well as Wilhelm's, and then lifted his hands up in the air, showing how they would help lift up the poles.

The Indian looked at the poles and then back at August. He paused, then nodded as if he understood.

The brothers helped the Indian lift the teepee poles. It took them a good half hour to erect them. Soon, squaws and Indian maidens mysteriously appeared and gathered round them to help. August wondered where they had been hiding. The women wore moccasins, knee-length leggings of blue and red cloth, a skirt and a cloth thrown over one shoulder. Their long hair was parted in the middle, the part colored with vermilion. The brothers and the Indian helped the women throw on buffalo hides to cover the poles, after which the squaws hung the buffalo meat out in the sunlight and open air to be cured, or jerked. No bugs or flies came around. The women left to scour the area for wild berries and plants.

The Indians offered the Kopczynskis a peace pipe in appreciation.

They sat down in a circle and didn't speak much, but passed the pipe back and forth. After a while, the brothers mounted their horses and returned to their camp on the sand hills. They smiled at their good fortune. The Indian made killing a buffalo seem easy, so they got up early the next day and got a fresh start.

Armed with needle guns, August and Wilhelm mounted their horses. With reins in one hand and their gun in the other, they charged at the buffalos. The herd immediately stampeded.

They rode after them. As soon as they got within shooting distance they dismounted and prepared to shoot. They fired directly into the bull's shaggy head, causing only a slight aggravation to the buffalo because of its matted hair and thick skull. They didn't know the best shot was at his heart, located behind the shoulder.

The buffalo they shot galloped off, joining the herd. They mounted their horses again and charged at the herd three more times, but finally gave up and they returned to Ellinwood empty-handed.

Seeing the disappointment in Marie's eyes, August visited a nearby neighbor and asked him for help. After he told him about their experience, the man graciously offered his advice.

"You're going about it the wrong way," he said. "You should be doing what they call 'still' hunting. In 'still' hunting, you need to be more cautious. A buffalo can pick up the scent of a man a good distance away. You need to walk within a quarter of a mile of the herd, drop to your knees and then crawl the remaining distance. The sight of a man walking upright usually starts a stampede, but the buffalo pays little attention to a man 'down on all fours.'"

"Why is that?" August said.

"Us old timers believe that a man 'down on all fours' is likely to be mistaken for coyotes or other smaller prairie animals. The crawling hunter can bring down a buffalo before the animal finally realizes what's going on and gallops away."

That afternoon the Kopczynski brothers rode their horses out to the buffalo herd again. This time they followed their neighbor's advice.

A large herd lay just beyond a hill, not far from the Arkansas River. Taking a southeasterly course, within a quarter of a mile of the herd, August and Wilhelm dropped to their knees and crawled "on all fours." August, an expert marksman, earmarked a buffalo on the perimeter which, to him, looked like a large elephant. He and Wilhelm agreed beforehand to both shoot at the same bull. When August gave the signal, they fired, but the bull went galloping off with the rest.

The beast was injured, however, and limped badly. They pursued him with their guns, determined to have a buffalo, and finally succeeded in shooting the fat bull through the loins.

The disabled bull fell out of the herd while the rest of the herd passed on. After about a dozen shots at the enraged bull, they brought him down. They followed the Indian's example and skinned the buffalo, bringing back the hide, hams and loins to Marie at the sod house.

Her face glowed with joy as she thanked them for their good deed.

Like other white settlers in Kansas, August and Wilhelm ended up slaughtering hundreds of buffalos. After all, the buffalo was a gift from God. Although the Indian killed only for what he needed of the meat and hides, August knew men who also killed for sport or profit, shipping thousands of buffalo robes to the east. And, because the Kopczynski brothers were farmers, like other white men in Kansas, they were determined to rid the Plains of the buffalo.

Chapter 25

Come harvest time in late July, August was still optimistic, hoping and praying that his crops would survive, that he would realize an average of 30 bushels of corn an acre, even though they were in the middle of a Kansas drought. After all, he had risked everything. Like the thousand other settlers who arrived in Kansas in the spring of 1874, he naïvely believed he wouldn't encounter any problems after the back-breaking work of turning over the soil and planting the crops was done. He didn't know it takes 30 inches of rain to grow corn properly. He had never experienced drought back in *Grabionna* and hadn't counted on bad weather. He figured God would somehow provide.

But weather, he was about to learn, was not the worst enemy of a farmer. One late morning, August stood by the door to his sod house in the dry, windswept prairie, after surveying his carefully tilled acres and corn fields. He noticed a peculiar smell and looked up in the sky. The hot Kansas sun was hidden by a greenish-brown, dark cloud that moved over the plains at a ferocious speed. *What in the world is that?*

He heard an incessant whirring and rasping, which sounded to him like a rainstorm. He focused on the cloud. *Ach du lieber Gott, enormous snowflakes falling from the sky. How could this be...so late in the spring?*

Then a flying grasshopper hit him in the face. Luckily, his mouth was closed. He realized what he thought were snowflakes were millions of flying grasshoppers, also known as Rocky Mountain locusts.[32] These insects with bulging eyes, fluttering wings and tiny legs swooshed with the wind, swarms of millions, raining down from the heavens, filling the air and covering the ground two to three inches deep.

August waded in grasshoppers, paralyzed by fear. He couldn't breathe, the air was so thick with grasshoppers. His eyes widened in horror as these hungry pests swooped down on his corn and wheat fields. A tear fell from his eyes as he watched them ravage his crop. *I've lost everything. Everything's gone. All my hard work for nothing!*

Soon hundreds of grasshoppers were dripping from the door of the sod house. August thought of raking them into a pile to burn or crushing them with his boots, but this seemed impossible because of their sheer numbers. What he saw felt surreal. The whole prairie, covered thick with winged creatures, seemed to slowly crawl westward.

His whole world was crumbling before his eyes, his ambition to get ahead thwarted. His head ached; the sight made him nauseous and helpless. *Mother of God, have mercy, what are you doing to us?*

"Marie, come quick!" he said, panic in his voice. "*Ach du lieber Gott*, it's a nightmare! There's millions of grasshoppers. They're destroying everything! We must save the garden. Where is Wilhelm when I need him? Help me take the quilts and the carpet from the house to cover some of it before I run to cover the well."

The carpet was heavy, almost too heavy for Marie, but she tugged and managed to help August pull it out of the sod house to cover part of the acre garden. There wasn't enough to cover the whole thing, so they also brought out quilts and laid them over the patch of green beans and peas.

When they finished, they stood back to inspect the damage. Unfortunately, within what seemed like an hour, the grasshoppers ate through the carpet, leaving only the green onions' outer shell.[33] Everything was gone in a matter of hours. These hungry pests ate all the corn stalks,[34] every blade of grass, all the tops of carrots, radishes, potatoes, peas, green beans, squash and watermelon in the garden until nothing was left except the bare earth.

August hung his head in despair. Marie started crying.

"It's no use," August said, throwing up his hands in the air. "We've done all we can do. It's in God's hands now."

Although he had heard priests preach that God is merciful and, like Job in the Bible, would give no man a burden he couldn't bear, August was beginning to have doubts. He felt he and his family were cursed. He wondered how they could possibly recover when it seemed likely they would die from starvation. *God, have mercy! I'll do anything you ask, just spare my family this tragedy.*

August's eyes opened wider as he swatted the grasshoppers off his clothes. He noticed they left tiny holes in his and Marie's clothing. He watched amazed as the creatures also ate the handles on pitchforks and axes, leather stirrups, bridles, and leather saddles. He and Marie later learned the grasshoppers piled so high on the train tracks making the rails slippery, they actually stopped the trains.

At night before going to sleep, Marie had to shake their bedding out to get rid of the pests and planned on shaking it again before morning, if needed.

After wading in millions of grasshoppers for a day or two, a strong, hot wind came up and the grasshoppers mysteriously vanished, just like they had initially appeared, rising high and fast in the sky, leaving behind barren land. The following morning, after surveying the damage, Marie, who was five months pregnant and just beginning to show in her long, black dress and apron, turned to face August. They had little money in reserve to tide them over. Their livelihood depended entirely upon whether they could harvest the corn, but it was all gone now; their dream wiped out overnight.

"We're ruined!" Marie said, crying, her voice cracking. "I thought you said we were going to be rich! You made farming sound easy. First the drought, now the grasshoppers." She stared at him with hostile eyes. "What are we going to do now?"

August tried to take Marie in his arms but she backed away. His face turned ashen; his smile turned into a frown. He began to question his own judgment.

Why did I ever take Henry's advice? 'The money is in agriculture right now,' he had said. Ha!

August's shoulders sagged. He looked at Marie with pleading blue eyes. "I never expected this," he said, in a low tone in defense. "I'm sorry."

Marie, eyes brimming with tears, picked up her year old toddler, who was playing with locusts in the dirt beneath her feet, and held him as she continued her tirade. She stomped her feet and glared at August. It was clear she had no intention of letting him get off this easy. More than just mad or upset, she sounded like she was zeroing in on her and Leo's new enemy.

"It was you who said 'think of the first couple years as an adventure.' It's an adventure, all right! I never imagined it would be an adventure into poverty! A great provider you turned out to be! What are we supposed to do now? We don't have enough to eat. You need to think of your family instead of that foolishness about freedom. You need to think of Baby Leo. How are we going to survive?"

He bristled at her lack of appreciation. If he hadn't married her when she was with child, he wouldn't be in this mess. But he knew this wasn't fair. He loved her then and he loved her now. He tried to put things in perspective, tried to make sense of his situation, tried to rationalize his actions. *This is further proof God is punishing me for not staying in Poland and fighting for freedom.*

He shrugged his shoulders and sighed. *I just need to live my life so that I take advantage of the freedoms offered here. Marie won't understand this. It will do no good to return her anger.*

He had a better idea. He got down on his knees in the dirt. A drop of perspiration rolled down his neck as the hot, Kansas sun began to warm the windswept prairie.

Marie looked at him with suspicion. "What are you *doing?*" she said, annoyed.

He put his finger to his mouth. "Shhhh," he said. He looked up at the sky and spread out his arms. "Dear God, please help my beautiful wife to know I love her and I would never do anything on purpose to cause her or Baby Leo harm. Please let her see that you are standing by our sides and will help us get through this very tough time. Please help us get enough food to eat. In God's name we pray." He made the sign of the cross. "*In nómine Patris, et Fĭlii, et Spĭritus Sancti, Amen.*"

His words softened her heart. She sniffed, set Leo down for a moment, and cupped her hands on August's cheeks and beard. "I'm sorry I got so mad." She kissed his forehead. "August, my dear, will you ever forgive me?"

"We'll get through this somehow, Marie. I never imagined I'd be put into a situation like this where I needed to ask for help. I'm a proud man. It hurts my pride to ask for help. But I promise you I will do what is necessary to put food on our table. We won't starve. I guarantee you that."

August applied for aid at the Appraiser's office in Lakin Township, one of three civil townships.[35] He was among 500 destitute people (100 were German immigrants) who lived in Barton County, which included 150 families, who were unable to provide employment for themselves and sustenance for their families during the winter. The average farmer's age was thirty-seven and most had arrived there less than two years ago.

The County Commissioners proposed a poor farm and poor house, but the proposal was voted down. Each indigent person applying for aid had to swear that it was on account of poverty and register in the "Poor Book." August listed himself as having four in the family including his brother Wilhelm, two horses, mules or oxen, two cows, three bushels of potatoes and $125. In January 1875, he received fifty pounds of flour.

Help also came from eastern states, especially because of the efforts of fifty-seven-year-old Mary Ann Bickerdyke, nicknamed "Mother" by soldiers she nursed during the Civil War.[36] She went east and gathered clothing, foodstuffs and other supplies for the settlers in Barton County which amounted to about 200 railroad cars that were shipped to Kansas. She also distributed them.

If it had only been for the drought, the easterners wouldn't have been motivated to send supplies because bad weather was just bad luck. However, since the grasshopper plague was considered a disaster, Pennsylvania, New York and other eastern states sent beans, pork and rice, winter clothing, rail cars full of barley and corn seed for next year's crops, grain to feed their work animals, and a myriad of other needed supplies. The Granges in Illinois, Iowa, and Indiana sent fellow farmers beans, coffee, flour, meal, apples and coal to carry them through the winter months. As a gesture of good faith, the railroad companies,[37] standing to profit if the settlers had produce to transport in better times, shipped the supplies free of charge.

August and Marie felt overwhelmed by the kindness and generosity of strangers. They never imagined that one day they would be the recipients of charity but they sucked up their pride and were very grateful for the help that came their way. They thanked God for their blessings during Sunday Mass at Sts. Peter and Paul Mission Church, a small, Catholic, country church located seven miles north of Ellinwood. They hoped and prayed they would survive through the winter.

Chapter 26

After the devastating grasshopper plague, many Kansas farmers abandoned their farms and moved east, but not August. He didn't have the money to move and, after all, the Kopczynski's were not quitters, they liked a challenge. So he resolved to try again, to plant crops once more in high hopes that this time God would help him realize his dream. The grasshopper plague was just a fluke. It couldn't happen again.

Most of the land in Kansas was barren after the plague except for buffalo skeletons and bones. When hunters killed the buffalo, they would strip off the meat and leave the bones behind. The bones, which were bleached in the sun and stripped of all remaining flesh by coyotes, dogs, wolves, and birds, were strewn everywhere about the prairie. The Kopczynski brothers needed to clear these bones in the month of August before they could plant wheat in September.

They also picked up buffalo chips. Since there was little money to purchase coal and not much timber to be had, they learned buffalo chips were also inflammable and would hold heat much the same as coke. It was a cheap and abundant source of fast-burning heat, a substitute for wood, for the sod house in the winter.

Mid-morning on Monday the following week, the hot, Kansas sun again engulfed the windswept prairie where the sod house stood. While Leo was taking his morning nap, August, Wilhelm and Marie trudged with buckets about a quarter mile from the house in what were fields of corn before the grasshoppers decimated them. The sweltering sun did not deter Marie from dressing in her long-sleeved black dress and apron.

"Ewww, the smell!" she said as she gingerly picked up a crusty buffalo chip with a poker while pinching her nose shut at the same time. She wrinkled up her nose.

"You'll get used to it," August said.

"No, I won't!" Marie said. She didn't have a rag so she used the corner of her apron to handle the chip instead. "Imagine—a pregnant woman collecting stinking buffalo dung! My girlfriends and grandmother in Chicago would be laughing if they could see me now. This is *undignified*!" She threw the buffalo chip on the ground.

"Dignified, shmignified!" August said. "It's what we have to do to survive."

"These things smell to high heaven," Marie said.

"You'll forget about the smell when you use them in the stove to heat the soddie in the winter. Your nose will become accustomed to it just like you no longer notice the smell of dirt from the sod."

Marie stood with her arms crossed. "You may have a point. I guess I don't have a choice in this matter," she said, pouting, as she put the buffalo chips into the pail. "I never dreamed my life would be like this."

August winked at her. "It's not so bad really. Like I said, you'll get used to it."

Marie soon got over her squeamishness and sense of pride, collected several buckets full to take back to the sod house and said she planned on giving her hands a thorough washing after handling them.

While Marie was busy collecting buffalo chips, August and Wilhelm worked from 7:00 till dusk, six days a week, picking up buffalo bones. Compared to farming, collecting buffalo bones was pretty easy work for the Kopczynskis and by gathering about one-hundred buffalo skeletons, they accumulated a ton, which comprised a wagon load, which earned them around $8. With a team and wagon, they gathered two or three tons a day. Twenty-four dollars a day was considered good wages in tough times like these.

Since they lost their crops, it was the only viable way they had to make money. They could have sold the bones[38] to bone dealers, who would in turn sell them to fertilizer plants and sugar refineries; however, August and Marie used the bones to barter for goods they needed, like medicines, seed, sugar, salt, cornmeal and flour, feed for their draft animals and lead for bullets.

August and Wilhelm continued using a breaker plow to turn the sod into farmland and by September they were exhausted. Although seed was scare, they still needed to plant five acres of wheat. Even Marie, who was six months pregnant, helped with the planting. By the end of the month, their backs ached yet they all felt good about their accomplishment and joined in singing the popular German folk song, *O du lieber Augustin:*[39]

O du lie-ber Au-gu-stin, Au-gu-stin, Au-gu-stin,
O du lie-ber Au-gu-stin, al-les ist hin.

Hut ist weg, Stock ist weg, Geld ist weg, al-les weg.
O du lie-ber Au-gu-stin, al-les ist hin.

The days turned into months and winter came with a bluster. The snow, although not a spectacular amount, drifted along the rutted, dirt roads in Ellinwood and the surrounding area, making it a treacherous eighteen-mile journey by horseback to town and back. August and Marie's store of food was dwindling. Although they lived in poverty, they would've paid a high price for a piece of fruit or some vegetables but there weren't any to be had. They still had some potatoes left, but they survived mostly on cornbread and the occasional treat of buffalo meat when August and Wilhelm went hunting and shot one, dragging the bloody, 1,500-pound carcass back home.

The nights were long in the winter months, the sod house was pitch black inside and after dinner Marie washed dishes by candlelight, tucked Leo into bed, and then sat by the cook stove with August and Wilhelm. Sometimes she would knit or crochet and August, sitting close by the lantern, spent time reading a German language newspaper[40] or playing poker with Wilhelm or just staring at the stove, deep in thought. Sometimes they danced around the room listening to a Viennese waltz in their heads or sang German folk songs.

After reciting the nightly rosary, during which they continued to pray for Poland's freedom and independence, they snuffed out the candles and lantern, retiring to bed by seven o'clock as there wasn't much else to do.

Then they listened to the sound of wolves howling outside before making love and going to sleep. "*Ja cie kocham,*" they said to each other.

Wilhelm, who slept in the same room, never uttered a word.

In late November, Marie received a letter postmarked from Chicago with no return address.

As she opened it, she turned to August and said, "It's probably Grandma writing to tell me when she'll arrive to help me with the birth."

August saw her face flush white, as if she had been spooked by something.

"Oh, my God! No!" Marie said.

"What is it?" August said.

"Grandma passed away and two days later Grandpa died of a heart attack. Their funerals were two weeks ago. I'm all alone now," she said sobbing. "I have no one left."

"You have me and Leo."

That last remark didn't sink in. "I feel so bad. I didn't even get a chance to attend their funerals."

August put his arm around her and held her close while she cried.

Marie wiped her eyes. "Grandma won't be here for the birth now. How can I do it alone?"

"You can do this by yourself, Marie. You've been through it before. You're a pioneer woman now. You need to be tough. You need to be strong. For me. For Leo. I'll pray that God gives you strength. Everything will be fine."

"It's all your fault, August," she said, bristling. "If we hadn't moved to Kansas, I would have been there when Grandma and Grandpa died."

"I'm sorry, Marie, and especially sorry for your loss," he said. "Please find it in your heart to forgive me."

Although the sod house palpitated with warmth, the cold wind moaned and ice formed on the windows as August and Marie climbed into bed on the night of December 4th. The odor of burning buffalo chips lingered in the air. After two hours Marie awoke with labor pains. She nudged August, patting his beard and mustache, and told him to wake up. He pulled the sheets and homemade quilts over her large belly, and then woke up Wilhelm and told him to ride his horse to a nearby neighbor, and ask her to come and act as a midwife. While Wilhelm was away and Marie screamed, August fretted over what to do. He felt inadequate when it came to female matters.

Leo began fussing. "You need to pick him up, August!" Marie said.

He tried to hold him, but Leo was squirming and Marie continued to scream during each contraction. A glob of mud fell from the roof onto Marie's pillow near her head.

"August, get a rag!" Marie shouted. "I can't believe I'm having a baby in unsanitary conditions like this!"

He found a rag and wiped the mud away. Then he gave Marie a kiss on the cheek and told her not to worry, that everything would be ok. Leo started crying and Marie screamed again. August's nerves were wearing thin and he felt helpless. *Where is Wilhelm?*

Twenty minutes later, Wilhelm showed up with the neighbor. She told August to boil water and then to sit by the cook stove and stay out of the way. The birth went smoothly. Leo had a new baby brother who they named August, Jr. August felt proud of his two young sons. He had always wanted *Stammhalters*—boys to carry on the family name—which he felt would make fine farmhands one day.

The next day Marie got up and fixed the men breakfast.

Chapter 27

Hardly ever stopping to rest, August and Wilhelm continued with their farm work, breaking up more sod to prepare the soil for cultivation. August soon gained a reputation in Ellinwood among farmers as a person with enviable talents. He could fix anything and, unlike most blacksmiths in town, he usually offered his services for free.

One day an old German farmer, his neighbor to his right, asked for his help. It was late in the morning after August and Wilhelm had put in back-breaking hours cultivating the soil for planting. Although August hoped to continue working in his field that day until dusk, he never failed to take time out of his day to help a fellow farmer. He had just taken a break to eat lunch at the sod house when the neighbor approached him.

"I need to drive to Ellinwood today and my wagon is broken. Could you help me fix it?"

"I'd be happy to, my friend," August said. "What seems to be the problem?"

"I don't know. I'm not very good when it comes to fixing wagons. I've hitched my horse up to it, but the wagon won't move. I've been trying to get it moving for over an hour, but it won't budge."

"Let's walk over to your house and take a look."

August inspected the wagon and diagnosed the problem.

"It's the front axle," August said. "It needs grease. Where is the wheel-grease container with the leftover meat greases and tallow?"

"I try to use it sparingly because I don't have much."

"Well, the axle needs grease. Axles are made of hickory. This dry weather, the low humidity and hot sun, removes moisture from the wood and is not kind to the wagon wheel. It shrinks it in size."

"The grease is in the ox-horn container on the rear axle."

The sun was hot and August wiped the sweat from his brow. Before he got the grease, August examined the large iron pin with a 'C' head that attaches the double-tree bar to the to the wagon tongue to see if he could remove it. It didn't seem rusty or anything so he pulled it and used the 'C' head-pin as a wrench to loosen the remaining nuts from the axle prior to removing the wheel for lubrication.

"There's not enough grease. Do you have any fatback? We could slice it and wrap it around the wheel spindles as a lubricant."

The neighbor went in his house to get some.

After August finished greasing the axle, he tightened up the nuts with the 'C' head-pin "wrench" and put the "wrench" back where he found it.

"Can I give you some money for your effort?" the neighbor said.

"I'm glad to help. My reward is your friendship. Besides, God gives back to those who give. I'm hoping for better crops this year."

"That's mighty kind of you," the neighbor said.

"It's nothing."

In 1875, they planted potatoes again on St. Patrick's Day, but less than they did the previous year. By April, because seed was scarce, they could only plant eight acres of regular sweet corn, instead of fourteen, and two of the Kaffir corn for the draft animals, instead of four. When June came, it was time to harvest the wheat, and in late July, the corn.

That year the crops failed because they received less than 26 inches of rainfall and 30 inches was required to grow corn properly. However, that was not the worst thing that happened. August learned that the grasshoppers had laid eggs in gray pods, thirty to forty grasshoppers to a pod, buried a couple of inches deep. When the eggs hatched, all the crops were destroyed, just like the year before. The land was barren again, as far as the eye could see.

It was a Thursday, in late July 1875, and August stood at the door to the sod house, surveying his ruined crops. His deep breath stopped by a sharp pain in his heart which lasted only a minute and then subsided. August felt God had pierced his heart once again after the last devastating blow. Tears welled up in his eyes.

Dear God, why again? The crops are gone. We have no food. Marie and Leo's bellies are aching from hunger. Why are you testing me? Why do you keep punishing me? Did I make a mistake by leaving Poland? You've left me with nothing. How can I possibly provide for my family now?

Please help me feed my family and give me the strength to get through this difficult time. I'll plant again. I know you will not abandon me a third time.

This time help didn't come. Bad weather was just bad luck. Many families simply left, but not August and Marie. And, if it wasn't bad enough that they had another crop failure, later that year, they gained another little hungry mouth to feed. Another son, George, was born in October. The one-room sod house, with three adults and three small children, was crowded.

Chapter 28

For the next two and half years, the family ate mostly cornbread and buffalo meat to weather the tough times. Yet, August and Marie did not suffer alone. The other men and women in the area also struggled to find enough food to feed their families.

Late one morning in July 1877, a man in tattered clothing showed up at the Kopczynski sod house and knocked on the door. August, having heard from neighbors and friends that strangers sometimes appeared who sought to rob folks like him, cocked his rifle before he answered the door. He cracked the door open and peered out. A man with disheveled hair and dirty face and hands stood before him. The man's mouth curved into a smile.

"What do you want, my friend?" August said.

"We lost all our crops," the man said.

"We lost ours, too," August said. "We've been picking up buffalo bones to survive."

"I hurt my back and haven't been able to work," the man said. "My wife and kids are hungry. Could you spare some food?"

August wondered if it was a ruse for the man to enter the house and rob him like the stories he heard from friends and neighbors. He paused and studied the man's face. *He doesn't seem to have a gun and he is thin like he hasn't eaten in a while.*

"Wait," August said, as he shut the door.

He rushed to the kitchen where Marie, in a family way again with their fourth child, stood at the cook stove, her belly protruding, warming up two slices of day-old cornbread for lunch for August and the boys.

"Marie, there's a man outside who is begging for food. What can we give him?"

Marie bristled. "August, we don't have enough for ourselves. Leo cries himself to sleep every night because he's hungry. Why should we give some food away?"

August's eyes narrowed as his eyebrows knit together in an anguished expression. He pleaded with Marie. "The man is thin as a rail. He hurt his back and can't work. He has a wife and kids to feed. They're hungry, too."

She looked up at him. "But, we'll have to go without."

He put her cheeks in his hands. "We can miss one meal. I'll get Wilhelm to go hunting with me tomorrow."

"But, we don't have any bullets, remember?"

August shrugged his shoulders. "Marie, God gives back to you when you give."

"Ok, I'll get the last of the cornbread." Marie grabbed a tin plate to put it on.

August took the cornbread from Marie and went to the door. He handed the cornbread to the man.

"I'm sorry we don't have more to give you, but this is all we have."

The man's eyes teared up. "Are you sure you can spare it?"

August nodded. "We'll be okay. What's your name, sir? I don't think I've seen you around these parts before."

"I live closer to Ellinwood. I've been walking for miles and miles, knocking on doors, but you're the first one who has given me anything. My name is Jimmy. Jimmy Bates."

"Nice to meet you, Jimmy. My name is August." He held out his hand and the man shook it.

"I'm much obliged to you."

"Glad to help. I know you'd do the same for me if I was in your predicament. Stay in touch, my friend. God bless you."

August closed the door. He locked eyes with Marie, who stood by the cook stove with a frown on her face.

"What will we do now for food? You have three young boys and a wife to feed, besides Wilhelm."

He glanced at Marie with her expanding belly, and looked at his sons, ages four, three and two as if it was the first time he had laid eyes on them. Two-year-old George was at her feet, playing on the carpet which covered the dirt floor. August felt a pressure on his shoulders as if the weight of his responsibility had settled there. He tried to calm her fears, saying, "Marie, God will provide," but his voice sounded doubtful, not confident.

"August, you need to do something to help God help us," she said. "There are plenty of God's other children in this area who are starving."

If only there was a way to hunt a buffalo...but my neighbor and I are out of bullets. Wilhelm and I can pick up buffalo bones tomorrow and barter them for bullets at the store, but the store is closed until Monday, and that will mean we'll be without food for several days. I can't make Marie and the boys suffer like that. Please God, help us.

"Let's pray the rosary," August said. He took the amber rosary from his nightstand, the rosary his father had made for him, the only remembrance he had of his father or Poland. He and Marie knelt down in the kitchen and began reciting the prayers.

Halfway through, when he came to the Third Mystery, he got an idea. *The Indians. They don't need bullets. I'll trade them something to get some meat. But, what can I trade them? We don't have anything of value like gold coins or jewelry.*

After they finished praying, he fingered the amber rosary beads and amber cross and put it back on the nightstand. He stared at it for a minute. There before him he had the answer: the rosary.

He wrestled with the idea. *How could I give up something that means so much to me? How could I not? It's only a thing, after all. What good is a precious rosary if you die from starvation? I owe it to Marie and the kids.*

While Marie wasn't looking, he pocketed the rosary and left the sod house.

"Where are you going?" Marie called after him.

He saddled his horse. "I'll be back," was all he said.

He rode his horse over to the Indian camp near the sand hills by the Arkansas River, the place where he and Wilhelm had helped the Indians erect the teepee poles. Over the past year or so, he had two other peaceful encounters with the Indians, and now considered them friends, as everyone was his friend, even though the Indians remained suspicious of the white man.

When he got to the camp, he dismounted and met a squaw who was hanging buffalo meat out in the sunlight and open air to be cured. His stomach growled. The sight of the buffalo meat made August salivate.

The squaw ran inside the teepee and mumbled something August didn't understand. An Indian came out. When August saw him, he raised his hand in a greeting. The Indian stared at him as if not comprehending why he was visiting them.

August smiled, pulled out the rosary, felt a tug at his heart because he was giving up a precious item which had sentimental value.

He lifted the rosary into the air, then pointed at the buffalo meat with the other hand and brought his hand up to his mouth to show he wanted to eat it. The Indian took the rosary in his hands. It glistened in the sunlight. After a detailed inspection, his face lit up. He put the rosary over the squaw's petite head and the two of them grinned. He nodded his head and said something to the squaw. She went back inside the teepee and came out with a single serving of dried buffalo meat and offered it to August.

August shook his head several times. *This is not what I meant. How can I make him understand that I want the whole thing or at least half?*

He tried again. This time he held up six fingers and pointed his thumb to his own chest, hoping the Indian would realize there were six people he was talking about. He pointed to the buffalo meat, made a sweeping gesture of the whole thing, held out six fingers again, then cupped his fingers over his mouth and opened and closed them like he was chewing with his hands.

The Indian paused. A bead of perspiration trickled down August's face. The Indian looked again at the rosary around the squaw's neck, as if trying to decide if this trinket was worth it.

August held up his hands in a prayer position, his eyes pleading for help. He didn't know how to show his family was hungry, so he held up six fingers again and then rubbed his stomach.

The Indian nodded as if he understood. He walked over to where the buffalo meat hung and gave it to August.

August carted it back to the sod house and the joy he saw in Marie's face made it all worthwhile. When he later explained he had traded the rosary for it, Marie hugged him and kissed him on the forehead. "*Ja cie kocham.*"

Chapter 29

Marie, strong, fit and healthy, told August she always felt blessed during her pregnancies, and appeared even more so on April 6, 1878, when she bore another child—a daughter they named Malinda. Now she would have someone to help her with housework and cooking, another female to converse and share her womanhood with. Marie glowed as she cuddled the newborn in her arms.

The 12 x 14 ft. sod house they lived in, which was less than 200 sq. ft., grew even more crowded with the addition of Malinda. Along with a cook stove and a table, it housed a double bed for August and Marie, constructed by nailing a couple of boards together into a frame with ropes stretched from side to side with a bed tick, homemade quilts and pillows placed on top. The bed tick, a variety of colors and fabrics made of scraps from worn clothing, was filled with buffalo grass, and acted as a mattress. The bed stood in the corner and was partitioned off with a curtain of thin muslin.

On the opposite wall stood a single bed for twenty-eight-year-old Wilhelm which he shared with five-year-old Leo and three-year-old August, Jr. Two-year-old George and the baby, Malinda, slept with August and Marie. The beds often doubled as a couch or chairs when the family ate a meal or when local farmers came for a visit. Life was hard on the prairie, but the door was always open to others, whether they might be friends or strangers, in need of a meal.

In early May, August and Wilhelm felt the strong wind on their backs as they walked back to the sod house, their shoes dusty, after surveying their wheat and corn fields.

August wiped his brow with his handkerchief. "Wilhelm, do you think Katy Hanauer is *the one*? Are you getting serious with her? You know you are always welcome here, but it's high time you get married, move out and start a family of your own."

Wilhelm shot him a quizzical look. "How do you know a girl is *the one*?"

August smiled and kept walking. "Well, as I've told you, it was love-at-first-sight for me with Marie. I never expected to see her again after I lost contact. But, God had other designs for us. Later, I got Marie in a family way so I agreed to marry her, but I think I would have married her anyway. We've had our disagreements, but we love each other. You'll have disagreements in your marriage, too. Everyone does. But, you need to marry someone who shares your faith, your values and your goals." August paused. "I don't think I could've found a better pioneer wife."

"You got lucky!"

August nodded. "Yes, I did," he admitted.

Wilhelm's shoulders tightened. "I agree that I should marry, and I have been courting Katy for a while now, but courting her hasn't exactly been easy what with her family living in Raymond. Even though it's not too far away, there never seems to be any time for us to be alone. The kids are always around. Besides, I need money to buy land and build my own sod house before I can move out."

"Thankfully we've had good crops this year," August said, smiling. "The last two years were dismal because of the hot, dry summers. This year we averaged about 23 bushels of wheat per acre, compared to 20 last year. Why, some of our acres even yielded 40 bushels!"

Wilhelm turned his head to face August. "Do you think it was because of the Turkey Red wheat?"

"Yes," August said. "I'm so glad I talked to that farmer from Marion County who told me about the seed. He told me about its resistance to disease and the fact that it was better suited to withstand Kansas' cold and dry winters. It may just revolutionize wheat production here."[41]

"I heard that they loaded kitchen crocks and trunks and suitcases with Turkey Red wheat seed to bring to the U.S. and they planted their first crop in Goessel.[42] Do you think that Mennonite legend is true?"

August rolled his eyes. "I'm not sure. I don't think it was likely that they transported enough wheat to plant a large first crop, but I feel fortunate to get the seed." He cleared his throat.

Wilhelm looked out over the corn field. "What will the yield on corn be?"

"Last year we got 30 bushels per acre. [43] I hope it does as well as wheat this year, since we planted more corn than wheat, but I'm not too optimistic. Wheat always does better because it matures sooner and is harvested before the dry months set in."

"Plus it seems like we need more rain in these parts for the corn to grow properly."

August scratched his head. "You're right. Whoever said there is more freedom in farming has never farmed a day in his life. We're forever at the mercy of the weather. Every day I ask God to bless us with good weather."

"Well, like I said, I need money to buy land before I can move out, so how much are you going to pay me for this year's crop?" Wilhelm looked at August expectantly.

"Since wheat is priced at a dollar a bushel, we should make over $1,000 before expenses, thank the good Lord, so I'll give you a third of that since I've been paying all your expenses. How's that sound?"

"I'll definitely be able to buy some land with that."

Within a month, Wilhelm, or William as he called himself, made his first attempt at moving out of August and Marie's house. On June 3rd, he purchased 80 acres of choice land from the Atchison, Topeka and Santa Fe Railroad Company, paying the U.S. government $200 which amounted to $2.50 per acre. The land bordered August's in Lakin Township, ten miles north of Ellinwood.

On October 8th, four months later, the day was sunny with no clouds overhead, the cool air wafted with odors of oxen, horses and cows along with the smell of dirt from the fields, and Wilhelm married Katy Hanauer at the sod house on his brother's nearby farm. Katy looked stylish in the new black dress she had bought for the occasion and Wilhelm appeared handsome in the black homespun clothes Marie had made for him.

Father Felix S. Swemburgh, a Catholic Missionary, who ministered on horseback to both the Plains Indian tribes and the white settlers in Kansas, married the couple and said a

Latin mass inside the sod house. Because the priest rode horseback and didn't carry any wafer hosts with him, he gave the adults bread, which Marie had baked, for communion.

August, Henrietta and Stolz, and their four young children, as well as Katy's family from Raymond, Kansas, attended the wedding. They ate on tin plates, drank from tin cups, and feasted on buffalo meat, potatoes, gravy and cornbread as well as green beans, carrots and peas from their new vegetable garden. For dessert, Marie even baked a white wedding cake. As they had been surviving on a daily ration of cornbread, johnnycakes or biscuits and a little bacon, the children were relieved to finally have a good meal. They remarked that they had never seen such a large amount of good food, even on a holiday. At the end of the celebration, everyone joined in singing Catholic wedding songs as well as the familiar folk song, *O du lieber Augustin.*

In November, the wind howled outside as August sat reading a German newspaper inside near the cook stove and lantern. Then Marie brought in the postal mail which included a letter from August's stepmother, Rosalia, postmarked October 2, 1879. August opened the letter and read it out loud to Marie.

My dear August,
Please share this letter with Henrietta and Wilhelm. I have some bad news. Your father died today of a heart attack, at age 66, one month shy of turning 67. There was no warning. He wasn't sick. I think he had been

*working too hard in the field this summer and lately in
the blacksmith shop.*

August paused while reading the letter to wipe away a tear.
Marie gasped, put her hands over her mouth and said, "Oh, no!"
Then August continued reading.

*I am overcome with grief. I never imagined I would be a
widow at age 50. I don't know how I will survive. Albert
is only 17 and Theodor only 6. Although they can help
farm, they are hardly able to be breadwinners for the
family. And among the six girls—Emilia, the oldest, is
26, and Pauline, the youngest, is only 9. How can I feed
them? We may have to sell the horses. Anything you can
do to help would be very much appreciated.*

*I also wrote Mary in Chicago today. Please give my
love to Henrietta and Wilhelm. I'll write more after the
funeral which is Saturday.*

All my love,
Mama

He folded the letter and put it back in the envelope. "I'll
take this to Wilhelm and Henrietta later."

Marie got up from her chair and went over to where
August was sitting and reached down and gave him a hug.
"I'm so sorry," she said. "I know how much he meant to you."

August took Marie in his arms and held back tears. "No
one lasts forever," he said, his voice sounding sad. "But, no one
is ever prepared to lose a father. I am so sad I never saw him

again. He was the best father I could have ever hoped for and the main reason I believe in God and the Catholic Church. I owe him so much. I would be nothing if it weren't for him."

They sat there for a while, holding each other, not saying anything.

August couldn't bear the thought of dwelling on his father's death, so to take his mind off it, he changed the subject. "Our neighbor in Rice County abandoned his farm. It's 161 acres."

She stopped what she was doing and looked up at him with suspicion. "Oh? Are you thinking of moving there?"

August felt nervous bringing it up. He fidgeted. "They've got 135 acres that are cultivated already." The tone in his voice became impassioned. "It would mean we could plant more crops and *really* get ahead! I'd like to put more wheat in next September since it usually does better than corn."

Marie frowned. "But, we've got money in the bank in case we have another crop failure. Why don't we just stay here?"

August folded the German newspaper he had been reading and looked at Marie. "We could give this land to Henrietta." *I owe it to her for stealing money from her in my youth.* "The land in Rice County is better land and we wouldn't have to turn over the soil. We could make a whole lot more money."

Marie shook her head. "But, what if we have another drought?"

August didn't let on that he also feared another crop failure, leaning forward closer to Marie, reassuring her, "We had a record crop this year. I expect to have an even better one next year."

"By the way, why should we give our 80-acre farm to Henrietta? Why not Wilhelm?"

"Wilhelm already has 80 acres. He can't farm 160 acres by himself. Stolz said his own land is worthless after the plague. He and Henrietta deserve a break. He's a very hard worker and he's helped us out a lot. Besides, I owe it to Henrietta for what I did to her in my youth."

"What did you do to her?"

"I'd rather not say. That's between me and God."

"Well, if it puzzles me, it will certainly puzzle Henrietta and Stolz."

So, August told Marie what he had done. "I've carried this guilt with me all these years. It's time I repay her. I want to finally make things right. I don't feel I'm a good Catholic if I don't."

"Oh, August, my dear. But, 80 acres?"

"The land doesn't mean that much to me, especially since it's been plagued by grasshoppers. Even though I applied to homestead it, I wasn't able to improve or cultivate the land. As long as I'm going to abandon it anyway, I may as well give it to Henrietta and Stolz. He can put in a claim to homestead it. I hope he will be able to turn things around and make a profit off it someday."[44]

Although Marie usually offered an opposing argument, she always gave in and followed what August wanted to do.

August left the house then to report the bad news first to Wilhelm and then rode over to Henrietta and Stolz's place.

"I have bad news and good news," August said after a loving greeting and a bit of small talk.

"*Oh?*" Henrietta said. "What's the bad news?"

"Papa died of a heart attack." He handed Rosalia's letter to her.

Henrietta's face went blank. "Land sakes, almighty, what next?" She read the letter. Her face softened. "I am so sorry for Mama. She must feel all alone. And with so many mouths to feed!"

"I feel bad," August said. "Neither of us are in any position to help her, but I'll try to send what little I can."

"So, what's the good news?" Henrietta said.

He told them about the new farm they were planning to move to in Rice County and asked what they thought about taking over their 80-acre farm in Barton County.

"Are you abandoning this farm to take the other one?" Stolz said.

"Yes. I can't farm both."

"I think that's a good move on your part," Stolz said. "That's mighty generous of you, though, to offer us your farm. Why wouldn't you give it to Wilhelm?"

"He's already got more than he can handle. You've helped us out and besides, Henrietta is my sister. I owe her more than you could ever know and you both deserve a break. So, what do you say? It's yours if you want it. You could apply to homestead it."

"You've got yourself a deal."

August and Marie planted seventy acres in Rice County in the fall with the help of Stolz and Wilhelm. The wheat and corn fields looked promising and things went well until May 31, 1880, when August decided against inspecting the fields after dinner at noon because it was overcast and cloudy. By three o'clock the sky was covered with black storm clouds. He saw a flash of lightning and heard a deafening rumble which sounded to him like a huge herd of buffalo stampeding over the Plains. Suddenly hail as large as baseballs rained from the sky with the force of a tornado, bouncing high off the ground, pounding the wheat and corn fields, as well as the sod house.

Soon the lightning was so blinding the interior of the sod house was lit up like a Christmas tree. But what scared little Leo, August, Jr., George and the baby even more was the booming thunder. Its hammering caused the baby to scream and the other children to wail, putting their hands over their ears. As August, Marie and the children huddled on the floor near the double bed, as far from the cook stove pipe as possible, the roof started caving in and the windows crashed inward from the force of the hail. August warned the children to stay away from the windows while Marie swept up the glass.

When the hail stopped, August opened the door and looked out. The fields were blanketed in white, the crops all destroyed from the hail. He felt sick to his stomach. He remembered *bad weather is just bad luck*. He swallowed hard. *God, are you cursing me?* He sighed, wiped tears away from his eyes, and closed the door.

"What is it?" Marie said, staring at him.

He shrugged. "It's all gone. The crops—they're ruined! All our hard work." He looked away, avoiding eye contact with her.

She stamped her feet. "*You* thought this would be a record crop," she screamed. "That we would make more money if we moved to this farm!" She gave him a stern look of resentment.

He felt her hostility. He tried his best not to return her anger but he couldn't help feeling defensive. "Well, I thought *wrong*, ok? This area is jinxed. If it wasn't the grasshoppers, it was the drought. Now it's the hailstorm. This is the last straw. I'm through with farming."

She put her hand on his shoulder. "You can't mean that."

"I do. I've been doing a lot of thinking lately. I told myself if this crop failed, I'd go back to my old blacksmith trade."

"But, there are no jobs for blacksmiths here. You said yourself the blacksmiths in Ellinwood have loyal customers and there's no room for another blacksmith here."

He sat down at a chair by the kitchen table. "Yes, but there's a need in Westphalia."

Marie's voice rose. "*Westphalia?* Where's Westphalia? Why would we go there?"

August smiled, lost in his own dream. "It's a small town where only a handful of people live in eastern Kansas. Father Swemburgh told me some German Catholics have started a colony there. They've advertised for a blacksmith in the pamphlet he left with me. He encouraged me to look into it. My father always said, 'Never trust anyone except the priest and the doctor.' My father was right. Like the priest in *Grabionna*, Father Swemburgh knows what's best for us."

Marie threw her hands up in the air. "Land sakes! What will we do for *money*?"

"Don't worry. The good Lord will provide." He smiled again.

Marie gave him an exasperated look. Then she rolled her eyes, crossed her arms and stared him in the eye. "Then he can provide for us here."

"Marie...don't you see?" He paused to get her reaction.

"No," she said, shaking her head.

He locked eyes with her. "We're ruined. It's too much work to save this farm. Besides, we'd starve. We should have just enough money to move and buy a shop. This is our only chance. We can live above the shop until we make more money. Once we get ahead then we can buy another farm there and you and the children can run it. It's the best I can offer you. We'll survive, I promise you."

"Moving *again*?" Marie asked, resigning herself again to giving in to his wants. Her voice rose. "*With all these kids? How* are we moving?"

"By covered wagon, pulled by teams of oxen. We can load all the things we'll need and give the rest to Henrietta and Wilhelm."

"What about the Indians?"

August didn't want to hear anymore from Marie. He knew how smart and capable she was. He felt he always had to rebut her arguments. "I told you not to worry your pretty head about the Indians. I make friends with everyone including Indians. Besides, they've been put on reservations years ago and, anyway, they never show their faces unless they want to be seen, unless there's trouble. We don't intend to cause any trouble. We're just passing through on the cattle trail. The road to Westphalia will be smooth sailing, wait and see."

She sat down in a chair beside him. "So, you think Westphalia is our only hope. You're sure?"

"Yes. We'll get a new start." His shoulders tightened. "It will be better, I promise." *Oh God, I sure hope I can keep my promise.*

Chapter 30

Quiet hung over the prairie on the morning of June 21, 1880 as the Kopczynskis prepared to leave their sod home in Rice County. The grass-covered land was flat as far as the eye could see with a horizontal line running in the middle between the sky and earth. Thirty-four-year-old August woke up early to the sound of birds chirping and went to feed the oxen and horses, milk the cow, and prepare them for the long, two week journey to Westphalia.[45] Twenty-four-year-old Marie hurriedly dressed the three boys, ages seven, six, and five, and fed two-year-old Malinda.

Wilhelm helped August load the wagon. The wagon, known as a prairie schooner because the canvas cover top billowed in the wind and looked like a sailing ship from a distance, had a flat, rectangular wagon box below an arched frame of hickory, bowed hoops covered with a white heavy-duty canvas. August had waterproofed the taut-stretched canvas by soaking it in linseed oil, which protected them from the sun and rain.

August and Wilhelm packed the heavy items which couldn't easily be replaced, wrapped the plow, the cook stove, bags of seed and a chest of drawers, placing them on the bottom of the wagon box. He gave the beds he had made out of boards to Wilhelm. Next came the clothes and the bed ticks which were strapped down. On top were items they needed along the way including a large water keg, flour and salt, hardtack, lots of dried fruits and vegetables, salt pork, a cooking pot, kitchen utensils, homemade quilts, and a spare axle just in case one of theirs broke along the way. August's rifle was essential for shooting game for food. Besides the teams of oxen they used to pull the wagon, they also brought along a milk cow and two horses.

Although the wagon could carry a load of a ton and a half, August and Wilhelm were careful to keep the weight down to a ton because a lighter wagon would not bog down in a muddy stream or tire the oxen pulling the load. On one side of the wagon was a water bucket and brake lever, on the opposite side, a toolbox. A grease bucket, filled with animal fat and tar, which was used to keep the wheel hubs greased, hung from the rear axle.

Wilhelm helped August hitch the oxen to the wagon. The three young boys climbed up the back of the wagon. August helped Marie swing up to the wooden seat in front and Wilhelm took Malinda and handed her to Marie. They said their goodbyes to Wilhelm and the Stolz family who came to see them off. August climbed up, took the reins and sat beside Marie who held Malinda on the wagon seat.

With clean clothes and scrubbed faces, August and the children were excited to get going, glad to be leaving Rice County and the crop failures behind. The sun rose in the east, blanketing the flat land of the prairie in sunlight, on the dust-covered cattle trail. The scent of oxen wafted in the air as they spied carefully-tilled soil in the distance and a neighbor's sod house about a mile down the road.

Marie looked like a sturdy, pioneer's wife in her long-sleeved black dress and matching prairie bonnet. Unlike August who appeared optimistic and hopeful that things would be better in Westphalia, Marie, although glad to leave the crop failures behind, seemed apprehensive and skeptical about what their new life would bring. Moving to Kansas from Chicago had been disastrous. Moving east might also be a mistake, but things couldn't get worse, could they?

Along the wagon roads and cattle trail to Westphalia were high steppe-like, treeless plains, and a few hills. The air was hot and dry. Fresh water was scarce. Lack of food and water made the cattle trail very risky. During most of the trip, they traveled only fifteen miles a day.

They started out riding in the covered wagon, but the seats were uncomfortable in the hot sun and the oxen moved very slowly because of the load. So, they stopped to let the oxen rest and when they continued on, August carried Malinda while Marie and the three young boys followed him, walking beside the wagon as the oxen pulled it.

They traveled slowly on foot over the cattle trail for six long and suffering hours, gaining only ten miles, rarely encountering other travelers. Lost in thought about his responsibilities as a husband and father as well as keeping his family safe, August spoke few words while Marie tended to the children who broke the silence with their mindless chatter. After the boys complained that their feet hurt and they were tired of walking, the family climbed back in the wagon to ride.

The covered wagon glided easily over cattle trail bumps and dips with its six-foot-diameter rear wheels as well as the four-foot-diameter front wheels. Time passed by quickly until they came upon a patch of sand and mud. Luckily, the wagon wheel's wide rims prevented the wagon from sinking. They weren't so lucky when, after riding in the covered wagon for an hour or two, the boys in the back started fighting.

"Mama, Leo poked me," five-year-old George said, tattling.

"I did not!" said Leo, the oldest.

George's large green eyes lit up with anger at his brother. "You did to!" he said.

Holding Malinda in her arms, Marie turned around to look at them. "Stop fighting, you two! Leo, you're old enough to know better."

"But, he started it," blond-haired Leo said. "He's a baby-faced liar!"

George punched Leo in the stomach. Leo punched him back.

"Quit, you two!" Marie said.

"But, he called me a name," George said, whining. "Mama, he keeps looking at me. Tell him to stop looking at me!"

Then Leo snatched George's toy gun which he had fashioned from a buffalo bone.

"Leo stole my gun," George said, sobbing.

Marie turned toward August. "August, do something! These boys are tired and cranky and getting on my nerves."

"I need to pee," Leo said.

"Hold on, son," August said. "We're stopping. We need to feed the oxen and let them have a rest anyway."

"Are we there yet?" six-year-old August, Jr. said.

"No, we have many more days to go," Marie said. "We're just stopping for supper."

The hot, Kansas sun was setting in the distance, and while August tended to the animals, giving them Kaffir corn to eat and water from the large keg, Marie spread a homemade quilt on the buffalo grass near the wagon where the children could sit. Then August helped her start a fire to cook the food in the pot she had brought.

"What are we having to eat?" said August, Jr., his sandy hair blowing in the wind.

"Salt pork and potatoes," Marie said.

"Thank goodness it's not cornbread again!" August, Jr. said.

"You can say that again!" Leo said, laughing.

"Me, too!" George said. "I'm glad, too!"

August glanced at Marie and then back at the kids. He seethed. The stress and strain of this journey came to a head and made him snap. "You'll eat what we tell you to eat. Do you understand that?"

The boys looked frightened. "Yes, Sir," they answered, sheepishly.

"You should never complain about your mother's good cooking. You should be grateful for any food at all. There are poorer people than us who are starving."

"You can always give my helping of cornbread to the poor," August, Jr. said.

"One more word out of you and you'll get a whipping. Do you understand?"

"Yes, Sir," said August, Jr.

"August," Marie said, "don't be so harsh on them. They're just boys."

He scowled. "And boys need to be disciplined!"

Marie silently dished up the salt pork and potatoes on the children's tin plates.

"Now, let's say the meal prayer before we eat," August said. He made the sign of the cross. Marie and the children followed suit. *"In nómine Patris, et Fīlii, et Spĭritus Sancti, Amen. Segne, Vater, diese Gaben...Bless us, oh Lord, for these thy gifts..."*

When they finished eating, they bedded down outside in homemade blankets underneath the full moon. After a long and tiring day, August made sure his rifle lay by his side underneath the blankets, while the family prayed the rosary together. He thought about the amber rosary his father had made which he traded with the Indians. He had a new rosary now, black beads, however, not near as special as the amber one. The children drifted off to sleep before they finished their prayers.

Marie elbowed August and pointed to the kids. All his anger gone, he smiled like the proud papa he was and put his arm around Marie.

"What a lovely night, my dear," he said. "We'll remember it forever." He kissed her cheek. "Goodnight, my dear. *Ja cie kocham.*"

She pulled the covers up to her neck and turned on her side. "Goodnight," she said. *"Ja cie kocham."*

They were asleep about an hour when August woke up with a start. He opened his sleepy eyes and glanced around the arid plains. The sky was pitch black, but ominous clouds had moved in. He noticed the air seemed humid and smelled the heavy scent of impending rain. The wind picked up, whistling, giving a warning signal like a howling wolf in the night.

For a moment, everything was quiet. Even the wind held its breath. Then, a jagged streak of white hot lightening cracked the darkened sky, and seconds later the silence was broken by rolling booms of thunder.

It woke Marie and the kids. Another streak of lightening darted across the sky followed by reverberating thunder. Bam, bam, bam, it continued, relentlessly.

"Papa, I'm scared," said George, sobbing.

"So, am I," Marie said. "August, what should we do?"

Soon the rain fell, slow at first, and then as if from buckets, in torrents, unforgiving. In the middle of nowhere, heading east on a cattle trail, there was no place to take shelter besides the wagon.

Paralyzing fear lined August's face; he tried hard not to panic. "This huge storm reminds me of my journey over here," he said, as he herded Marie, the two youngest boys and two-year-old Malinda to safety inside the wagon with their blankets to sleep on the load, while he and Leo took cover underneath the wagon.

"*Ach du lieber Gott*, let's hope the livestock won't get spooked by the storm."

After more thunder and lightning, an ox broke loose from the rope where he was tied and stampeded away from the wagon in the dark of night. Feeling violated by the storm, August got out from underneath the wagon, attempted to run after the ox with his gun in the soggy rain, but decided his efforts were futile in the heavy darkness. He vowed to hunt him when the sun came up tomorrow. He returned to the wagon and secured the remaining three oxen, and went back underneath the wagon to join Leo and get some sleep.

At the crack of dawn, August woke seven-year-old Leo and the two of them set about scouring the area for the missing ox.

August took his rifle just in case. Unlike the flat terrain back in Ellinwood which had smooth sandy surfaces, this ground had a lot more rocks and small hills.

After an hour of looking, Leo spotted the lost ox. "Papa, over here!" he shouted.

The ox was lying on the ground and appeared to be dead. As he inched closer, August noticed a rattlesnake nearby.

"Don't touch that snake, son!" he said. "It's poisonous!" He cocked his rifle and fired several shots. If it wasn't dead before, it was now.

"How did you know it was poisonous?" Leo said, inspecting the dead snake.

"Our neighbor in Rice County told me many people have died from snakebites. You can see the rattle here at the tip of his tail."

"It looks like it has eyes, but no ears," Leo said.

"That's right, son. It can't hear sounds. The old-timer said they sense vibrations in the ground. He also said the snake's eyes see well even in low light, and there is a place between the eyes and nostrils that helps the snake hunt in darkness by detecting body heat. The ox was probably its prey."

"What should we do with the dead ox?" Leo said.

"Leave it for the wolves and birds. We'd better get back to the wagon. Your Mama will be worried if she gets up and finds us both gone."

"Can the three remaining oxen pull the wagon?" Leo said.

"They'll have to, son," August said. "They'll have to."

Chapter 31

August and Leo returned to camp, and packed their belongings. Walking alongside the wagon to lessen the load for the oxen, the family headed east on the wagon-rutted, dirt road. They were about forty miles west of their destination. It would take them at least another three days to get there.

The sun peeked its head over the horizon and the sky appeared bright and blue, dotted with white clouds. The morning air felt cool and crisp until around noon, when the hot sun made them sweat and thirst for a drink of water. They stopped only long enough to refresh themselves with food and water and let the remaining oxen rest.

After the second day, the oxen started to tire and moved slower, so to lighten the load, August abandoned the plow and the chest of drawers alongside the road. When the oxen began moving again, August walked alongside holding Malinda while Marie held hands with George and August, Jr. and Leo trailed behind.

Then, in the middle of the wagon-rutted road, out of nowhere, August spied two ruffians five feet away. They appeared to be in their early twenties, the tall one pointing a rifle at the approaching wagon and at both August and Marie. Dressed in black, tattered clothes that looked like they hadn't been washed since the Civil War, with grease-backed hair, the tall one had a large, pointed nose and a scar on his face and dark, bushy eyebrows that knit in a permanent frown. The short one had a beer belly on him and large hands.

August thought about his own rifle which was hidden inside the wagon near the front seat. Instead of panicking, he tried to defuse the situation.

"*Guten Tag, meine Freunde,*" he said. "*Bitteschőn?*"

The tall one with dark hair sneered at August, then spoke to his companion. "Did you hear that, Johnnie? The man wished us a good day and wants to know how he can help us."

"That's so funny, Richard," Johnnie said, laughing. They both walked toward August, Richard, the tall one still pointing his rifle.

"Hey Mister, have you got any gold on you?"

August shook his head. "Sorry, no."

"How about in the wagon?" said Richard.

As soon as they got closer, August smelled heavy alcohol. "No. We're poor folks."

"What about jewelry?" Johnnie said. "I'll bet your fine-lookin' Missus here has some."

Marie's face grew pale. She grimaced and looked away. August saw gripping fear in her eyes. He stepped in front of Marie to shield her. He wasn't about to let Johnnie touch her.

"We don't have any jewelry either," he said, blocking Johnnie's view. He stared at him, blank-faced, not revealing the disgust and rage he felt inside.

"Maybe you've got a drink for us," Richard said, grinning. He was missing some teeth. "Mind if we search the wagon?"

"Suit yourselves."

"We'll take the boy here for security," Richard said, pointing the rifle at Leo.

Marie gasped.

"It'll be ok," August whispered to reassure her.

The two hooligans were at the back of the wagon foraging for gold and jewelry inside, making a mess of August's carefully organized load. August, who was near the front, heard one of them say, "Where's the gold and jewelry, Sunshine?"

"Papa told you," Leo said. "There ain't none!"

Meanwhile, August climbed up the front seat, quickly retrieved his hidden rifle and pointed it at the two robbers inside the wagon.

"Run, Leo!" he said. "Run!"

Johnnie, the short one, was holding onto him with his large hands, but Leo was able to break free. Johnnie ran after him. Richard, still holding his rifle, turned around and shot at Leo, missing him by a half inch.

In the same minute, August fired a single shot to Richard's head, killing him.

Marie stood by, horrified, holding on to the two youngest boys and Malinda.

August took off after Leo. Johnnie had Leo in an arm grip. They were only a few feet away when August, brandishing his rifle, yelled, "Your friend is dead and you will be, too, if you don't let my boy go!"

August inched closer. Johnnie looked puzzled and scared.

"You won't get hurt if you let him go," August said as calmly as he could under the circumstances.

Johnnie released his grip on Leo and fled, stumbling as he went.

August threw his arms around Leo and they walked back to the wagon. Marie and the children watched as August dug a shallow grave for Richard. Leo helped him lift the body from the back of the wagon.

"God may punish you for this, August," Marie said, wiping blood from the back of the wagon.

Even though he was thinking the same thing, wondering if he had done what was right, August recoiled at Marie's words. It was tough hearing that from her. Wasn't a wife always supposed to be on her husband's side? "Marie, God is merciful. Our family was in danger. There was no other way. The killing was justified."

"But what about those you killed in the Danish-Prussian War? Maybe God continues to punish you for that."

August and Marie returned to the front of the wagon and climbed up the seat. August took the reins. "Although I'm not proud of it, sometimes killing is justified. Besides, I had no choice. I had to join that war. And I had to kill that man today to save my son."

Marie touched his arm. "Listen, I thought you hated killing, hated war. Isn't that why you avoided service in the Franco-Prussian war?"

August had mixed emotions. He did hate war and killing, but life sometimes wasn't as black and white as that. How could he possibly defend his actions to Marie? How could he make her understand his viewpoint? "Bismarck only wanted able bodies to fight his Prussian wars. We weren't fighting for Poland or freedom. We were Bismarck's slaves. It was not a just war. And I was wise to avoid it."

She nodded. "You are wise," she said. "I just pray that God thinks so, too!"

On July 4, 1880, thirteen long and tiring days after they started, the covered wagon came across a gently sloping upland prairie, located east of the Coffey county line near the head of Thomas Creek in east Kansas. The Anderson county, six-block town site of Westphalia, known formerly as Cornell, had just been renamed by Anton Flusche, who was postmaster and railroad agent, and one of the six Flusche brothers who came to the U.S. from Westphalia, Germany. [46]

Upon their arrival, as the three remaining oxen pulled the wagon into town, August and Marie met with the three youngest Flusche brothers, Anton, Emil and August, who had taken up colonization activities, and spent a great deal of money advertising for would-be German immigrants in Catholic newspapers and pamphlets. The Flusche brothers made a profit by helping those immigrants find suitable farming locations. The brothers were responsible for establishing seven Catholic colonies, including one in Westphalia, Kansas. [47]

August Flusche sold the first resident lot to August Kopczynski from the land he purchased from Smith P. Cornell, the original homesteader who platted the town.

At thirty-four, August's dream to own his own business and be his own boss came true overnight. No more working in undesirable conditions at a factory where the bosses took advantage of "green" workers. No more starving due to poor crops in Barton or Rice counties or being at the mercy of weather conditions.

The pride in his heart showed on his face. His future looked bright. He could not stop smiling.

He started construction of his blacksmith shop on the lot the next day. He hauled rough lumber from LeRoy, several miles away. He also built new beds out of boards, dug a six-foot hole and covered it with a four-by-four foot wooden square, seven-foot tall outhouse, and constructed a 200-square-foot dwelling above the blacksmith shop, with outside stairs. Luckily they had brought with them the cook stove, but they bought a table and a chest of drawers, to replace the one they abandoned on the trail, from the Flusche Brothers Store, a large storeroom filled with general merchandise.

During construction, August discussed a new name for the shop when he and Marie were in the Flusche Brothers Store to get some supplies. August was known in town as a Polander and as "Mr. Ski" because most people couldn't pronounce his last name.

"How about Mr. Ski's Wagon Repair?" Marie said, standing at the counter.

"Sounds like a great name," said Anton Flusche who was waiting on Marie.

"Well, it won't just be for wagon repair or horseshoes," said August. "We'll also make iron pots and pans."

"Then, maybe Mr. Ski's Iron Works?" said Anton.

He stood scratching his beard. Like other men in the West, August had let his dark beard grow long. Although Marie preferred his clean-shaven look, beards were in style and Marie cared a great deal about fashion and style, so she gave August her approval.

"I'm thinking maybe Kopczynski Iron Works," said August.

"He's very proud of his last name," said Marie.

"I hope you are, too, dear," August said, glancing at Marie.

After construction was finished, August felt giddy, like a kid in a candy store, and could hardly contain his excitement when he erected the sign out front:

KOPCZYNSKI IRON WORKS

His heart beat so fast he thought it would pop out of his chest. Since his was the only blacksmith shop in town, he soon gained customers. He was amazed by the speed at which his luck had changed.

The family lived above the shop for the next two years. Their new home always smelled of iron from the shop as well as dried buffalo dung which they used to heat their home in the winter.

The Kopczynskis became dependent on the Flusche brothers who sold them land, clothing, furniture and other assorted items they needed, as well as for the practice of their Catholic faith.

Every two weeks, on alternate Sundays, Father Anastasias, Prior, a Carmelite superior, said a Latin Mass in the south living room of the Flusche brothers' family home[48] east of town. The Mass was said only when he would come from the monastery in Scipio, located thirty miles from Westphalia.

On one Sunday, August, Marie and a dozen other adults as well as the Kopczynski's four children and their friends' children gathered in the living room when the priest knocked on the door.

August was in a hurry for the priest to hear his confession to relieve the heavy weight and anxiety he felt in his heart over the grave sin he committed, but first he needed to begin with pleasantries.

"Good morning, Father," August said as he opened the door for the priest.

"Good morning," the priest said. "Isn't it a gorgeous day? No wind. No rain. And it looks to me like today will be sunny, praise the Lord."

August decided not to wait further. "Father, I was wondering if you could hear my confession before Mass."

Normally, after Mass, things got more chaotic, so this was not an unusual request. "I'd be happy to, praise the Lord. Is there a room where we can have some privacy?"

With the crowd seated in the living room, the only other possible rooms were the kitchen or a bedroom, but since this was the Flusche residence, not August's house, the bedroom would have been too private. "Yes. Let's go in the kitchen."

They went to the airy kitchen and sat in chairs by the wooden table covered with a flower-covered tablecloth.

"Bless me Father, for I have sinned, it has been a month since my last confession," August said in a soft tone of voice.

Two young teenage boys stood near the door. One of them turned to the other and snickered. "Let's listen. August is sayin' his confession."

August heard them. "Quiet, you two!" he said. "You should be ashamed of yourselves for listening in on a private confession. I'll tell your parents about what you did if you say one word. Now, get away from that door!" The boys scrambled.

August turned to the priest. "It's hard to get privacy in a house full of people. Now, where was I? Oh, yes, I broke the fifth commandment, Father. I'm afraid I've murdered a man."

It felt good to finally get this off his chest. He could feel his heart becoming lighter already.

The priest looked startled. "Oh, my!" he said. "Killing a man is a grave mortal sin. The Bible says 'those who kill by the sword will perish by the sword.' You don't seem to be the murderous type. Why did you do it? How did it happen?"

He told him about the incident during their trek to Westphalia. He felt relief at getting this burden off his chest. "I'm not proud of killing a man, but I felt I had no other choice."

"God is a God of mercy, praise the Lord," the priest said. "You killed him in self-defense in order to protect your family. God will forgive you. Please say a rosary in reparation for your sin. Now say your act of contrition."

August prayed, "O my God, I am heartily sorry for having offended Thee, and I detest all my sins because of Thy just punishments, but most of all because they offend Thee, my God, Who art all-good and deserving of all my love. I firmly resolve, with the help of Thy grace, to sin no more and to avoid the near occasions of sin. Amen."

"I absolve you from your sins in the name of the Father, the Son and the Holy Ghost. Now go in peace!"

A sense of peace washed over August, the heavy weight had been lifted from his heart. *Forgiveness is wonderful!* He nodded at the priest.

They returned to the living room and the priest began saying the Latin Mass.

Feeling blessed, August said a silent prayer, thanking God for his children and his new friends, for enough food to eat, as well as for the prosperity they now enjoyed. He couldn't possibly foresee the trouble to come.

<h1 style="text-align:center">Chapter 32</h1>

A year later, in December 1881, with a foot of snow on the ground, Wilhelm and Katy, who left Barton County on August's advice, arrived in Westphalia and bought a residence lot, which included more than two acres, from Emil & Anna Flusche. Katy, who had lost a child in childbirth, looked at Marie's pregnant belly with a faintly jealous eye. Marie bore her fifth child on January 8, 1882, another girl, who they named Mary.

The blacksmith business had prospered, and on August's birthday, February 14, 1882, the Kopczynskis paid August Flushe $40 for the lot on Division Street where he built a new blacksmith shop. The Kopczynskis also purchased school relinquishment land, located close to town, which included a small 80-acre farm that had an old shack on it. August remodeled the shack and the family moved to the small farm.

Things went well until four days before Christmas of that year, when seven-year-old George came down with aches and pains and a high fever. When the fever didn't go away after three days, Marie sent August to get the local doctor, fifty-one-year old, Swiss-born, Jacob Affolter.

"I'm afraid young George has smallpox, an acute, highly contagious disease. He's very sick. Keep your other children away from him."

Marie's face went pale and her brows knit in worry.

"Oh God, smallpox? I heard it's…incurable," August said.

"Yes. But people do pull through."

Marie gasped. "What causes it?"

"We don't know that much about Smallpox[49] or what causes it."[50]

"Then how do you know George has it?" August said.

"There is an eruption or two on his body. They will quickly spread over his entire body. The lesions will become blister-like and pustular within a week. In another week or two, you'll see pockmarks on his skin."

"Is George going to die?" Marie said, her voice cracking and tears brimming in her eyes. August walked over to her and put his hand on her shoulder.

"I don't know for sure. I don't want to scare you, but it has killed more people over time than any other infectious disease."

"What should we do?" August said as he squeezed Marie's shoulder.

The doctor sighed. "Pray."

After Dr. Affolter left, the Kopczynskis recited the family rosary that night and prayed for George's recovery. *Surely he would get better. God would see to it.*

On Christmas day, things were gloomy at the Kopczynski house. The children wanted to play with George and when they were told not to, they sensed things were bad.

They sat at the table and chairs at the shack to eat their oranges, their Christmas gift, which usually was a source of utter joy. The fruit was expensive and hard to get, and August had insisted on getting it even this year, although George was so sick. It was meant to be a beacon of hope. He peeled four-year-old Malinda's orange for her and the boys peeled their own.

"These are juicy," Leo said, tasting one. "I wish we could have oranges every day of the year."

"Me, too," August, Jr. said. "Thank you Mama and Papa. Are you going to give Georgie one, too?"

"Not today," Marie said. "I'm afraid he's too sick to eat it. Georgie just needs rest."

After the Kopczynski children finished eating their oranges, Wilhelm and Katy stopped by to wish them Christmas cheer.

"Merry Christmas!" Wilhelm said, smiling as he came through the front door to the shack. "Do you have a hug for Uncle Wilhelm and Aunt Katy?"

Leo and August, Jr. ran to him and opened up their arms for big hugs.

"How is Georgie?" Wilhelm wanted to know.

"Still sick," Marie said. "Dr. Affolter was here yesterday. He said George has smallpox."

"I was afraid of that," Wilhelm said, then paused, as if unsure how to go on. "There's an epidemic of smallpox in Barton County. I got a letter from Henry Bockemoehle yesterday. I brought it with me."

"Have people died?" Marie's voice was barely audible.

"I don't know. All I know is they are trying to keep it away. Here's what the letter says:

Town leaders in Ellinwood have taken stern measures to protect Ellinwood's population from the smallpox epidemic in Great Bend.[51] They closed schools and didn't allow travelers from Great Bend to pass through

Ellinwood. They constructed a guardhouse, which cost almost $12, and erected a signboard about a mile west of Ellinwood. Round-the-clock guards included J. Batchman and Theo Iten, Jr. They also instructed the Marshall to meet every train to prevent any passengers coming from Great Bend from getting off in Ellinwood. They increased his wages because it constituted 24-hour duty. The city had to pay a lot of money for the guardhouse, guards, their wages and the sign. I tell you, this is the greatest scare Ellinwood has ever had!"

Three days later, on January 28, George died.

August, fighting the muscles in his face, tried to show no emotion, remaining strong for Marie and the boys who sat sobbing, but he was angry with God. *Why did you take my son away from me? What did I do to deserve this? Have I not been a good husband and father? I have tried to provide. And I have tried to live by your rules. Are you punishing me?*

The house was consumed by sadness. Marie continued to sob as August carried George's dead body, wrapped in a blanket, out of the house, and placed the small corpse in the wagon while the frightened boys looked on in horror and shock.

August, Jr., who was just a year older than George, asked, "Am I going to die, too?"

Marie, through elephant tears, tried to comfort him. "No, not anytime soon. Georgie was very sick. His time on earth was up and God called him to heaven. That just shows we should never take life for granted."

August nodded. "I'm going to contact Father Broccard, that Carmelite priest in Scipio, so he can perform funeral rites for George at St. Teresa's. I'll ride over to Wilhelm and Katy's. I need Wilhelm's help in digging a grave. I can't do it on my own in this foot of snow we have."

The cold wind blew as August hitched the oxen to the wagon and Marie, who held Baby Mary, climbed up the seat in front while the other children climbed in the back.

"Don't touch George's body, unless you want to get small-pox and die like Georgie."

"August! Don't be so blunt," Marie said. "You'll scare them for life."

"Nonsense," he said. "They won't listen unless you put the fear of God into them."

As protective as a mother bear with her cubs, August thought, sure that her sympathetic attitude would do his kids more harm than good. This was a matter of life and death, after all. The kids needed to be fearful.

"We've just lost one son. We don't want to lose another child."

The children sat still and quiet in the back of the wagon. Dressed in warm winter coats and hats, they rode over to Wilhelm's first, then to St. Teresa's Church for a funeral mass, and then to the cemetery, a five-acre plot lying a half mile northwest of the church. Although digging in the snow and ice proved a challenge, Wilhelm and August shoveled a two-foot shallow grave.

Sprinkling holy water over the blanket-wrapped corpse of George, the priest began:

"A reading from the book of Matthew 18:1-4: At that time the disciples came to Jesus, saying, 'Who is the greatest in the kingdom of heaven?' And calling to him a child, he put him in the midst of them and said, 'Truly, I say to you, unless you turn and become like children, you will never enter the kingdom of heaven. Whoever humbles himself like this child is the greatest in the kingdom of heaven.'"

He read another verse—Matthew 19:14: "But Jesus said, 'Let the little children come to me and do not hinder them for to such belongs the kingdom of heaven.' ...and let the perpetual light shine upon him."

Why pray? August wondered as the ceremony drew to a close. *It's no good when God never answers your prayers.*

The priest made the sign of the cross, then August and Wilhelm shoveled dirt on the grave and stuck a small wooden cross in the ground to mark it.

Then the family left the cemetery.

Chapter 33

Two years later, in January 1884, the snow and ice piled up high outside the shack on the small farm while the Kopczynskis faced another crisis. Marie was eight months pregnant with her sixth child when Leo, their oldest son, came down with a high fever, headache, stomach pain and diarrhea. On New Year's Day, fearing Leo might have something akin to smallpox, August went to town and fetched Dr. Affolter.

After examining Leo, Dr. Affolter came out to the kitchen and stood near Marie. "How old is Leo?" he said, his voice even-keeled so as not to raise immediate alarm.

Marie, who had been washing dishes, wiped her hands on a towel. Two-year-old Mary was at her feet, wanting to be picked up. "He's eleven years old. He'll be twelve May 1st." She raised her fingers to her mouth and bit her nails. "Does he have smallpox?"

"No, his symptoms are different. He has stomach pain and he's got rose-colored spots on his abdomen and chest and is suffering from diarrhea. I'm afraid he's got typhoid fever.[52] Are any of your other children sick?"

"No, only Leo," Marie said.

"Well, then he probably wasn't infected at home. He may have been infected at school. At any rate, it was probably two weeks ago or more when he was infected."

August had been standing by the doorway listening. "Will it kill him?"

Dr. Affolter turned around toward him. "It's a common illness. The bacteria are spread through contact with the stool and urine of a person who is infected or who carries the bacteria. The main source is drinking water or milk or eating food that has been contaminated. Contaminated with the feces of an infected person."

"Will it kill him?" August repeated.

"Well, sometimes people live if they get round-the-clock care as well as a high calorie diet to prevent wasting of the body."

Marie looked at the doctor, her eyes glaring with fright. "Is it contagious? I'm eight months pregnant. I can't catch what Leo has."

Dr. Affolter turned around toward Marie and locked eyes with her. "Yes, it's highly contagious. You can get it by eating food or drinking water contaminated with the bacteria or consuming food or water which Leo has prepared, since he carries the bacteria, if he does not wash his hands properly. It's important for everyone in the family to wash their hands good and frequently. Keep him isolated from everyone else."

"Will it kill him?" August asked a third time.

The doctor looked at August, but then turned back to Marie and put a hand on her shoulder. "It's a life-threatening illness. Right now there is no treatment for typhoid fever.[53] We will just have to hope and pray."

Five days later, on January 5th, when the wind blew fiercely and icicles formed on the window panes, Marie came down with a headache, fever and vomiting. August, who had quit praying after George's death, panicked. *Not Marie, please don't take Marie from me. I am nothing without her.* Sure he was being punished for doubting God, he began to pray. *Heavenly Father, I am sorry for my actions. I'll do anything you say, anything, but please don't take Marie or my firstborn, Leo.*

August rode over to Wilhelm's and Katy's residence and even though he knew it would be the ultimate sacrifice, he asked Katy to come and help take care of Leo, the other children, and now Marie, too. He didn't know what else to do or what he would do if Katy refused. Katy, who was the kindest woman August had ever met, readily agreed. She rode back with August to the small farm, fixed the children and August dinner, let Marie get some rest and tended to Leo's diarrhea.

Marie's condition got worse so August went to town and brought back Dr. Affolter.

"She's suffering from the stomach flu. I am concerned about her being pregnant, and also catching typhoid from Leo, but with proper nourishment and rest, I think she'll be better soon. Keep Leo isolated. Let me know if Marie's not better by tomorrow."

He left then. Katy brought Marie some chicken broth and made sure the kids were quiet so Marie could get some rest.

"You're a godsend, Katy," he said. "I couldn't have handled this without you."

"I'm glad to help," Katy said. "Marie seems better. But, you need to talk to Leo. He won't eat. I'm afraid he's wasting away."

August took some bread and cheese for Leo to eat. It was noon and the sun shone through the window, so he didn't need a lantern. He climbed up to the loft where Leo was resting and sat down beside him on the bed. "Leo, you must eat! It will help you get better."

"What's the use, Papa? It all comes out the other end. I'm going to die, aren't I?"

"Son, don't talk like that. You must continue to hope!"

"Georgie died and now I'm going to die."

August bit his lips to remain calm. It was harder than he imagined to be positive and hopeful. He pulled the blankets up to Leo's chin and tried changing the subject to something more pleasant. "Son, remember when I took you fishing in the Arkansas River?"

Leo smiled. "Yeah, that was one of the best times of my life."

"Mine, too. You were young and afraid to put the worm on the hook. But I showed you how and you ended up catching a catfish in those waters. You are a good fisherman. Why, those catfish didn't have a chance!" His eyes popped wide.

"I remember," Leo said. "That was fun!"

August smiled, knowing he was making headway. "Do you remember when I taught you how to hunt with a rifle? You shot an antelope when we traveled by covered wagon from Rice County to Westphalia."

"Those were good times, weren't they, Papa?"

"Yes, they were. You'll have more good times in the future. You just need to eat!"

"I...can't, Papa."

August felt choked up. His hopes for Leo taking over the farm one day seemed dashed, but put his hand on Leo's cheek and continued. "I want you to remember one thing. I love you, Leo. Always have. Ever since I first laid eyes on you. You were our miracle baby. You were breech and it was a miracle from God that you were born. Remember that, son!"

"I will, Papa. But now I just want to go to sleep."

"Get some rest and then maybe you'll feel like eating."

Three days later, Leo started to hemorrhage. Dr. Affolter was called again, but he couldn't do anything. Leo died on January 8.

That night, August stepped outside and cast his eyes toward heaven. *Why are you tormenting me? Wasn't it enough that you took George from me? You needed to take my firstborn too? How have I displeased you? What have I done to deserve this? Answer me.*

August had had high hopes for Leo, that he would succeed in taking over the farm and realize more wealth. He had hoped that Leo would follow in his footsteps and be known throughout his community as a kind and generous man. And he had hoped Leo would appreciate music and dancing as much as he and Marie had. It was not to be. August's hopes were dashed.

The next day, August and Wilhelm buried Leo in St. Teresa's cemetery next to George. A small wooden cross marked the grave. August didn't shed a tear.

A month later, on February 1, Marie gave birth to her sixth child. August had hoped for a boy to join the only son he had left—August, Jr. His hopes for another *Stammhalter* were crushed. They named the baby Kathleen and nicknamed her Kate, after Katy. That is the least and the best they could do to honor her help.

After Leo's death, August poured his heart and soul into his work. The town had grown to almost 500 people. To keep up with the competition from a new blacksmith in town, William Coldsmith, who was not only a blacksmith but also a wagon maker, August built an addition to his blacksmith shop to add wagon and carriage manufacturing. He couldn't afford to lower his prices, though, because he also hired Herman Helm, a twenty-year-old German from Prussia.

One day in late April Vincente Highberger stopped by the shop to see if August could repair his wagon. Herman waited on him.

"Did you know we also sell wagons?" Herman said. "They're better quality than the one you've got. August is proud of his craftsmanship. Where did you buy this one?"

"I bought it from Coldsmith," Vincente said. "His wagons were cheaper than August's."

"Cheaper, yes, but they're a piece of junk!" Herman's voice rose. "And now you expect August to fix it? *Shame! Shame!* You should have bought one from August in the first place!"

August stood by listening. *Ach du lieber Gott, having Mr. Highberger buy a wagon from Coldsmith and then asking me to fix it is like putting salt in a wound. But still you don't treat customers like that.*

August walked over to where Herman and Vincente were standing. "That's enough, Herman." Then he turned toward Mr. Highberger. "Herman is in training. I'd be happy to fix your wagon, Mr. Highberger. So, what's the problem? Let me have a look."

"The wagon box cracked. I think I need a new one."

After inspecting it, August said, "Yes, it looks like you do. I have another one just that size. I can switch it out in no time. I'm glad you came in today. I've seen you at church on

Sundays but we've never had the chance to get to know one another. Didn't I read in *The Westphalia Independent* that you moved here a couple years ago with your family?"

"Why, yes. You may have also read that Miss Mary Highberger was the one who opened the parochial school for the children of St. Teresa's parish. She teaches twenty-two children in the church building, maybe even your kids."

"My son, August, Jr. goes to that school. I lost two of my other boys. One to smallpox and the eldest one to typhoid fever." His voice always cracked when he spoke about Leo.

Herman shot a look at August to show his concern for his boss.

"That must be very hard," Mr. Highberger said. "I can't imagine losing a child, much less two boys."

"It is tough. I can't sleep at night. It's been my worst nightmare. The ache in your heart never goes away, the pain never stops, but..." He sighed, held back tears and continued in almost a whisper. "They say it gets easier with time."

There was an uncomfortable silence. Then Mr. Highberger changed the subject. "Who does your farm work now for you?"

"Marie and the kids. We own a small, 80-acre farm. I hire someone to do the heavy work but Marie and my son and the girls do all the planting and even help with the harvesting. They also milk the cows. We have twelve now so that keeps them pretty busy."

"I keep busy, too, with my hardware store and me and my brother's grist mill and hay press. Business has been good. How about yours?"

"We do a fair amount of business. I came here from Ellinwood and had a hard time of making it as a farmer there so I went back to my old blacksmith trade. It was a new start for me and so far I've been satisfied. Thank the Lord! Say, do you remember Ferdinand Goebel? Did you ever know him?"

"Yes, I remember him. He was German and farmed here, didn't he?"

"Yes, for about three years. He arrived in Westphalia the same year we did and just moved to Idaho last year. He writes me occasionally. I got a letter from him last week. He lives in Cottonwood, Idaho now, up by a monastery there. Said he likes it there. Encouraged me to move there, but, of course, I'd have to start all over again. I think I'm too old. Plus I like the people here."

"I like it here, too. Well, if you've finished fixing my wagon, I think I'll be on my way."

"Thanks for your business, Mr. Highberger. It's been a pleasure."

After Mr. Highberger left, August took young Helm aside and gave him some advice. "Herman, you get back what you give in life. If you treat people right, treat them how you would like to be treated, it will come back to you. Maybe Highberger will tell his friends and family how I treated him and we'll get more business because of it. Maybe when Highberger decides to buy another wagon, he'll buy one from me. You never know what effect treating people with respect might have. Do you understand?"

"Yes, sir. I'm sorry, sir. It's just that I want our business to grow. I'm eager to get ahead."

August's blue eyes perked up. "If you really want to get ahead, I'd suggest you move out west."

Herman glanced at August. "Can you put me in touch with that Mr. Goebel?"

This young boy has been a good employee. I'd like to see him get ahead. "I'll write him a letter if you'd like and tell him you're coming."

Herman smiled. "I'd like that."

August patted Herman on the back. "We'll miss you around here. Promise me you'll write and let me know what you find there."

"I promise."

Chapter 34

On December 6, 1885, Marie gave birth to her seventh child. August hoped and prayed for another son to carry on the family name, to help on the farm and in the fields, and was sorely disappointed when he learned that it was another girl. He and Marie praised the Lord, however, because she had all her fingers and toes and was healthy. They named her Cecilia.

A year later, in 1886, after milking a dozen cows with twelve-year-old August, Jr. on a cool day in March, thirty-year-old Marie, dressed in a long-sleeved, ankle-length, black-and-white plaid cotton dress and black apron, her head covered in a scarf, finished nursing Cecilia who was just four months old. She put her in a basket and trudged out to the field at 10 o'clock in the morning along with her four other children to plant potatoes. It was a sunny day, but chilly as the wind had picked up. A neighbor, who August had hired, had already plowed the dark grayish brown soil two days ago to get it ready for planting.

That day, they somehow managed to lug buckets filled with potatoes which Marie and the two oldest children had cut into quarters, an eye of the potato in each piece. They carried these buckets, two shovels, a brown sack with their lunch, a jug of water, and a homemade blanket, along with walking four-year-old Mary and carrying two-year-old Kate, out to the field, which lay a quarter mile away from the shack.

To keep the rows straight, Marie tied a piece of string to a small wooden stick and pushed the stick in the ground at the end of a row and unrolled the 10-foot ball of string till she got to the opposite end where she tied the end of the string to another stick. With August, Jr.'s help, she tightened the string until it made a straight line. Then Marie took a shovel and dug a hole, starting at one end, removing the dirt while Malinda dropped in a potato piece, after which Marie covered it with dirt again. Marie and Malinda worked feverishly, and although they were slower at it, August, Jr. tried to do the same thing with young Mary.

By noon the baby was fussing, Marie's back was aching and August, Jr. was exhausted. They stopped and sat on the blanket while Marie nursed Cecilia and the children ate ham sandwiches and boiled eggs. Since the children didn't know Polish, they always spoke to each other in German and before they ate, they said a meal prayer in German: "*Segne, Vater, diese Gaben*...Bless us, oh Lord, for these thy gifts..."

Soon after, little Kate surprised Marie by saying, *"Mama, ein Käfer!"*

"Where?" Marie said.

"Under rock!" Kate said.

"That's a daddy longlegs," said Marie. "Don't play with it. Usually we see these around harvest time. Bad bug!" She shooed it away with her hand.

"Bad bug!" Kate repeated.

August, Jr. was fascinated by bugs and loved to catch them to study them up-close. "Don't hurt it!" he said. "It kind of looks like a spider. I think it's what my teacher called a Harvestman or an arachnid. They have eight long legs. Let me catch it."

"You'll do nothing of the sort," said Marie. "You don't have a jar to put it in."

"I bet the dog would eat it if we had one," said Malinda. "Can we get a puppy, Mama? A little wiener dog? *Please?*"

"Who would take care of it?" said Marie. "Who would train it? Who would feed it? I have enough trouble keeping up with all you kids, feeding you. I don't want another responsibility."

"I'd feed him," said Malinda.

"Maybe for a while," Marie said, "but a dog is a big commitment. You don't even get up early enough to help with the cows."

"But..." Malinda said.

"No buts," Marie said. "The answer is no. Wait till you're a little older, then ask your father." She switched Cecilia to her other breast. "Malinda, we need to go to town tomorrow and buy you a new First Communion dress."

"Ohhh," Malinda said to Marie, "that will be nice. I'd like that."

"Mama," August, Jr. said, "I still have the booklet my teacher, Miss Ahrens, wrote in German for me for *my* First Communion. I carry it in my wallet wherever I go.[54] I almost have it memorized. She said, 'Remember that you belong to God, you live to serve Him. And, blessedly, you will be united with God in Heaven.' Then she wrote twelve rules to live by."

"What are some of the rules?" Marie said.

"One is: 'Don't forget your good opinion about others during your morning prayer as you can earn yourself daily a huge treasure towards Heaven. Without this good opinion, each day will be lost for you.' I'd like to earn a huge treasure towards Heaven. I want to be rich in the next world, and not have to do farm work like now."

Marie held Cecilia up to try to burp her. "There are more important things than money, August, Jr. Your father and I would never have survived without our faith. We were very poor and God helped us through those tough times, and we sincerely hope all of our children will join us in Heaven." She smiled like a mother pleased with her children. "What else did your wise teacher write?"

"Number eight is: 'Don't let anyone lead you into temptation—the seducer is Satan's helper. His excuse is: "Others are doing the same." These are Satan's words.' Malinda needs that one. She always uses that excuse cause she does what her friends do."

"I do not!" Malinda said. "You HUSH!"

"All right, you two!" Marie said. "Let's not get into an argument over it! What's something else your teacher said?"

"Number nine is: 'Always show the deepest respect towards your dear parents as well as your superiors. Remember, they are standing in for God in your life. If you won't love or honor them, you are not loving or honoring God.'"

"Those are very wise words!" Marie ate a few bites of a ham sandwich, then looked at her watch. "It's time to get back to work. I'm hoping we can get an acre planted today. Then we have two more to go. When I think of all the hard work that has to be done, my head spins."

She knit her eyebrows together, then continued. "We need to plant 35 acres of regular corn this year, 5 acres of the Kaffir corn, and 35 of soft wheat." She gave an exasperated sigh.

"We'll help you, Mama," August, Jr. said.

"I know you will, son," Marie said. "I know you will. And, I love you for it."

They spent the next four grueling hours planting potatoes. At four-thirty, they trudged back to the shack as she and the kids needed to get cleaned up and ready for supper. Marie finished nursing Cecilia and was busy preparing a meal of pork roast and potatoes for supper when August walked in.

He tossed a small sack of hard candy at each of the three kids—one to August, Jr., one to Malinda and the other to little Mary. "For your help in planting potatoes today!" he said. The children squealed with delight.

After they finished supper, said the meal prayer and Marie put Cecilia to bed, August took his black-beaded rosary from a peg near the kitchen cupboard and he and Marie and the kids knelt down and prayed the nightly rosary. Afterwards, the kids went to bed, Marie did the dishes, and August lingered to talk about his day.

"Unfortunately, it was a slow day," August said, "No one came into the shop, and so I did what I usually do. I busied myself with making a new wagon. I'm so excited! You should see it! It's a real beauty! Almost anyone I can think of would be happy to own it. I used some pine wood to create the wagon box and the wheels are so sturdy they seem to glide over rocky surfaces. A pure bit of genius, if I do say so myself."

August noticed Marie didn't say anything. Normally, she would be happy for him. "Are you listening?" he said.

"I'm just tired, August. I've had an exhausting day."

August looked at her. "What did you do, besides plant potatoes?" he said.

Her voice sounded annoyed. "You wouldn't understand if I told you. Can we talk about it tomorrow? Let's get to bed. I'm tired and we both need to get up early tomorrow morning." She snuffed out the lantern.

They went to bed and even though August felt he would never understand women, he put his arm around her and kissed her on the mouth and told her goodnight and that he loved her. She surprised him by kissing him back hard. He couldn't remember when she had kissed him so passionately before. *If she's tired, she certainly has a funny way of showing it.* Soon one thing led to another, Marie took off her nightgown, and they were going at each other with a passion as deep as their first encounter. His mouth became glued to hers. There were countless *I love yous* whispered in Polish: *Ja cie kocham.* He felt breathless and like his world was ready to explode. At the height of their ecstasy, Cecilia woke up and began crying. In such a small house with five high-spirited children, interruptions like this frequently occurred, and while it didn't stop their passion for one another, it did pause their lovemaking. Marie sighed, put her gown back on and picked up Cecilia, rocking her back to sleep.

Then four-year-old Mary got up. "What were you and Mama doing?" she said to August.

"Nothing," he said. "Go back to bed."

Their voices woke up all the other children who had been asleep in the loft. It took an hour before everyone was back asleep. Before August dozed off, he said a silent prayer to God, asking Him to bless his beautiful, energetic wife and five loving children and keep them safe, happy, healthy, and prosperous. Still skeptical that God wasn't listening to or answering his prayers, he decided that no matter what, this time things would be different.

<h1 style="text-align:center">Chapter 35</h1>

Two years later, on a cool, windless night in early April 1887, after they finished supper and prayed the nightly rosary, Marie told August he had finally received a letter from Herman Helm.

"I miss him, Marie," August said. "But I'm happy to hear from him."

Sitting by a lantern, he read the letter out loud.

Dear August:

I've been thinking of you and Marie and remembered to write and tell you what I've found here in Cottonwood, in Idaho Territory. I recalled my promise when I met some members of the German Colonization Company that is here from Effingham, Illinois. It is kind of a secret society that is scouting this area for possible emigration, but although the Company is secret, its membership also includes women, so it won't stay secret for long. Henry Kuther, J. B. Forsmann and Hubert Hattrup from the Company are inspecting the country and reporting back to the German-speaking people in Illinois as to what they find. As a side note, you'll find most of the people in Cottonwood speak German. I'm hoping you and Marie will want to move here before that contingent of German Illinois people arrives.

This area is really God's paradise. It's quiet and peaceful here. You hear the sound of tall pine trees rustling in the forests next to creeks, streams and rivers with a spotting of deer here or there. You can hear your own voice echoing in the forests. You wake up in the morning to the sound of birds—bluebirds, wrens or sparrows. Small bands of buffalo, wild Cayuse ponies, and coyote can be found on this wide-open prairie at the foot of the Craig Mountains. They call it the Camas Prairie. It was named after the camas root (a bulb like an onion, only sweeter) which kept the Indians and early settlers alive in hard times.

You don't have to be afraid of the Indians here. The battles with the nearby Nez Perce Indians ended last year and dealings with them have stabilized. You'll find them to be friendly now.

Cottonwood consists of a hotel-stage depot, a saloon and several homes, in all about 200 people, on the west side of the Camas Prairie. It has a town well where you'll get the most refreshing drink of water you've ever tasted. Most of the people here are Catholic; however, there are no regular Catholic services in this area. The Jesuits, Fathers Diomedi and Morvillo, who are from the Indian mission at Slickpoo, near Lewiston, have occasionally said Mass here, usually at Ferdinand Goebel's home. Like me, most people stay at the Goebel cabin when they first arrive here.

The opportunities are unlimited. As of yet, there is no blacksmith here. I need to tell you about prices. You can *buy a cow for $35 to $40 and a horse for $100. Wagons cost about $125 to $150, and a self-binding harvesting machine costs $300. The land yields between 35 and 40 bushels of wheat per acre here and the price of a bushel is 55 cents. There are also 50 to 60 bushels of oats per acre. Heads of cabbage weigh 1 to 5 pounds each and average twelve to the bushel. Onions are huge, weighing 1 to 3 pounds and pumpkins are also large with an average diameter of 2 to 3 feet.[55]*

We don't have any insects here and other sicknesses like typhoid fever are entirely unknown here. We don't have a need for any doctors or apothecaries. In short, Idaho is the Promised Land, an area perfect in every way. You will not be unhappy if you decide to move here.

I hope you and your family are well and enjoying life.

Yours,
Herman Helm

Seated near the stove, August's blue eyes twinkled as he looked at Marie, waiting for a response. "Well, Mama, what do you think? This is our big chance." He winked. "Should we move?"

She looked up from her knitting and frowned. "Herman paints a pretty picture, that's for sure. It sounds almost too good to be true. No insects or sickness! I can hardly believe that!"

August grinned. "The prices and measures of produce he quotes are certainly good. And the area sounds beautiful. We might just be passing up the opportunity of a lifetime! I think you need to reconsider it, my dear!"

"Don't get any notion in your head about that, August," Marie said, raising her hand. "We're happy here. We've had good crop years and you're making good money at the blacksmith shop. Business has been very good. I don't see why we'd need to start all over again in Cottonwood."

August slumped down in his chair, cleared his throat and rolled his eyes. *A marriage, as they say, is full of compromise.* "I suppose you're right about this, my dear, but I'll keep this letter just in case."

"So, how was work today?" Marie said, changing the subject.

August straightened up. "Can't complain. Business is good. Shoed five or six horses and sold a wagon to Emil Flusche. By the way, Peter Endres came into the shop today. Said their brass band just got new instruments. Call themselves The Westphalia Concert Band. Invited me to hear them play sometime."

Marie went back to knitting. "Who's in that band?"

"Endres, Sattler, Brees, Huffman and Allman, all good friends of mine."

"You consider everyone your friend! Will they be playing at the new Opera House? I heard there's to be a grand opening April 14 with over 300 seats."

"Endres said the Garnett String Band will be furnishing the music that night. I hope we can go. The ball is June 10. I remember how you like dancing. When is the baby due again?"

Marie touched her belly. "In June. Probably the first week. And the way the seams on my clothes are bursting and the fact that my belly is pointed, not rounded like the last two, I'm certain this one will be a boy."

August beamed. "I hope you're right. We could use another hand on the farm."

She leaned forward. "I know," she said. "And another boy to carry on the family name."

"Yes, that would please me, too," he said, smiling.

Almost every day in April, Marie went out to the fields with her children to plant corn, even though her belly was enormous. Digging a trench and bending over to put seeds in the brown-gray soil was difficult and uncomfortable for her, her face often covered in sweat. She came in each day exhausted, but the work had to be done, and she was grateful for the children's help. Fortunately, she was strong enough to work right up to the day of her delivery.

On May 10, a warm, beautiful, early morning before August went to work at the blacksmith shop, Marie went into labor, a month before her baby was due. As soon as Marie started having contractions, August rode over to a neighbor's house and asked his neighbor's wife, Rose, to come and act as a midwife. She rode with August back to the shack, and immediately went to the bed where Marie was lying. Experienced in giving birth by now, Marie breathed deeply and rested after each contraction. She smiled at Rose, looking pleased that she had come.

"You're not alone," Rose said to Marie. "I've come to assist you. You're going to have a great delivery. Everything will be ok."

"Thank you, Rose," Marie said. "You're a godsend!"

Compared to the birth of her previous seven babies, it took less time for Marie for this one to get to the point where she could start pushing. Three pushes and the baby was out. Rose shouted that it was a boy. Rose massaged his chest to help him breathe, then wrapped him in a blanket and held him up so Marie could see him.

"He's so little!" Marie squealed. "I've never seen a baby that tiny before."

August, who had been sitting in the kitchen, glowed and smiled like a proud papa. "Is it all right to come in and hold him?" he asked.

"Just a minute," Marie said, in a panicked tone of voice. "I can't believe it! I'm still having labor pains! Is something wrong?"

"Oh, my gosh!" Rose said. "I think you're having another baby!"

"You mean she's having twins?" August said, astounded, his eyes widening.

"Yes, I think so," Rose said.

August looked dumbfounded. Neither he nor Marie had counted on twins.

Marie caught her breath and rested again after each contraction. Rose checked the position of the next baby by feeling Marie's tummy and asking her permission to do a vaginal examination. Then Rose broke the waters surrounding the second baby. Marie delivered the second child, a girl, twenty minutes later. The boy was blonde like August had been at birth, and the girl was dark-haired like Marie. After helping the tiny, wrinkled girl breathe, Rose wrapped her in a baby blanket and handed both of the sweet babies to Marie so she could hold them for the first time, each one nestled in an arm.

August walked over to the bedroom, excited, his heart bursting with pride. "Thank God, you and the babies are ok." He kissed Marie on her forehead.

"This is the most special day of my life. To think I actually carried both of them. They're so tiny and fragile-looking! Never in my wildest dreams, did I ever think we'd have twins."

August took his turn in holding the tiny, crying newborns to keep them quiet and contented all night while Marie struggled, juggling each baby trying to feed them and keep them happy. Unfortunately, the babies didn't suckle. Rose did what she could to help Marie with the two tiny babies and even stayed overnight. The babies kept Marie and August up all night. They barely got a minute or two of sleep.

The next morning both babies were dead.

Chapter 36

The children were up in the loft, asleep; August sat next to Marie on their bed. He found it difficult to listen to Marie's sobs for he was wrestling with his own grief. *God, why do you continue to punish us? You've taken away four of our children and three of them were boys! Please, stop! Have mercy on us!*

Although August felt like his own heart had broken, he did his best to console Marie. "Everything will be all right," he said, stroking her hair.

Marie shook her head. "No, it won't. They weren't even baptized." She blew her nose in a handkerchief, her voice high pitched. "They'll go to limbo and I'll never be able to see them again. We don't even have any names picked out for them." She rubbed her swollen eyes.

August tried to be helpful. "My grandfather, Jacob, and his third wife, Anna Christina, had a set of twins they named Adam and Eve," he said. "Why don't we call them that? Those are nice biblical names."

"I don't really care what we call them. It doesn't matter now. They're dead. How could God do this to us?" her voice cracking, her sobs overtaking her. "Why did God give me babies and then take them away?"

August put his arm around her. "God works in mysterious ways, my dear. Maybe God wants to teach us something.

Maybe God wants us to love the children we have left. Maybe God's punishing me for leaving Poland."

Marie paused, sucking in air between sobs. "The babies' deaths are my fault. Maybe I wasn't a good enough mother. I don't want to live anymore, August."

"Don't talk like that, Marie. Better times are ahead."

"You always say that!" Tears trickled down Marie's cheeks. "There is no reason to go on living."

August raised his eyebrows and glanced at Marie with a softness in his eyes. "What about your other children? What about me?"

Marie sobbed. "I can't think of anything right now besides the death of my two babies. Westphalia is full of death. First George, then Leo, now the twins. I feel like this place is jinxed, like Ellinwood was. It was crop failures there. This town has only brought us sickness and death. Let's get out of here. Let's move to Cottonwood." She wiped her eyes.

August shifted in his chair and rolled his shoulders. "Marie, are you sure? We'll need to sell everything, sell the farm, sell the blacksmith shop."

"I'm sure, August. Let's get away from here, get a new start. We need to leave here. Now!"

She got out of bed and went to their dresser, rooting around in one of the drawers. "I need to find that picture Leo made for me in school one year. It's not in this drawer where I usually keep it." She panicked. "*Where* is it?" She kept looking in other drawers.

August got up from the bed, stood next to her and stared at her for a moment or two. He knew Marie would never have said that she wanted to move to Cottonwood if she hadn't lost the twins. He also knew that picture from Leo was one of her most prized possessions. "*Ach du lieber Gott*, Marie, we're not leaving yet. That can wait. Let's talk about it later. We have things we need to do right now."

He looked tired and worn out, like he hadn't slept in two weeks rather than just one night. He was on edge, each tiny undertaking or responsibility he was now faced with caused him frustration and set him off. All color had drained from his face and his eyes were red and puffy. He wrung his hands and combed them through his hair. Having his wife obsessed over a piece of artwork from Leo tipped him over the edge. A wave of sadness washed over him, a sadness in not just losing the twins, but also Leo and George. He backed away from Marie and looked out the window, staring into space, lost in his thoughts. He poured his heart out to God.

My dear Lord, you who are all powerful, why have you abandoned us in our time of need? I have been a faithful servant, remaining true to my Catholic faith. All I've asked you is to bless my family and help us get ahead. Not only have all my dreams evaporated, you've made us suffer. We ended up with nothing. Have you no mercy at all?

Marie stopped what she was doing and looked at him. "What are you thinking, August?"

He turned to face her. "I've had it! God has abandoned us!" he said, balling his hand into a fist. "We've suffered enough! First the drought which left us penniless, then the grasshopper plagues which left us starving, and then the hail storm which I thought was the last straw. And now the loss of four children! It's too much."

He wondered if it would be any different if they moved to Cottonwood. He decided it might not. After all, God hadn't answered even one of his prayers. He decided he needed to make a change in his life right now.

"I'm never going to pray or go to church again."

His words frightened Marie. She forgot her obsession with Leo's picture and mustered up the will to be strong. "That sounds almost blasphemous," she said. "August, you will never forgive yourself if you do that. You'll wish you hadn't said it. If you can't do it for the love of God, then do it for the remaining children you have. You'll be setting a bad example for them if you give up your faith."

His voice rose. "This is between me and God, Marie!" he said.

Marie covered her mouth with her hand and took a step back. "I'm angry at God, too," she said, "but our faith is what has always gotten us through the bad times. We don't know yet what God's plans are for us. Maybe He has something better in store for us."

Marie's attempt at seeing both sides was lost on him. "We both know nothing is worse than losing a child," August said in almost a whisper. "Not to mention four." Tears trickled from his eyes.

"August, I know you're hurting but I need you to be strong for me right now, strong for your remaining children. You're right. We have things we need to do now before we prepare to leave for Cottonwood. You need to go to the church and invite Father Schmandt to come and pray the rosary with us tonight. I hope he can say a funeral Mass for the twins tomorrow at St. Teresa's, although maybe because they weren't baptized he won't agree to it." She lowered her eyes to the floor.

"I won't be going anywhere that reminds me how great God is supposed to be," he said in a sarcastic tone.

"Please, August, this is no time for self-pity," Marie sobbed. "Please go see Father Schmandt."

He bristled. "How can I go see the priest?" August said. "There is no way he'll say a funeral Mass for the twins."

"August, he needs to see that we are devout Catholics, that we love God and obey His rules. We intended to have the twins baptized. There just wasn't time."

"And if I refuse to go?" he said, arching an eyebrow.

She gave him the look a wife gives her husband that makes him realize that he'll have hell to pay if he does not give in to her wishes.

"Oh, all right," he said, touching her shoulder. "If that will please you." He stifled his doubts about God for the moment and took charge of the situation. His mind raced with tasks that needed to be done.

Marie wiped her swollen, red eyes with a handkerchief. "Thank you," she whispered.

"While I'm gone, can you wash and dress the twins and prepare their bodies for burial? They should be buried tomorrow. I'm going to go to town to the General Store and buy some wood to make small caskets and then I'll go see Father Schmandt."

August reached over and hugged her, then he took the wagon and rode into town, and after he bought two pieces of wood for the coffins, which he planned to make no larger than shoe boxes, he rode over to St. Teresa's Church to visit Father Schmandt. He met him at the door to the sacristy, where the vestments were kept.

"I have some terrible news, Father. Yesterday Marie gave birth to a set of twins and this morning we found them dead."

"My word! How tragic! I'm so sorry for your loss. Did you have time to maybe pour water over their heads and baptize them?"

"We were up the whole night with them and didn't think of it. We hoped they'd survive."

Father Schmandt didn't offer a whole lot of comfort. He seemed too preoccupied with Church rules. "That's a shame. They'll end up in limbo, you know. Only people who are baptized go to heaven."

August's blue eyes locked with the priest's. "We were hoping you could come over to the house tonight and pray the rosary with us and also say a funeral Mass for the twins tomorrow."

The priest scowled and scratched his beard. "This is a highly unusual request."

August could not erase the image in his head of Marie sobbing, her eyes swollen. "Please, Father. It would make Marie feel much better. She's taking it really hard."

August could see that the priest didn't understand what it was like to have a wife and be so in love with her that a man might consider breaking rules.

"Again, they're not Catholics. God has rules."

The priest looked uncomfortable. To that priest, August realized, rules were rules and they should be obeyed. Though he disagreed with the priest, August remained polite out of respect. His father's words cut like a knife. *Never trust anyone besides the doctor or the priest.*

"Please, Father. I'll do anything you say in reparation—attend Mass, say rosaries, anything! This is very important to us. I'm sorry we made the mistake but we intended for them to be baptized and I think God is a merciful God and He will forgive us!"

The priest had a high regard for those who owned up to their mistakes. "Very well. You're right. There is such a thing as baptism of desire. The Church says funeral rites may be celebrated for children whose parents intended for them to be baptized but who died before baptism so I *will* say a Latin Mass in honor of the twins tomorrow."

"Thank you, Father."

The priest went over the order of the Mass with August and explained what would be different because the babies weren't technically Catholics because they hadn't been baptized. "There will be no sprinkling of holy water or pall because the babies had not been baptized."

After they finished, Father Schmandt told August he would see him at the house that night for the rosary.

Chapter 37

Early morning the following day, the church was full of people and flowers for the funeral Mass. Like always, the Mass was held early because people had to fast before taking Communion. There were so many flowers Marie whispered to August that, "I will never be able to smell flowers again without thinking of the twins' death."

Wilhelm and Katy attended as well as the Flusche and Highberger families. Thirteen-year-old August, Jr. who had been taking lessons to play the organ, played for the Mass. There was a brief address to the parishioners in German, followed by an Entrance Procession. The parishioners were quiet as the priest stood at the lectern and the organ music stopped. Father Schmandt prayed to God to help August and Marie get through this difficult time and gave the homily he had promised. He spoke in German.

"Purgatory," he said, "is a time when your sins are purified in preparation of spending eternity with God. In purgatory, your sins are cleansed in order to gain entrance to enter heaven. Purgatory is entirely different from the punishment of the damned.

"As far as limbo is concerned, the word was coined in the early Church. Unbaptized, but otherwise sinless, infants and children go to limbo, not heaven, a dominant belief held by Saints and theologians going back to the earliest Church."

After the Mass was over, people came up to August and Marie and told them how sorry they were about the twins' deaths. But to August and Marie, the day was a blur; they felt emotionally spent, exhausted. They walked around in a fog, and later wouldn't even remember who attended the funeral. Then they all went to the cemetery and August and Wilhelm dug two four-foot graves near where George and Leo were buried. They marked the graves with wooden crosses with the names Adam and Eve. Then everyone went to the Kopczynski farm for lunch and a reception, prepared by the ladies of the church.

Within a month, August and Marie sold the 80-acre farm for $500. Westphalia had grown to 1,019 people. The sale was mentioned in the June 9, 1887 edition of *The Westphalia Times*: "A gentleman from Kansas City bought the Kopczynski property south of town." August couldn't remember when he had seen such a promising corn crop, some of the stalks towering to twelve feet. He felt his luck had changed and God was blessing his family, however, because scarcely ten days had gone by from the time when they had sold their farm till the weather turned unbearably warm, and the scorching hot winds dried everything up within three days, ruining the crops.

The family stayed with Wilhelm and Katy until two months later, on August 10, 1887, when August and Marie sold the blacksmith shop and town lot to Vincente Highberger for $585. Although Highberger was not a blacksmith, he invested in local properties which proved to be profitable and hired help to keep them running smoothly. He and August had become good friends after August had repaired his wagon, and August couldn't have been more pleased as to how things turned out in the end. He made a mental note to tell young Herman Helm about it when he arrived in Cottonwood.

Cottonwood, where the Kopczynski family was headed, was located first in Walla Walla, Washington Territory, the latter created in 1853. Ten years later, Idaho Territory was founded from lands in eastern Washington, and included Cottonwood.

The discovery of gold near Walla Walla in 1860 had attracted many prospectors and because of this trains were routed there. The family boarded the train for Walla Walla on August 16, 1887 at one o'clock in the morning. The Westphalia Concert Band, all fourteen of them good friends of the Kopczynskis, showed up at the train station and saw them off, playing band music with their brass instruments.

The train passed through the states of Kansas, Nebraska and South Dakota and looking out the window, August noticed everything was burned by hot winds. *Ach du lieber Gott, we are blessed. Thank you, Lord, for enabling me to sell the farm when I did.*

When they reached the Rocky Mountains, they finally saw green forests. Crossing the Rockies, they went through a sleet and snow storm.

They had to stop along the way and stayed overnight in a hotel. Marie had sewn $1,000 into her petticoat for safekeep-ing. They went for a walk down the street past the rows of businesses in a small town in South Dakota. It was around noon and they could feel the warmth of the sun. When they crossed in front of a bank, August turned to Marie and said, "Got your money, Mama?"

"Oh my, I'm not wearing the petticoat with the money sewn in it. We'd better go back to the hotel."

"I hope the money is safe," August said. "We'll be in big trouble if it isn't."

Their hearts fluttered as they quickly ran back to the hotel, returned to their room, and both Marie and August gave a sigh of relief when they discovered the petticoat with the money sewn in was still there. Once more, proof that the tide had turned and God seemed finally on their side.

Chapter 38

At the end of August in 1887, August, Marie and their five children, ages three to thirteen, finally reached Walla Walla, Washington Territory, their shortest route to their destination of Cottonwood. The temperature was over 100 degrees[56] and the air was so dry the roads were full of dust. The seven family members rode in a buggy from the train depot about one mile to the town of Walla Walla, with August and Marie and three-year-old Cecilia sitting with the driver on the front bench and the rest of the kids on the bench in the rear.

"This is a dirty road," said August to the driver. "There are dust holes almost up to the axle of the buggy."

"It's typical in Walla Walla," the driver said. "We don't get much rainfall here, and it is often windy. Walla Walla is located in a valley with the rolling Palouse hills and the Blue Mountains to the east of town. In the distance are the Cascade Mountains which is why we don't get much precipitation."

"Why do they call it Walla Walla?" Marie said. "Seems like a strange name for a town."

"It's an Indian name," the driver said. "It means place of many waters. The original name was Steptoeville, named after Colonel Edward Steptoe. I like the name Walla Walla better."

"How many people live in Walla Walla?" Marie said, running her fingers through Cecilia's hair.

The driver snapped the reins on the horses. "Over one thousand. The town is little more than a military fort for U.S. soldiers with its officer's quarters, troop barracks and stables. It also includes blacksmith shops, a granary and a saw mill. There are wheat farms and vegetables, including Walla Walla sweet onions, cattle, sheep, and orchards."

The driver glanced at August. "Have you ever heard of Marcus Whitman and his wife Narcissa?"

"No," August said. "Who are they?"

"He was a physician and they were missionaries here in Walla Walla. They got killed in 1847 by the Cayuse Indians. There was a disease epidemic and the Indians believed the missionaries were poisoning them."

They rode the rest of the way in silence with August wondering if Marie had second thoughts about their move given what the driver had just said. They stayed overnight in a rustic hotel and the next day took the steam-engine train to Riparia, Washington,[57] on the Snake River, but while on the train for Riparia, the Railroad Company received a telegraph saying that the main shaft on the boat engine broke, so the family had to go back to Walla Walla while it was being repaired.

Since Fort Walla Walla was only a small army post, the first day they did nothing but sit around at the train station, hoping for good news. The kids grew tired and restless, yet the family sat around the next two days, too.

Luckily, the following morning, they boarded the train again, crossed the railroad bridge at Riparia[58] and rode the boat to Lewiston, Idaho. Mr. Goebel, his friend from Westphalia, had black hair graying around the temples and a stocky torso, and awaited them in Lewiston.

"It's good to see you again," said August, shaking Mr. Goebel's hand. "You have more gray hair than you did in Westphalia." He winked.

"You as well," Mr. Goebel said. "And that beard of yours? I had no idea a beard could grow so long!" He winked back at August. "Welcome to Lewiston! It's not the capital anymore. They moved it to Boise in 1864. Now it is mainly a mining outfitting place with about 900 people living here.[59] Let's load the baggage and get going. Cottonwood awaits us!"

August nodded. They gathered their baggage, loaded it into a Schuttler covered wagon and started their journey to the Camas Prairie, a 200,000 acre, wide-open prairie in north-central Idaho, surrounded by the Craig Mountains.

Riding in the covered wagon along the wagon-rutted, dirt road from Lewiston, they camped the first night at the Stevens' place. Most of the camping sites had no houses and travelers always made sure they made it to the next camping place, never between, so that they could get drinking water and water for their horses.

They started out bright and early in the exciting new territory. The weather was seasonably hot and dry, offset by a cool breeze of air rustling through the evergreen trees at times. On the third day of their journey, the covered wagon jutted over the steep and rough terrain of Fountain Grade.[60] After climbing Fountain Grade, they stopped at Mill Creek to feed the horses and get some dinner for themselves.

August climbed down from the front seat of the wagon and breathed in the fresh air. He locked eyes with Mr. Goebel. "We're not used to such hills and mountains. They're such a stark contrast compared to the flat land of Kansas. *Ach du lieber*

Gott, what a country! I love it here! Reminds me of home back in Poland. What I like best though is how fresh the air smells."

"It's the scent of evergreen trees," Mr. Goebel said, smiling.

Mr. Goebel and August chopped some wood from fallen trees, making an open fire pit so Marie could cook dinner. She took some salt-cured meat and new potatoes from the wagon and with the men's help stuck the roast on skewers over the open fire. While Marie was busy cooking, the children were laughing and playing, their excited voices echoing in the vastness of the evergreen forest.

Marie caught Mr. Goebel's eye. "What a thrill it is for our family to eat outside underneath the big pine trees!" she said. "Just look at the children. They're having such a great time."

"Do you see that?" August shouted to the children, pointing. "Look, over there! That brown animal with white spots and four long legs just peeked out from behind the bushes! It's bigger than any dog I have ever seen." He turned his head to face Mr. Goebel. "What kind of animal is it?"

"Why, it's a deer!" Mr. Goebel said. "Haven't you ever seen one before?"

"No," August said. *"Ach du lieber Gott,* what a beautiful creature!"

"They're plentiful here," Mr. Goebel said. "Sometimes people kill them for their meat. Deer meat is very tasty."

"I can't imagine killing one, with those eyes staring back at you," August said.

"May I remind you, buffalo have eyes, too, and how many of them did you kill?" Mr. Goebel said.

"Speaking of killing," Marie said, "have there been any Indian wars in Cottonwood[61] where we're heading?"

"Some," Mr. Goebel said. "The Nez Perce Indians won most of the wars on the Camas Prairie. You don't have to be afraid of them though. They're peaceful now. The only thing you'll have to worry about is cattle stealing, but you have wild horse and cattle roundups to look forward to."

"Tell me about that," August said.

Mr. Goebel's eyes lit up at the prospect of telling his story. "The roundup corral in Cottonwood is built mostly of logs and is quite a good size with smaller corrals attached to the big corrals, as well as branding chutes. It has a snubbing post in the center, used for holding horses or cattle when roped. About sixty to one hundred, hard-working cowboys attend. There are usually two roundups a year—one for horses and one for cattle—with as many as four thousand head of horses or cattle in one bunch."

August's and Marie's eyes were wide and they were all ears. They leaned closer to Goebel as he continued his story.

"The cowboys start out in the morning, each in a given direction, covering about fifteen square miles. It isn't possible on the brakes of the Salmon River, but on the Camas Prairie it is. It's always a pleasure to see such a large amount of stock brought together in a day and you see some bronco busting, too."

"I like the sound of the name Camas Prairie," said Marie. "It sounds beautiful. What is camas?"

Mr. Goebel relished being an expert of the region. "Camas is a bulb-like root which the Indians ate to survive. It's nutritious. The camas plant is a type of lily that produces beautiful blue flowers in the spring."

"I didn't mean to interrupt you, Ferdinand," Marie said. "Please continue with your story."

"Well," he said, "With so many cowboys gathered together, you can imagine there are always some who dare the others to ride a certain horse in the bunch. That's when the fun begins, usually after the work of cutting out the stock and the branding is done for the day. Towards evening, the sport of riding takes place and, believe me, it gets very interesting.

"One time I especially remember was when I watched a six-foot tall cowboy boast that he could ride anything with hair on it. The other cowboys gave him his chance, picking out a real small, extremely vicious pony. The cowboy who made the dare got on the small pony, and at every jump the animal took, the cowboy's feet touched the ground. The pony finally jumped out from under him. We all laughed, including all the other cowboys."

"What about the cattle roundups? Are they like the horse roundups?" said August, taking a sip of water after finishing his supper.

"The cattle roundup is quite a bit slower," Mr. Goebel said, "as cattle don't drive quite as fast as horses unless they are stampeded. Then, look out, for when cattle stampede, it becomes impossible to handle them. One cattle roundup I remember well was when the cowboys dared one another about riding a certain bull in the bunch. Someone was always ready to take a dare like that. They roped and saddled a bull. The cowboy got on, but was finally thrown, and, by doing so, stampeded the whole herd of cattle. You can imagine the confusion it caused and the cowboy was minus a saddle for about three weeks after that."

"Cottonwood sounds like a wild, western town," Marie said. She began scraping the food from their tin plates and washing them in the nearby creek. "I can listen to you while I wash these. Tell me more. Where does the name come from?"

"It's named after a grove of Cottonwood trees," said Mr. Goebel, "and it's a hotel-stage depot, a stopover place for those traveling by wagon train, horseback, stagecoach, or horse and buggy. Many miners, which include Chinese,[62] are in search of gold on the Salmon River and stop at Cottonwood to get supplies."

"How big is it? How many people live there?" Marie said, shouting from the creek. "Are there any stores or shops there?"

"About 450 people live there now, most of them farmers," said Mr. Goebel. "The town, which is on the western side of the Camas Prairie, consists of a store, a post office, a saloon, the Cottonwood Hotel and a medical doctor, Dr. J. W. Turner. The majority of people speak German like us."

August and Marie were mesmerized by Mr. Goebel's tales of this new territory. Their faces glowed with excitement.

Mr. Goebel, proud of the place he now called home, continued his sales pitch. "You can view the whole Camas Prairie from a spot on the Cottonwood Butte. It's very quiet and peaceful there and the sky lights up with spectacular pink sunsets in February every year. I think you'll enjoy living there."

"Is there a Catholic church in Cottonwood yet?" August said.

August loved attending the routine weekly Sunday Mass, not only for religious reasons. He knew that in a small town like Cottonwood, his contact with other local farmers would depend on gathering at the Church door after Mass.

Mr. Goebel shook his head. "There currently aren't any religious services of any kind, but most of the people are Catholic and more German Catholics like you and I seem to arrive daily. The Jesuits from the Indian mission at Slickpoo, near Lewiston, Fathers Diomedi and Morvillo, occasionally say Mass in my home. I'm betting there will be a Catholic church in Cottonwood soon."

"There will be if I have anything to say about it," August said, raising an eyebrow. He had every intention to return to his daily practice of religion. Now that things were going well, he wanted to thank God in any way he could. If he could help build a church, by God, he would.

After Marie finished washing the dishes, they soon were on their way to Cottonwood. The children were tired and cranky when the covered wagon arrived at the Goebel cabin about 10:00 p.m. on August 28, 1887. The one-room, dark brown, rustic log cabin sat back several feet from the wagon-rutted, dirt road. The grass surrounding it had yellowed under the hot, August sun.

Since there were only two beds in the cabin, some of the kids slept in the wagon that first night. No matter. The Kopczynskis quickly fell asleep that night listening to the sound of wolves howling and awoke the next morning to sights and sounds different from what they had experienced in Westphalia. Although the temperature was about the same, there were no hot, dry winds like in Kansas. The air was fresher and the skyline included curves from the hills and the mountains. The land on the Camas Prairie was flat like it was in Kansas, but here they could see the Craig Mountains in the distance. They also noticed how deafeningly quiet it was, yet they could hear the sound of birds chirping—bluebirds, wrens and sparrows. After a hearty breakfast of eggs, sausage and potatoes, they looked out the wooden front door of Ferdinand Goebel's log cabin and the whole family was terrified by the sight of a large, hungry moose.

August and Marie had never seen their kids so excited, their faces so happy about this new location, and it made them excited and happy, too. August also noticed a definite difference in Marie. Her depression after the twins' death seemed to have lifted and she seemed cautiously optimistic about their future, happy to start a new life in Cottonwood. There was hope again in her eyes. There was hope again in his, too.

The Kopczynskis continued to live with the Goebel family for several days until they moved nearby to the old Gibson log cabin which was near the culvert at the turn to the old monastery in Cottonwood. Marie and the girls did their best to clean and fix it up. With seven people to one room, the temporary quarters were cramped. They hoped to get a new home soon.

During the fall of 1887, August helped Mr. Goebel harvest his crop, using the old method of threshing grain by flailing it out. August took the flail, a piece of round timber about three feet long and three inches thick with a strap of rawhide nailed to it for a handle, and beat the wheat with it, which was spread out on a clean patch of ground. It was a hard day's work to swing it. Even though August thought it was a pretty good farm implement, he did not like swinging the flail as he had done quite a bit of that in Poland, so he suggested using horses, which would take less work.

They cleared about a thirty-foot circle and spread the wheat around, then drove the horses around over this circle till the grain was tramped out, then scraped the grain to the center and put a new layer of wheat on top. After that, they had quite a pile of shelled grain which they ran through an old farming mill and cleaned. They were able to get enough wheat threshed for flour and seed and a few extra bushels for feed.

August helped Mr. Goebel plant in the spring and made plans to build his blacksmith shop in Cottonwood. They had plenty of work to do. He thanked God for his faith, his family and his many blessings.

Chapter 39

During the winter of 1888, the Camas Prairie had the least snowfall ever—about three or four inches total. The ground had moisture to a depth not to exceed four inches, all the moisture they got during that winter and spring. So, during the winter, besides getting paid for work done for Mr. Goebel, August split some rails and fence posts for the 160-acre farm he and Marie had purchased for $1,000 east of Cottonwood. He also cut some heavy timber to construct a blacksmith shop at Cottonwood. Mr. Goebel helped with the construction and August managed to acquire the other necessities for his blacksmith shop—the anvil, horseshoes and blacksmith tools—which he had shipped from Lewiston.

In front of the blacksmith shop was an old-fashioned town well, with a rope eight or ten feet long tied to an oaken bucket that sat next to it on a platform. Although there were other wells in town, including one at the stage barn and one at the hotel, the well in front of the blacksmith shop became the most prominent. Both men and beast drank here, and sometimes the men passed around a bottle of whiskey, often joining in song.

Mr. Goebel stopped by the blacksmith shop one hot, July afternoon. August stood at the well and dropped the bucket in, pulled it out and had a refreshing, cool drink of water.

After he got a drink for himself, he also watered Mr. Goebel's nearby horse from a trough, a log with the heart burned out.

"Care for any whiskey?" Mr. Goebel said as he pulled out a bottle.

"Don't mind if I do," August said, taking a swig.

"How's that new log cabin?" said Mr. Goebel. "Have you moved in yet? I imagine Marie has been busy fixing it up."

"The log cabin was pretty run down and needed a lot of work to get it in shape, but we finally managed to finish it," August said, handing the bottle back to Mr. Goebel.

"How big is it?" Mr. Goebel said, taking a sip of whiskey.

"Well, of course, it's just two rooms—a kitchen and a bedroom, twelve-by-eighteen feet.[63] Rather cramped for seven people, but we'll make do. We've got two beds in the bedroom and the kitchen has a stove, a table, a few chairs and an organ in it."

"An organ?" said Mr. Goebel, wide-eyed. "Who plays that?"

"August, Jr. is taking lessons. He's got a real ear for music. Speaking of music, last night Marie and I and the kids were over at the neighbors—Henry Terhaar's who bought 160 acres from McCafferty north of my place—and, like always, someone started playing the mouth harp, or jaw harp[64] as it is called, and also a small accordion. Both the younger folks and the older folks danced around the kitchen to the tune of Jenny Lind's polka. Marie loves to dance and the kids love it, too. They all take after her."

"We danced to the polka at my house, too," Mr. Goebel said. "It seems whenever there are people gathered, someone always pulls out a jaw harp and plays a polka. Say, did you hear George Seubert is building a barn?"

"Oh?" August said, scratching his beard. "Didn't he buy the Chenoweth place? Will there be a barn dance?"

"Yes, he did," Mr. Goebel said, "and, without question, there will be a barn dance. George said he wasn't willing to go the extra mile of laying a floor to dance in the barn, but was relieved as he found some young men who were willing to do that work for him. He's furnishing the lumber since it won't be any loss to him as he can use the lumber again to finish the barn. The younger men are donating the work and the women are calling it an Apron Party. Of course, it will be around the time of harvest. Speaking of harvest, how did you do this year?"

"Not well. Marie and the kids planted fifteen acres of grain. It grew to about six to eight inches tall and then dried up, so we cut it for hay. It was pretty light hay and not much of it. We also cut some bunch grass for hay."

"Bunch grass?" said Mr. Goebel, standing near the platform of the well with August, taking another swig of whiskey, then handing him the bottle.

"Yes, bunch grass hay. It was all we could get. Since the land is all open country, there were spots where the cattle hadn't grazed last year due to lack of water close by, and, of course, it was mostly old grass from the year before, but it proved to be real good feed."

"So, how are you getting by?" Mr. Goebel said.

August took another drink. If anyone besides Goebel asked him this question, he wouldn't be so frank to admit that he was still struggling, which he was not proud of, but he considered Goebel a close friend, so there were no secrets between them.

"Mostly by trade. I trade the iron kettles I make and smoked pork bacon at the store for groceries."

"Well, I'm driving hogs to market again this year," Mr. Goebel said. "Some men from down south are coming to buy what few hogs we have here and drive them to Lewiston or Uniontown. They come only once a year, usually in the fall."

"How hard is it?" August said. *If it's easy, I think I will try it myself.*

Mr. Goebel winced. "Driving hogs is not as easy as you may think. Last fall we drove about 400 to 500 hogs in one bunch and it took us about three days traveling a total of 60 miles to get to Lewiston. We had to have wagons to haul feed and also to carry the hogs that got lame. It was by no means all sport. They say if a hog only had two heads you might drive him the right way." He took a swig of the whiskey.

"And, talk about cattle stampedes! Have you ever seen a hog stampede?"

"I didn't know hogs would stampede," said August, taking the bottle from Mr. Goebel.

"Yes, hogs will also stampede," Mr. Goebel said. "And, you have to watch out, run and keep up with them. Sometimes, oh my, you will get out of breath, but run you must or you'll lose the hogs. Run, I say, and you will. You will laugh about it in the evening around the campfire but during the chase it sure is *no* laughing matter."

"Well, hogs are hogs in more than one way," said August.

August wondered what Marie would think about driving hogs to market, whether she would give him permission, not that he needed her permission, but if she wasn't happy, he knew it would cause conflict in their marriage.

He knew Marie supported him in his effort to build a Catholic Church. She had supported him in most things he wanted to do. He loved her for that. They both tried to live up to their faith and she was as much for building a new Church as he was. He just needed to come up with a way to fund it, but he had already thought of a plan. He shared this with Goebel.

"I've been talking to some people like Seubert, Terhaar, and others, about how they feel about building a Catholic Church in Cottonwood. Brueggeman and List both live out on Moughmer Point but they're in favor of a Church in Cottonwood. What do you think we should do?"

"It's a coincidence you should ask," said Mr. Goebel, taking another sip of whiskey. "Hendricks, Rad, Forsmann and I got together last week. We talked about getting the lumber for it from the government land on the Cottonwood Butte. We figure it would take between 20,000 to 30,000 feet of lumber and decided we should go ahead and do it. We'll donate our time and teams and haul the logs over to Forsmann's sawmill and help him saw them. There are more and more Catholics settling here. All we need now is Bishop Glorieux's permission to build."

August smiled. There was nothing Goebel could have said that would make him happier. His heart fluttered and he felt like he was walking on air. His dream might come true. And yet, there was one problem.

"Several people have already approached him," said August. "He's leaning against it. After all, he's from Boise. I don't think he understands this area. Said he's afraid it would disrupt the older Keuterville parish. *Ach du lieber Gott,* it is seven miles to Keuterville. It takes a half a day to get there with a team of oxen. I'm exaggerating, but I don't know why we can't have two parishes—one at Cottonwood and one at Keuterville."

"What about the cost for a priest?" said Mr. Goebel. "Maybe that's why he's inclined to say no."

"Nonsense," said August. "We can raise the money."

Chapter 40

In late September 1888, thirteen-year-old August, Jr. and ten-year-old Malinda, who had been milking cows, spotted a covered wagon rumbling down the road at their farm east of Cottonwood. Their cousin, Edwin Stolz, hopped off the wagon and said goodbye to the settlers and their girls he had ridden with. Then the settlers drove off in hopes of reaching their next camping place before dusk.

August, Jr. and Malinda ran out to greet their cousin, squealing with delight.

"What are you doing *here*?" Malinda said. Then noticing he was not with his parents, a puzzled look came across her face. "Where are Stolz and Aunt Henrietta?"

Edwin smiled and hugged Malinda and shook hands with August, Jr. "It's a long story," he said. "I have a letter here from Mom explaining it to your Dad. It's been a long ride. Let's go into the house. Do you have anything to eat? I'm starving."

"You need to wash up first," said Malinda. "You smell."

"You would, too, if you had been riding as long as I have."

"How is Otto?" August, Jr. said. "Is he still fishing in the Arkansas River?"

"There hasn't been much time for that now that harvest season is on. Dad keeps him pretty busy harvesting corn."

"And how are Lizzie and Berthie?" Malinda said. "I miss them."

"They're fine. Mischievous as ever."

August and Marie sat in the kitchen, waiting to eat the noon meal. August let out a small yelp when he saw Edwin at the front door. Marie ran up to him and embraced him.

"Aunt Marie! How good it is to see you!" Edwin hugged her hello. "And, Uncle August, I have a letter from Mom for you." He handed August the letter.

My dear brother, August,

I hope you and Marie are well and enjoying life in Cottonwood with your kids. I miss all of you. Although it has only been a year since you left, it seems like six.

You've always been kind to me and I need to ask you for another favor. I'm sending Edwin to live with you. There is no other possible way. He can't stay here.

My husband expects Edwin to do the work of two grown men. Last winter when there was a blizzard with snow piled high, wolves howled in search of food, often preying on frozen cattle in Rice County. He expected Edwin to ride an hour or more in the bitter cold north wind, driving the cattle so the cattle wouldn't freeze to death. He drove the cattle a mile south in the direction of the storm, then back again, against it. At the end of an hour, we had to lift Edwin off the saddle as he nearly froze to death. I wrapped a warm blanket around him to comfort him but Stolz dismissed my efforts, saying Edwin should grow up and "take it like a man."

Edwin tries hard to please his Dad but he always falls short of Stolz's expectations. Whenever he does, Stolz punishes him. Today was no different. Harvesting for corn wasn't going fast enough and it was all seventeen-year-old Edwin's fault.

Stolz stood over Edwin with a glassy stare, eyes hardened with hate. He slammed Edwin's head against the wall of the dugout. Then he started choking him. Edwin grabbed at his father's hands to try to stop him. Stolz tightened his grip. He squeezed Edwin's neck. Edwin couldn't breathe.

Stolz punched Edwin in the stomach and slapped him across the face. Edwin slid to the floor and curled up with his knees to his chest.

I stood by in horror. I am afraid Stolz might kill Edwin. He yelled at me when I tried to stop him, telling me that "my bastard son is no man."

Stolz left in a huff, returning to the cornfield to work. I tried my best to comfort Edwin.

Stolz is not a bad father. He's a good provider, but gets overwhelmed and frustrated sometimes by all the farm work that needs to be done. He takes his frustrations out on the kids. I fear for Edwin's life here at home, and that's why I sent him out west with a few settlers heading your way.

By now, I'm sure you've heard of Katy's death and Wilhelm's new marriage to Mollie Deckert on July 3. Edwin was his Best Man at his wedding. Although I miss Katy dearly, Mollie is a good woman and will make a nice wife for Wilhelm.

Praise the Lord, we're looking forward to good crops this year. I will send you money for Edwin's keep when I can.

I miss and love you,
Henrietta

August paused after reading the letter, then handed it to Marie. He turned to Edwin. "I understand your father has treated you harshly."

"Yes, sir," Edwin said.

"That's most unfortunate. Well, you're welcome to live with us until such time as you can homestead a place of your own. Our quarters are small, and you'll have to share a bed with August, Jr. I'll expect you to help us farm and do chores like my kids until you can be more independent."

"Yes, I'll work hard," Edwin said. "I'd be eternally grateful. You can't know how much this means to me, Uncle August."

Chapter 41

Although August had signed a Letter of Intent to become a U.S. citizen on December 24, 1873 at the Cook County Courthouse in Chicago, it didn't happen until fifteen years later when he went to the Courthouse in Grangeville, which was near Cottonwood, and finally became a citizen on April 23, 1889. And because he declared his new U.S. citizenship, Marie was automatically given hers. It gave August another freedom—the freedom to vote.

August and Marie and their children were now Idaho citizens as Idaho was granted statehood on July 3, 1890. Statehood also meant that the Bishop of Boise now oversaw the Catholic Church in nearby Keuterville.

The Kopczynskis and Edwin Stolz, as well as other Catholics in Cottonwood, drove oxen six miles to worship at the Church in Keuterville, for three years until the Bishop visited Cottonwood in the fall of 1891. A group of men, including August went to see him at the sacristy in the Keuterville church. After hearing an explanation of how the men had already gotten the necessary lumber ready to build the Cottonwood Church, the Bishop spoke.

"Dear me," he said, putting away his vestments, "I see you have everything in readiness to build, now if I should refuse your request, what would you do then?"

"Your Lordship," August said, smiling mischievously, "if we cannot build a church, we will build a dance hall." *The Church hierarchy thinks there are no morals in dance halls. I wonder what the Bishop will say now.*

The Bishop gave August a wide-eyed look. "I'll consider your request," he said, "only if Cottonwood and Keuterville each subscribe an amount of $300, together $600, for a steady priest between the two parishes."

So, August Kopczynski and George Seubert left the Keuterville church, riding on horseback, and contacted twenty other men in Cottonwood and the surrounding area. They gave the men their best sales pitch, telling them how much more convenient the Church in Cottonwood would be, especially in the winter months when they had to navigate the ice and snow with their teams of oxen on muddy, dirt roads. After much negotiations, August and George were able to get the men to sign the following Subscription List:

We the undersigned of Cottonwood and vicinity are willing to double as salary for a steady priest in case our prayer is granted by the Most Reverend Bishop such sums as is opposite our names:[65]

Aug. Kopczynski	$30	Wm. Hanley	$10
J. B. Forsmann	$30	James Carnes	$25
Geo. Seubert	$30	Heinrich Kohler	$10
Bernard Geise	$20	Joseph Schmidt	$15
Henry Terhaar	$30	Anton Boeckman	$5

H. H. Nuxoll	$25	Frank Goeckner	$5
H. W. Schmidt	$20	Edwin T. Stolz	$10
Barney Stubbers	$20	Henry Bieren	$10
H. J. List	$10	Joe Uhlenkott	$5
James Welsch	$20	Joe Nuxoll	$5
Frank Hanley	$10	George Terhaar	$5

After the Sunday Mass the following week, August and the group of twenty men presented the Bishop the donation list in the sacristy of the Keuterville Church.

An altar boy helped the Bishop put away his vestments. After looking over the list, he nodded. "I'll grant you permission to build," he said, smiling.

The men hooted and hollered.

"What about a priest?" August said when it was quiet again.

The Bishop turned to him. "I'll assign Father Kroeger as the first resident priest. He'll say Mass at both Keuterville and Cottonwood each Sunday."

"We can build a lean-to for him next to the church," said Seubert. "He can take his meals at the hotel."

The Bishop nodded in approval. "When you think of a name for the church and it is built, I'll come back for the dedication."

August felt overwhelmed. *Praise be to God. My dream for a Catholic Church in Cottonwood has come true, more proof that God is blessing me. Thank you, Lord, with all my heart for the opportunity to be with other Catholics and to share my faith.*

After the Bishop left that day, August and Ferdinand Goebel visited the Cottonwood Hotel for lunch. They sat down at a table and the waiter took their orders.

"Who did the Bishop say donated the land?" Mr. Goebel said, taking a sip of water. "I didn't hear."

"T. J. Rhodes. He owns and platted the Rhodes Addition at the north end of town."

"My wife and I will donate a bell," Mr. Goebel said, reaching for a napkin. "I assume the carpenters will be Henry Nuxoll and Barney Stubbers. They can see to it that all the men who donate their time have work to do."

"The food here is pretty good, don't you think?" August said, tasting the roast and potatoes.

"Not as good as Marie's home cooking. George Seubert overheard some of the regulars here say, 'Let's go to Kop's to eat. It won't cost us anything."

August laughed. "Yeah, we get a lot of visitors. Now I know why. Hey, what should we call the church? My church back in Poland was called *Parafia Podwyzszenia Krzyza Swietego or Elevation of the Holy Cross Parish* and Keuterville's, of course, is *Holy Cross.* I don't think the Cottonwood Church should be another version of Holy Cross."

"What about *St. Mary's?*" Mr. Goebel said, cutting the roast with a knife.

August wiped his mouth with a napkin, then took a sip of water. "Chicago has a *St. Mary's,* so I think Cottonwood's should be different."

"What about *Our Lady Help of Christians?*" said Mr. Goebel, raising his brows.

"That's a great name. Let's suggest it to the other men and to the Bishop.[66] I'm glad we won't have to drive oxen to Keuterville anymore. Those trips were brutal especially when it was muddy or the dirt road was icy. Had to bundle the kids then and they would complain to high heaven about having to go to church."

There was a comfortable silence, then August continued, "I've always liked going to church, gathering with other people who believed what I do. And, the music and homily are good for the soul. I feel God speaks to me, or at least my soul, in church. It makes me have a good heart toward people."

Mr. Goebel put his fork down and pushed his plate away. "You definitely have a kind heart. I heard you fixed a man's wagon in Westphalia even though he hadn't bought it from you."

"That was Mr. Highberger. Herman Helm must have told you that story."

Goebel nodded. "And what about that time you fixed a man's wagon for nothing because he had just arrived in Cottonwood with ten kids and couldn't afford to pay you. I forget his name. Do you remember who I'm talking about?"

August's eyes perked up. "I remember him, but I can't remember his name right now either. I guess maybe I have done some good in life. I think being kind is what's most important. It's what gives life meaning."

"You're right," said Goebel. "It doesn't matter how much money you make, how successful you are or how pretty your wife is. It's how kind you are."

August cleared his throat. "These kids today don't know what's good for them. They don't appreciate going to church because they've never had to go without. Last Sunday Malinda refused to go to church."

"What did you do about it?" Goebel asked.

"I told her if she didn't go Sunday, she wouldn't be allowed to ever go. She started crying and said she wanted to go."

"You've got good kids. You should be proud of how you raised them. They're kind like their old man."

"You should be around them sometimes. Kind is not necessarily the word that comes to mind," August said, rolling his eyes. "But, yes I'm proud. I'm very proud."

Chapter 42

On Tuesday, November 8, 1892, the day of the presidential election, August met his pal, Ferdinand Goebel, at Kopczynski Iron Works on Main Street. They saddled up their horses and rode fifteen miles to the courthouse in nearby Grangeville to vote.

August wore a warm, homespun black jacket Marie had made for him and felt the tug of wind at his back with the sun beginning to peek out over the horizon of the flat prairie. His nostrils flared as he took in the chilly, fresh air.

"Haven't seen you since spring, my friend," August said, looking over at Goebel and pulling on the reins. "How'd your crops come out?"

"Not spectacular," Goebel said, puffing on his cigar. "Just pretty fair."

"My corn did real well. Thirty bushels to an acre." *Proof again that God is blessing me.*

"That *is* good," Goebel said, raising his brows. "You're fortunate. I hope next year my crops do the same. So, what else have *you* been doing?"

"Got word in August that my stepmother, Rosalia, died the end of July. I guess she had been sick. I miss her. She wrote me almost every month. Now I've lost the connection to Poland."

August felt a lump in his throat. It was as difficult to talk about his Mama's death as it was to talk about the death of his firstborn son, Leo.

Goebel touched the tip of the cowboy hat he was wearing. "Sorry to hear that. How old was she?"

"Sixty-three. She was a strong woman like Marie. Mothered me since I was six after my natural mother passed away."

Goebel's horse whinnied. "Is your father still alive?"

"No, he passed away in October of 1879 when we were still living in Barton County, Kansas. Hard to believe that thirteen years have gone by since."

August thought about how proud his father would be of him being able to vote in the election. That certainly would have pleased his old man. He would never have imagined that one day his son would have this opportunity.

"It's not easy losing a parent, that's for sure."

August didn't want to dwell on his parents' deaths. This was supposed to be a happy occasion, after all. He changed the subject. "So, Ferdinand, this is my first time voting. How do I go about it?"

"It's real easy. When we get to the courthouse, they'll give you a written ballot with the candidates' names who are up for election. You mark your selection and then drop it in the ballot box to be counted. This year the vote is secret."

"Hasn't it always been like that?"

"Gosh, no. Years ago, an old timer told me that before the Revolutionary War I think, votes were made public. Believe it or not, back then men cast their votes at a local carnival, by saying their votes out loud. Heck, I'm sure some of them were drunk if they were at a carnival. There was a lot more foolishness and corruption back then. Ever since, voting has mostly been public, although privacy was up to the individual."

"Who are *you* voting for in this election—Cleveland or Harrison?"

Goebel puffed on his cigar. "As you know, one of the 'hot' issues is whether the currency should be backed by gold and silver, or just by gold alone. Although we taxpayers pay in silver, the dang international creditors ask for payment in gold which only depletes our gold supply."

August shot Goebel a furtive glance. "I thought most Republicans are for coining silver."

Goebel nodded. "They are in the West, but the northeasterners of both parties want the gold standard. Cleveland opposes the free silver, but President Harrison advocates for it."

"I'm with Harrison on this one," August said in a matter-of-fact tone. "You can find more silver in this part of the country than you can gold."

By now they were almost to Grangeville and were riding through the small town of Fenn which included only a handful of people. The temperature was a few degrees colder; they could see white puffs of air coming from the horses' mouths.

Goebel straightened up in the saddle. "So, where do you stand on the protective tariff? That's another big issue."

"You mean the taxes on foreign goods entering our country, don't you?" August said.

"Yes."

Since Goebel had arrived in Cottonwood earlier than August, and even though they were just friends, Goebel was somewhat of a father figure to August who he looked to for information, guidance and advice.

"How high are the tariffs now?" August said.

"About 47 percent."

August's eyebrows slanted in strong disapproval. "Gee, that's high. I'm with Cleveland on that one because the tariff has brought in so much revenue that the government is now running a surplus. Like Cleveland, I think it should be for revenue only."

"I'm with Harrison," Goebel said. "I favor high federal spending instead and think American industries will fail without high tariffs."

August's eyes perked up. "Someone said Harrison was also for voting rights of Negros, is that true?"

"Yes, I think so. Does that matter to you?"

August smiled. "I think everyone should have the freedom to vote. Even women. This is America, after all."

Goebel's jaw dropped. "Land sakes, women don't know anything about politics. They were born to breed babies. That's all."

August shook his head. "Some women are smart, like Marie. They could learn. So could Negros. We're all equal in the eyes of God, my friend. We all deserve the freedom to elect our leaders."

They were at the courthouse now and tied their horses up to the hitching posts out front. After they went inside, August felt giddy and lightheaded, proud about the new task before him. His eyes twinkled as the court official handed him his ballot and he felt stronger, more confident about the future, and that his life had new meaning and purpose. Voting was not an option either in Prussia or Poland. After his angst-filled journey to America and the heartbreaking crop failures in

Kansas as well as the loss of four kids, he never imagined that he would be standing here with the privilege of electing those who would have power over his livelihood. *Ach du lieber Gott, what a country! If only my father could see me now!*

He hesitated marking his ballot. *Cleveland or Harrison?* After he marked his choice, he put the ballot into the ballot box to be counted.

Goebel gave him a thumbs-up. August winked at him and smiled as if he had just finished doing something he had been prohibited from doing before and what could be the single most important thing in his life.

They unhitched their horses and rode back to Cottonwood.

Not long after the election, they found out former President Grover Cleveland who was a Democrat and had been the 22nd President of the United States was also elected to be the 24th President, beating incumbent Republican Benjamin Harrison.

Taking full advantage of his rights to privacy, August never told anyone how he'd cast his vote.

Chapter 43

On November 24 in 1892, August, Marie, their five kids and Ed Stolz, who was also invited, sat around the kitchen table, eating a Thanksgiving meal which Marie and the girls had prepared. They roasted a turkey, made dressing, mashed potatoes, gravy, baked sweet potatoes with brown sugar on top, creamed carrots and peas, baked fresh rolls, as well as pumpkin pie with whipped cream for dessert.

They said the sign of the cross in Latin and then the meal prayer in German. "*In nómine Patris, et Fĭlii, et Spĭritus Sancti, Amen. Segne, Vater, diese Gaben...* Bless us, oh Lord, for these thy gifts...May all the souls of the faithful departed, like Mama and Papa, through the mercy of God, rest in peace."

Then they passed around the dishes from right to left, while Marie spoke.

"I'm surprised we have no guests today."

"Funny you should bring that up. George Seubert told Goebel he overheard regulars at the hotel say, 'Let's go to Kop's to eat. It won't cost us anything.'"

Marie chuckled. "I wondered why we always have guests at our table."

"Well," August said. "I invited several people over for today, including Ferdinand and his wife, but they already had plans."

"Thank God!" said thirteen-year-old Malinda. "I'm tired of having strangers at our table. After all, they're not family."

August bristled at her remark. "We are all God's children. You were too young then, but I remember some tough times we went through in Ellinwood when we received charity from strangers. You need to learn to share your blessings with those less fortunate."

Everyone was silent for a few minutes.

"Please pass the turkey," Kate said, changing the subject.

"If we were in Poland, we'd be eating duck today instead of turkey," August said. "They are plentiful in the forests around *Grabionna*."

Even though Cottonwood was now his home and that of his children, he never let his children forget their roots.

"With all due respect, we're tired of hearing about *Grabionna*," said Malinda. "We live in America, not Poland."

August glanced at Marie. "These kids today! They don't have an interest in their Polish heritage!"

"Our heritage is German," Malinda said, curtly.

"Just because you speak German doesn't mean your heritage is German," August said. "We're Polish."

Marie gave August a knowing look as if to say she agreed with him. To avoid an argument, she changed the subject. "I was over at Mabel's today. She is expecting any day now. Do you remember when I had Leo and Grandma told me what to do to turn the baby? I was so frightened. But, we were able to get the baby's head turned down."

"That was a long time ago, Marie. You've come a long way since. I think it's wonderful that you are a midwife to ladies here in Cottonwood. They can really learn from your experience."

"I don't want anyone to have a baby and then have him die the next day. No one should have to go through what we went through with the twins."

An uncomfortable silence fell and August was compelled to change the subject. "Eat your peas and clean your plate, Malinda."

Malinda balked. "Why should I?"

"There are many children poorer than you who would be glad to eat what you leave on your plate," August said, calmly.

Malinda rolled her eyes and crossed her arms. "I don't give a horse's petute!" she said.

August felt his daughter was being disrespectful, which sparked a frown and an angry tone of voice from him. "You'll clean your plate if I say so! The Fourth Commandment says you should obey your parents."

"I don't believe in rules," Malinda said, defiantly.

Her answer startled August. He could see shades of himself in her. She was rebellious like him. "I didn't believe in rules either when I was your age," he said. "I used to think freedom was the most important thing in life, but I feel differently now."

Marie glanced over at August. "I can't believe you're saying this. What about that Prussian officer who whacked you across your face because you were belittling Prussia. You left Poland because you were galled by the lack of freedom of speech. You were against rules then."

"I've come to understand a person needs rules and structure to live by."

"Haven't you traded political rules for religious ones?" Marie said.

"Woman, it's unnerving how you see both sides to everything. I became disillusioned with the political rules in Prussia. I felt suffocated by them. But, I've come to understand a human being needs morals to become a good person, like the rules of the Catholic Church. It creates a more stable society."

Marie raised an eyebrow. "With age comes wisdom," she said.

"Nevertheless," August said ignoring her tease, "I still hope Poland becomes a country again. It's sad to think we've lost our Polish language and heritage. The kids aren't interested in it. They don't want to speak anything but German or English." He looked over at August, Jr. and Malinda and sighed. They avoided eye contact with their father, looking down at their plates.

"They're too young, August," Marie said. "They probably won't be interested till they're in their forties, or fifties, until after they've started families of their own."

"By that time, we'll both be dead, so our Polish heritage will be lost forever." He sighed again. "If only the Polish people would revolt. But, alas, I don't think it will happen in my lifetime."

"It may never be a country ever again!" Marie said. "Have you thought about that?"

"Don't talk like that, Marie. We must always have hope."

"Tell me, do you still consider Poland your home?" Marie said.

He sighed. "I've moved seven times now in my life, each time I thought it was a new beginning. I had hoped each move would be better than the next but it didn't always turn out that way. Chicago was not better than *Grabionna*. Kansas was certainly worse. I continued to long for Poland, for home. I always hoped the new place would feel like home. It never did.

He looked up at Marie with a smile. "Although it always felt warm and cozy where you are, no matter the surroundings."

Marie beamed at him. "What a sweet thing to say, my love!"

"And Cottonwood—the land, the weather, the people—they're like what I had in Poland, only better. I like the countryside here—the flat land of the Camas Prairie stretching as far as the eye can see, the wagon-rutted, dirt roads situated near groves of green Cottonwood trees. The smell of apple and plum orchards as well as dirt from the wheat fields, and even horse poop, cow dung, or chicken and bird droppings in the barn. It smells like home. And, if you travel down to the Salmon River, you can hear the sound of rushing water, so clear and pure, and see beautiful forests of evergreens on either side."

Marie nodded. "I feel that way, too."

"The weather is like *Grabionna*, too. I thank God for the four seasons we have here. The temperature over 100 degrees in August, leaves turning beautiful reds, yellows and browns starting in September, snowflakes beginning towards the end of November, and the snow doesn't let up until March or April. I couldn't ask for more variety in weather."

"Although I could do without the winter months, I do appreciate when the lawns and trees turn a lush green here."

"And, the people in Cottonwood are friendlier. There are more Catholics moving in and there are more Catholics here than there were in *Grabionna*. I don't feel like I'm an outsider or a minority like I was in *Grabionna* where Lutherans were the majority. Catholics are the majority here."

"I never thought about that before," Marie said, "but you're right, my dear. We are very fortunate."

"I feel free here," August said. "Everyone in America is pretty open about voicing their opinions about politics or religion. I love it! You can be for or against the President or government leaders without fear of repercussion. *Ach du lieber Gott,*[67] it's a great country!

"And, Marie, the most wonderful thing is that people look up to me here because I'm a pillar of the community. I'm a leader here. I didn't have that status in *Grabionna*. As a Pole in Prussia, I was nothing.

"I'm American now. Cottonwood is my home. I am home. I am finally home."

Epilogue

Time passed quickly. In 1906, sixty-year-old August, who was still working hard at his blacksmith trade, stood at the well in front of Kopczynski Iron Works on Main Street, and lowered the bucket to draw a refreshing, cool drink of water. He breathed in the fresh September air and noticed the temperature remained cool this morning after it had dropped down during the night. He hoped the rising sun would soon warm up the surrounding area.

August saw his pal, Ferdinand Goebel, riding his Arabian horse down Main Street and beckoned him to stop and have a quick drink with him.

"*Guten Tag,* said August. "*Wie geht's dir, mein Freund?*"

"*Sehr, gut,*" Mr. Goebel said. "Can't complain. I've had decent crops this year. How goes it with you? I brought a bottle of whiskey with me." He pulled it out of his satchel. "Let's have a real drink."

August took a swig and handed the bottle back to Mr. Goebel. "Life is good, my friend. Our home is a happy one, with music, song, and dancing."

"Music? Do you play an instrument?" Mr. Goebel said, sipping the whiskey.

"No, but August, Jr. and his four sisters, formed an orchestra which often plays for dances in and around Cottonwood."

Mr. Goebel smiled. "Is that where August, Jr. met Lena?"

"*Ach du lieber Gott*, I have a story about that. At a New Year's dance three years ago in January. I think the year was 1903. Yes, it was. Anyway, August, Jr., was playing the piano in the orchestra and saw his girlfriend, Lena Seubert, dancing the waltz with his rival, Clem Wemhoff. Clem even bought Lena's basket at the Basket Social at an event a week or two later. At the Social, the music started playing after lunch, and when the announcer said, 'Ladies Choice,' Lena promptly asked my son for that waltz, much to Clem's dismay. Clem was unaware that my son had already proposed to sweet Lena, but he soon found out that they were engaged."

Mr. Goebel smiled, chuckling. "What a great story! I do remember a horseman went house to house announcing their wedding."[68]

"That whiskey sure tastes good. Let me have another sip." Mr. Goebel handed August the bottle and August put the bottle up to his lips and took a gulp. "Aahh," he said, wiping his mouth. "Lena was the first woman in Cottonwood to wear a white wedding dress. My bride wore a black one like all the others. Of course, August, Jr. wore a tuxedo. This new generation has it better than we did."

"Speaking of new generations, I heard you now have grandkids."

"*Nur Einkelinnen.*" *Only granddaughters.* Marie was midwife to them. Johanna was born in March two years ago and then in August of last year they had another girl they named Alvina. They asked me to be a baptismal sponsor for each of them, but I refused. I won't do it unless I get a *Stammhalter.*"

"Why, you're as stubborn as I am!" Mr. Goebel took another drink. "Say, did you hear about Bill and Georgia Bash? You know them, don't you?"

"I think I remember him. He's been in my shop before. He's in his late 40s or early 50s and his wife is twenty years younger."

"That's the one. His wife just died giving birth to a set of twins. Marie probably knows about it. John Aichlmayr adopted the little boy. The little girl named Betty died at birth."

August remembered his own twins who died at birth. "I'm sorry to hear that. I'll have to ask Marie about it."

"Bill is left with four young boys—Lloyd, George, Frank and Merle. A man can't take care of small children like that so I've heard he's giving them up for adoption. Might be your chance to get a *Stammhalter*."

"That's a great idea. I'll look into it."

Mr. Goebel left and August finished up work at his shop and then rode his horse to the family farm east of town. Marie, who had been stirring chicken soup for dinner, met him at the door.

"I have some news," August said, dismounting. "I saw Goebel at the well today and he told me Georgia Bash died in childbirth. Did you know about that?"

"Yes, it's so sad. Really tragic. She was giving birth to a set of twins. It makes me think of our twins that we lost in Westphalia. Luckily, I survived, but Georgia wasn't so fortunate."

"Goebel said Bill Bash is left with four young boys and he's giving them up for adoption. I think we should adopt one of them."

"At our age? You're sixty years old, I'm fifty."

"The boys need a good home. Bill's not able to care for them. Besides, it doesn't look like August, Jr. is going to have any boys to carry on the family name. I would be extremely disappointed if the Kopczynski name died out."

"But, you and I might die soon. What happens to the child then? Have you thought about that?"

"Oh, Marie, don't think like that. My grandfather Jacob in *Grabionna* lived to be 89 years old. Longevity is in my genes. Let's adopt the youngest one. Please....Marie."

"Oh, all right. If you say so."

"Things will work out. You'll see."

August and Marie adopted Merle on March 9, 1906, when Merle was one-and-a-half years old. Frank and Mary Rad adopted his brother Frank; his brothers, George and Lloyd, continued to live with their father.

Ten months later, the Kopczynski family, like other families in Cottonwood, celebrated Christmas on Wednesday, December 25th in 1906. Every year August and his son would scour their timber land for the perfect fir tree, chop it down and haul it back to their home east of Cottonwood. Keeping with German tradition, Marie and the kids sang *O Tannenbaum* and *Stille Nacht, heilige Nacht* while they decorated the tree with real candles, as well as popcorn-cranberry garland and old fashioned wooden Christmas ornaments. They kept a bucket of water nearby to douse any flames. The scent of evergreens wafted in the air.

On Christmas Eve, the family attended Midnight Mass at the Catholic Church. At the front of the altar stood a large crèche with statues of Mary and Joseph, as well as shepherds, and a manger for the Baby Jesus. August, Jr. played the organ and the choir sang *Silent Night* as the priest and altar boys came down the center aisle carrying the statue of the Baby Jesus to put in the Crib. After Mass, the choir sang Christmas carols like *Adeste Fideles*, and *O Little Town of Bethlehem*.

The family returned home at one o'clock in the morning using a horse-drawn sleigh to navigate the icy roads, and drank hot chocolate before going to bed.

On Christmas Day, little two-year-old Merle awoke early and squealed with delight as he saw his gifts under the tree—an orange, some hard candy and a brown teddy bear with black button eyes Marie had made for him.

The Goebel family joined the Kopczynskis for a Christmas dinner. They feasted on honey-glazed ham, cheesy potatoes, green beans, Apple Waldorf salad and White Christmas Pie for dessert. Afterwards, August couldn't stop coughing and went to bed early, telling Marie he was exhausted because of all the excitement.

The day after Christmas, August woke up with a high fever and teeth-chattering chills, so Marie called the doctor. The doctor diagnosed pneumonia and lung fever and told August to stay in bed. Like other homes in the area, the house wasn't insulated very well, and the cold only worsened August's condition. Ignoring the doctor's orders, August sat up in a chair in the living room instead to conduct his personal business. He had a Last Will and Testament drawn up and on Friday, December 28, George Stubbers, Herman Nuxoll, and Frank Wimer came to the house to witness August signing it.

The will stipulated that all his personal property and real estate be given to Marie which amounted to 400 acres of farm land, 160 acres of timber land and six town lots. Upon her death, the land was to be divided among their children: 80 acres to Katherine (Crosby), a total of 360 acres to August, Jr. on condition that he divide the land he homesteaded (160 acres in Greencreek) and give 80 acres to Mary, 80 acres to Cecilia, and that he pay Melinda (Nuxoll) $1,600 ($20/acre times 80 acres) within two years after Marie's death. Of the 160 acres of timber land: 40 acres to be given to August, Jr. and 30 acres each to Malinda, Mary and Cecilia. As his legacy to his adopted son, Merle, he willed $100 to be paid when Merle reached the age of 21.

The following day, Saturday, December 29, August complained of chest pain and that he couldn't breathe, although he continued to cough. Marie felt his forehead. He was burning hot yet his teeth still chattered. She covered him with another blanket and went to the kitchen where all the kids were waiting: August, Jr. and his wife, Lena; Malinda, and her husband, Tony Nuxoll; Kate, and her husband Lloyd Crosby; Mary; Cecilia; and little Merle.

"Papa's failing," she said. A tear rolled down her cheek. "I don't think he's going to make it through the night."

August, Jr. put his arm around her. "Mama, this is hard on all of us. Let's all of us go in and pray the rosary with him."

After they finished praying the rosary, Marie looked at August's hands (they were blue) and at his feet. Marie knew the signs of death from seeing so many of her children die.

She gasped. Then she stroked his head. "It's okay, August," she said in a soothing tone of voice. "You can go now. We'll be fine."

Pretty soon August's breathing changed. He took a deep breath and then didn't breathe for a minute or so. The kids all sat around the bed. Between crying and blowing their noses, they watched August's upper chest rise and fall. Then all of a sudden his chest stopped moving. Everyone was silent and they all stood up, moved around and started talking.

Kate asked her mother, "Did he die?"

"Yes," she said.

After his death, Marie and Merle moved in with August, Jr. and Lena, who were Merle's godparents. They raised him along with their own children. When Merle was old enough, August, Jr. and Lena gave him a choice of whether he wanted his last name to be Bash or Kopczynski and he chose the name Kopczynski.

August Sr.'s wish for *Stammhalters* came true as August, Jr. ended up with a dozen kids of his own—five girls and seven boys (eight boys counting Merle) to carry on the family name. Led by August, Jr.'s son, Gus (August III), the boys created The Kopczynski Jazz Orchestra of Idaho which played for local dances, numerous proms, and Fair Dances in and around Cottonwood, playing Big Band tunes such as "In the Mood." They made $750 per year which kept the Kopczynski family alive during the Depression.

At sixty-four years of age, Marie died on February 18, 1920, from heart trouble. The property was not distributed until long after Marie's death, thirteen years after the will had been written, and caused a dispute which almost destroyed family ties among the Kopczynski children. Things had changed, like the price of land rose to $75/acre, and Malinda was supposed to get $20/acre but wanted more money. Shortly after Malinda was paid $75/acre, the price of land dropped to $10/acre. Also, included in the settlement were hogs and cattle. Marie owned the animals but August, Jr. had to pay for the feed and take care of them. During those thirteen years Marie lived with August, Jr., she often gave his sisters butchered hogs or beef, which August, Jr. considered part of their inheritance but the girls argued that it was gifts from their mother.

August and Marie remained true to their faith and never imagined the effect their lives would have on future generations. August's kind and generous nature, his work ethic, and his love for music and dancing carried over to the lives of his five remaining children, his 35 grandchildren, 129 great-grandchildren and over 350 great-great grandchildren. It was his and Marie's hope to give their offspring a better life, a life filled with freedom and prosperity.

Although not all remained devout Catholics, most of their descendants were hard-working and generous, many of them musically inclined. They include pilots, teachers, engineers, a lawyer, a realtor, stockbrokers, accountants, business owners, insurance agents, carpenters, hairdressers, authors, artists, an opera singer, a priest, and even a famous mountain climber. Several became millionaires.

Their lives became a testament to the love they shared, the hardships they endured, the freedom they never took for granted, and the economic success they achieved due to their unending, though continually contested, faith. It is hoped their adventurous spirit will never be forgotten.

A Conversation with the Author

What inspired you to write this book?

My cousin, Dawne Drake, suggested I write a historical novel because she and her husband, Larry, were avid readers of historical nonfiction and told me there wasn't much written about Polish history during this time period. They sent me two books to read: *The Polish Way*, A Thousand-year History of the Poles and their Culture, 1987 by Adam Zamoyski (Hippocrene Books) and *God's Playground*, A History of Poland, 2005 by Norman Davies (Columbia University Press). I also read *Poland*, 1983, by James Mitchener (Random House) which was suggested to me by Kryzsztof Kopczynski (not a relative), a Polish American living in New York City.

What inspired you to get interested in genealogy?

When I was twenty-one, I visited my Frankfurt cousin, Ursula Kothe, (now deceased), who was forty-four and lived in West Germany. She asked me a million questions about my relatives, questions I couldn't answer. I started research in the 1970s when genealogy wasn't as popular as it is today. I spent the next twenty years researching our family history (before

Ancestry.com was invented) aided by my brother, Don, who was also interested in genealogy. I enlisted the help of Marek Koblanski, a professional genealogical researcher in Salt Lake City, Utah, Lukasz Bielecki of the Poznan Projekt in Poland, and also Brother Herbert Osborn, at the Latter Day Saints (Mormon) Church Library in Spokane Valley where I spent numerous hours researching. That culminated in writing The Kopczynski Family History book, a huge book complete with photos which we self-published in 1991 and sold for $50 per book which only covered printing costs. We published 120 books.

How were you able to capture the personalities of August and Marie, your great-grandparents?

I had no information about their personalities from oral family history, so since I believe in astrology, I fashioned them after their astrological signs. August was an Aquarius. A typical Aquarius considers everyone his friend, loves puzzles, values conversation more than a woman who is fashionably dressed, and cherishes freedom and independence. Marie was a Libra. Libras tend to see both sides to everything, have trouble making decisions, enjoy fashion and love gardening.

What cities have you visited in order to do research for this book?

New York City in 1985 and 1986, where I got goosebumps touring the first immigration center, Castle Garden. **Chicago** in 1988 where I mistakenly visited St. Mary's Church, thinking it was the church where my great-grandparents were married. **Ellinwood, Kansas** in 1990 where I visited St. Joseph's Church. **Hamburg, Germany** in 2015, where just by chance,

I discovered the BallinStadt Emigration Museum on Vedder's Island and took a tour of the harbor by boat. I felt chills down my spine seeing the water in the harbor and tasting the salty sea air knowing my great-grandfather stood on this same spot and embarked on a clipper ship in this same harbor more than 145 years earlier. **Grabionna, Miasteczko Krajeñskie, Piła and Bialosliwie, Poland** in 2015. I drove to Poland with Christel, my cousin who lived in Munich, and met new cousins, Anita and Kryzsztof, who lived in nearby Usjie. They helped me find the Kopczynski house and barn on Grabionna Way, the Catholic Church in Miasteczko Krajeñskie as well as the railroad stations in Piła and Bialosliwie. Upon seeing these places I almost wept. **Walla Walla, Washington** in 2012 where I did a book signing. **Cottonwood, Idaho** where I grew up and returned to visit in 1991, 1993, 2005, and 2013.

How did your life experiences help you in writing August's spirituality?

I grew up in a devout Catholic family. My father studied to become a priest before he married my mother. Many family members remained devout Catholics. I also belonged to an Evangelical Church for ten years and was informed by my own moments of doubt.

What helped you in making August and Marie's Kansas and Idaho farming experiences realistic and historically accurate?

Google was my friend, and also Wikipedia. I retrieved a lot of information from the U.S. Census records and read some fascinating books about Kansas and the local history in Ellinwood and Westphalia. For expert advice concerning farming in Kansas, I contacted Bob Sterneker, a farmer in Cunningham, who is a descendant of August Stolz, as well as Robert E. Yarmer of the Ellinwood Historical Society, and Karen True in Westphalia. For advice about Idaho farming, I contacted Cliff Tacke, a farmer who lives near Cottonwood, as well as my sister, Connie, who is married to a wheat farmer in Moscow, Idaho. The information about wild horse and cattle roundups and hog stampedes in Cottonwood came from an unpublished manuscript my grandfather had written.

How did you research prices of land and crops in that era?

I obtained land deeds by contacting the Register of Deeds at Anderson County Courthouse in Garnett, Kansas, the Barton County Courthouse in Great Bend, Kansas, the courthouse in Lyons, Kansas and at the Grangeville Courthouse, in Grangeville, Idaho. I researched the prices of crops in Kansas using Google for various websites and obtained prices of crops in Idaho from a news article written in a German newspaper, *The Effingham Volksblatt 1884-1886*, translated and compiled by Dorothy A. Brumleve.

How did you research their interaction with the Native Americans?

I researched online for the various tribes in Kansas and have read several historical accounts of Native Americans. From oral history as well as from "Pioneer Days—Reminiscences of Mr. August Kopczynski (II)" by Sister Alfreda Elsensohn, OSB, published in "The Echo" of St. Gertrude's Academy, Feb., Mar.,

Apr., May, June issues, 1939, I learned my grandfather was friends with the Nez Perce tribe of Indians near Cottonwood, so I assume my great-grandfather also made friends with the Indian tribes in Kansas.

Acknowledgements

I wrote this book out of a love for family and a passion for writing. My initial goal in writing was to become the first millionaire in my family due to the success of a book I had written—like my mentor, Jack Hashian, (now deceased), who authored the first four TREVANIAN New York Times bestsellers, under his pen name, including *The Eiger Sanction*, which was made into a movie, and also like my writing coach for fifteen years, Robert Gover, (now deceased), who received a million dollars for writing the bestselling classic, *One Hundred Dollar Misunderstanding*, in the 60s when paperbacks cost 50 cents. Since then, I've learned that less than 1% of writers make more than $50,000, so I should have tried winning the lottery instead.

But, while writing this book, I came to the conclusion that the writing journey, the time spent bonding and critiquing with my writer friends (Marian Sheafor, Diana Wickes, Betty Deuber, Carol Senske, and at times Richard Smith and Gail Mangano—who are in their 80s and 90s), has been more important than the American dream of making a million dollars. I am extremely grateful for all your help as well as your friendship.

Special mention to Betty Deuber, a devout Catholic, who helped make sure the information about Catholicism in the book was correct and kept me grounded in the time period as she is writing her own book that takes place in the same time period.

I also want to thank the Eastern Washington University graduate students who were instructors for our group, The-Writers-In-The-Community, for their hard work: Elizabeth Dunham, a poet, Nahla Hobdallah, from Egypt who writes nonfiction, and Justin Eisenstadt, from Baltimore, Maryland who writes fiction.

I feel all the research and help from my critique group would have been in vain without the guidance and expert editing skills from the following who all get gold stars for their hard work: Sue Jostrom, Ashley Schwartz, and Helga Schier, who not only helped me write a better book, but also taught me invaluable lessons about the writing craft.

I am deeply indebted to Sister Alfreda Elsensohn, OSB, for interviewing my grandfather, August Kopczynski II. Both of them wrote down the first skeletal account of my great-grandfather's journey from Poland, his time in Chicago and becoming a pioneer in Kansas and Idaho.

This book would not have been possible without the aid of some genealogical researchers. First and foremost, I'd like to thank my brother Don who helped me with genealogy research for twenty years before Ancestry.com was invented. Several years later, Don and my coworker, Joe Booth, spent many hours on Ancestry.com and found several to-die-for gems. You have my heartfelt thanks for all your hard work. Kudos also to Marek Koblanski, a professional Polish researcher for the Latter Day Saints (LDS) Church in Salt Lake City, Utah, who

I hired to do research in 1991. (Thanks to my brother Allan who helped pay for it.)

Many thanks to Brother Herbert Osborn, head of the LDS Church Library in Spokane, who found my great-grandfather in the 1880 census on Ancestry.com. My brother Don and I had been searching for him for years without any luck. But, by a stroke of genius, Herbert found him living in DuPage County rather than Cook County. I also wish to thank Lukasz Bielecki of the Poznan Projekt in Poland for his genealogical research in 2018. (Thanks to my siblings, Don, Karen and Larry who helped pay for it.)

Credit also belongs to Kryzsztof Kopczynski in New York City, not a relative, who helped me with Polish translations, enlightened me with research on Polish history, and found the heir to the Kopczynski house on 28 Grabionna Way in Poland.

My cousins, Anita Majewska-Wychylewska and Krzysztof Wychylewski of Usjie, Poland also helped with Polish translations and guided me in Grabionna to help me find the former Kopczynski house (Many thanks to the present owners, the son of Alfred Krzeminski, for allowing us to visit.) and the church in Miastezcko Krajeñskie as well as the train stations in Bialosowie and Piła. Thanks also to my cousin, Christel Strumienski, who transported us.

And, thanks to my cousin, Johanna Kothe, and my editor, Helga Schier, who did the German translations in the book.

I'd also like to thank the following researchers: Rebecca Grabie, Reference Librarian, Patricia D. Klingenstein Library, The New-York Historical Society. Lesley Martin, Reference Librarian, Chicago History Museum Research Center. Nancy Wilson, Curator of Collections, Elmhurst History Museum,

Elmhurst, Illinois. The Chicago researcher at the Clerk of the Criminal Court of Cook County who found the Letter of Intent which I had been trying to find for ten years. Joyce Schulte, President, Ellinwood Historical Society. Vanessa Lopez, Parish Secretary and the staff at St. Francis of Assisi church in Chicago, Illinois. Karen True and the staff at St. Teresa's Church in Westphalia, Kansas. Uncle Joe Jacobs, Ellensburg, Washington who gave me valuable research on Adam and Eve, the Kopczynski twins born in Westphalia, Kansas. Muriel Konen, Naches, Washington, who provided needed information about Uncle Merle.

For copies of land deeds, I would like to thank Sandy Baugher, Anderson County Courthouse in Garnett, Kansas; Pam Wornkey, Barton County Courthouse, Great Bend, Kansas; and Rhonda Hunt in Lyons, Kansas.

For their farming expertise, I would like to thank Bob Sterneker of Cunningham, Kansas, Robert E. Yarmer, of the Ellinwood Historical Society, Cliff Tacke of Greencreek, Idaho, and my sister, Connie Esser of Moscow, Idaho, who is married to Garry, a wheat farmer.

Many thanks to Stolz family relatives who contributed research for this book: Bertha Stolz Hopman (now deceased), Ventura, California, for her write-up of the Stolz family history; Bob Zenziger, Lewisburg, Pennsylvania, for his information on August Stolz; Bill Stolz, Grangeville, Idaho, for the information on Edwin Stolz, his Dad; and Ivan Nuxoll, Greencreek, Idaho, for information on the Stolz family.

My brother Don deserves tremendous credit for all the work he's done for me. He read an early draft of the manuscript and provided important feedback and purchased several research books for me on E-Bay. Thanks to his wife Dena who helped with genealogical research, to my brother Larry who provided a valuable book from Teutopolis, Illinois, to my sister Maureen, who provided suggestions about children in my story, and to my sisters, Connie and Theresa, who gave me valuable feedback on portions I read to them over the phone. All of you have my deepest thanks.

Ginormous thanks to my siblings who gave me the surprise of a lifetime after I returned from a two-week research trip to Poland and Germany in 2015. As I entered my home, I saw a bouquet of red roses on the counter and found they had completely remodeled my bathroom, gave me a new washer and dryer to replace ones which were thirty years old as well as a new entertainment center and cleaned/organized my messy house from top to bottom. Thanks for your generosity and for saving me valuable time which I could use instead for writing.

Many thanks to my boss, Bill D. Smith, for funding a Pacific Northwest Writers Association Conference I attended in Seattle to pitch my book, and also to his wife, Sandee, for her inspiration and encouragement.

Thanks also to my cousins, Chris Kopczynski, a famous mountain climber, Dave Reed, a retired Delta Airlines pilot, Wayne Wimer, a retired Seattle attorney, Jim Reed, a retired electrician and member of a men's book club, and my sisters, Karen, Connie and Theresa, who inspired and encouraged me along the way.

Endnotes

1   Hajo Holborn: *A History of Modern Germany: 1840-1945*, Volume 3, page 165

CHAPTER 1

2   France's external military intelligence agency, the *Deuxieme Bureau*, was created in 1871 and operated as such until 1940.

3   Napoleon promised the Poles more than he ever intended to deliver, yet many Polish citizens believed that victories by Napoleon would result in the restoration of Poland's commonwealth.

CHAPTER 5

4   Translates to Elevation of the Holy Cross Parish. The Church was burned in 1890 and a new brick, neo-Gothic church was built in 1899 which stands today.

5   After the partition in 1772, Prussia, Russia, and Austria divided up Poland.

6   The enclosed confessional booth was created by Cardinal Charles Borromeo, former Archbishop of Milan, who lived from 1538 till 1584.

CHAPTER 6

7   *Bigos* is a national Polish favorite, containing cabbage, sauerkraut and a variety of meats, game and *Kielbasa* sausage is usually served with hard-crust rye bread.

CHAPTER 7

8   *Weisse Hohe* was formerly named *Bialosliwie*, and again since 1945. It is located 2.4 miles (4 kilometers) from *Grabionna*.

9   In 1874 at age seventeen, Albert Ballin took over an emigration company known as Morris & Co. from his father who had died. The memorial park and emigration center on Vedders Island, originally built in 1901, was named BallinStadt in Albert's honor. It is now home to an Emigration Museum.

10   Former residency has only been listed in the Passenger Lists of Hamburg, not other ports.

11   If he failed either medical exam, upon his arrival in the U.S., he would have been refused entry and the shipping company would need to pay for his transportation back to Europe.

12   Cottage Hill, first settled in 1837, was named after the Hill Cottage, an inn built in 1843. Renamed Elmhurst in 1870, its population today is 45,751 and it is an affluent western suburb of Chicago, comprised of 84% Caucasians.

13   Polish surnames show a person's gender. For example a female's name ends in "ska." A male's name ends in "ski."

CHAPTER 10

14 Originally opened in May 1852, the New Depot, near Sherman (now Financial Place) and Van Buren streets, a new train station named LaSalle Street station was built on the site fourteen years later in 1866 and still stands today.

15 Chicago's population tripled to 298,977 in 1870 according to the census; and the population today is 2.7 million (comprised of 44% Caucasians, 28 % Hispanics, 22% African Americans, and 13% Other)

16 St. Francis of Assisi was the first German parish in Chicago, located at 813 West Roosevelt Road, between Newberry Avenue and Halsted Street. The Church is now Spanish-speaking only (2014).

17 Elmhurst's name is derived from "elm," the local trees found there, and "hurst," a German word relating to "forest."

CHAPTER 12

18 The first circus in Chicago, the "Boston Arena Company," appeared on September 14, 1836.

19 The first minstrels to appear in Chicago were "Christy's Minstrels" and their songs like "Old Folks at Home" or "My Old Kentucky Home" were sung in every town and city, and many of their melodies were adapted to hymns.

CHAPTER 13

20   Sometimes called Reichsthaler, the Thaler was the
        currency of Prussia until 1857. The value is difficult
        to determine, since each area, duchy, kingdom, or
        principality set the value of its own currency.

21   In 1871, after Germany was united under the German
        Empire, a law was passed designating the German
        Mark as its single currency. At that time, one Thaler
        was equivalent to about 3 German Marks, which
        equaled 75 cents in U.S. currency. Therefore, 100 Thaler
        was equivalent to about $75, the cost of a brand new
        Peter Schuttler wagon.

CHAPTER 20

22   They were married September 15, 1872 in St. Francis of
        Assisi Church in Chicago.

23   65 hectares.

24   McCormick Machine Company was later named
        International Harvester.

CHAPTER 23

25   The founder and original settlers in Ellinwood were
        not German, however, they gave many of the main
        streets German names like Goethe, Schiller and
        Bismarck in order to entice German immigrants to
        settle there.

26   The Letter of Intent was found in Cook County
        Courthouse records, Chicago, Illinois.

27   Montgomery Ward's was established in Chicago in
        1872.

28   Ellinwood remained a small town. Its population today
     is 2,131, according to the 2010 census.
29   Kaffir corn is another name for the grain Sorghum.

CHAPTER 24

30   The state of Kansas derived its name from the Kaw,
     also known as the Kansa or Kanza Indian tribe.
31   Between 1871-1876, Congress passed several bills to
     protect the buffalo; however, they were never enacted.
     General Philip Sheridan, opposed the legislation
     stating his men "were settling the vexed Indian
     question by destroying the Indian's commissary.
     Let them kill, skin and sell until the buffaloes are
     exterminated."

CHAPTER 25

32   Plagues of locusts were recorded as far back as the
     time of Pharaoh and Moses in The Old Testament in
     the Bible (Exodus 10:4-6).
33   Recorded in diaries of Kansas women.
34   Crop damage was estimated to be $200 million across
     the Great Plains in 1874.
35   Barton County was divided into three civil townships:
     Lakin Township, Bend Township, and Buffalo
     Township.

36   Praised by President Lincoln, Mary Ann Bickerdyke
      was a nurse in the Civil War and had also been
      a missionary in New York and had several well-
      placed connections in politics and commerce as
      well as wealthy friends who helped in her various
      philanthropic relief efforts.

37   The Atchison, Topeka and Santa Fe and the Kansas
      Pacific railroad companies.

CHAPTER 26

38   In *Bone Picking on the American Plains,* Alicia Z.
      Klepeis, states that "buffalo bones were also used
      to make many domestic items, including buttons,
      umbrella handles, corset stays, crochet hooks, and
      even china."

39   The "Great Plague of Vienna" in 1679 gave rise to the
      legend of *Lieber Augustin.* Augustin was a popular
      street musician, who, according to the legend, fell
      into a pit with bodies of plague victims, late at night
      when he was drunk. The fact that he did not contract
      the disease may be owed to the alcohol. Henceforth,
      people who appeared to create fun for others, sort of
      like a clown would do, are called August or Augustin.

40   According to an exhibit at the BallinStadt Emigration
      Museum, "There were 70 German (language)
      newspapers in the U.S. in 1848 and that number
      doubled within the next four years." At one time there
      were more German language newspapers in the U.S.
      than there were in Germany.

CHAPTER 29

41   Due to the increased production because of the Turkey Red wheat, Kansas later became known as "The Wheat State."

42   The Kansas Historical Society noted some historians dispute this legend arguing that "Turkey Red was not the typical wheat variety grown by Mennonites in Russia."

43   In 2014, an average of 171 bushels of corn per acre were grown in Kansas, the increase due largely to irrigation.

44   Stolz applied to homestead the 80 acres in Barton County on March 30, 1880. On August 1, 1881, he sold the property to D.W. Moore. Later oil wells sprang up on this property.

CHAPTER 30

45   Population in Westphalia in 1880 was only a handful of people, in 1884 it was 500, in 1887 it was 1,019, and in 2010 it was only 163.

CHAPTER 31

46   Westphalia is a region in northwestern Germany between the rivers Rhine and Weser and is part of the state of North Rhine-Westphalia.

47   According to "Westphalia Kansas – The First 100 Years," the seven Catholic colonies included: Westphalia, Iowa in 1872; Westphalia, Kansas in 1880; Olpe, Kansas in 1884; Muenster, Texas in 1889; Lindsay, Texas in 1891; Pilot Point, Texas in 1891; and Mt. Carmel, Texas in 1907.

48   Mass was said at the Flusche residence in Westphalia for a year until St. Teresa's (of Avila) Church was built in May 1881.

CHAPTER 32

49   In the 1880s, Smallpox killed 40% of those who contracted it, including hundreds of Indians who had no immunity to it. A global immunization campaign led by the World Health Organization eradicated it in 1980.

50   Smallpox is usually caused by an airborne virus, however, the word virus only first appeared in 1898, with the discovery of the tobacco mosaic virus by Martinus Beijerinck.

51   Great Bend is 10.4 miles from Ellinwood in central Kansas.

CHAPTER 33

52   Typhoid fever is a bacterial infection of the intestinal tract.

53   Typhoid fever can be treated with antibiotics; however, penicillin, the first antibiotic was only discovered by Alexander Fleming in 1929.

CHAPTER 34

54 August, Jr. carried the booklet in his wallet his whole lifetime. It was passed down to August, III's family.

CHAPTER 35

55 Statistics are for Walla Walla territory, which included Idaho, printed in the German language newspaper, *Effingham Volksblatt*, Thursday, December 3, 1885.

CHAPTER 38

56 Over 100 degrees Fahrenheit is 38 degrees Celsius.

57 Riparia is now a ghost town. All that's left is a campsite.

58 Lewiston (population 31,894 in 2010) is across the Snake River from Clarkston, Washington (population 7,229 in 2010).

59 The 1890 federal census for Idaho was destroyed, so 900 is an approximate number.

60 Fountain Grade, which doesn't exist today, was a road on a hill with many twisty curves or switchbacks near Culdesac, Idaho.

61 Cottonwood, Idaho, is located 175 miles (280 kilometers) southeast of Spokane, Washington.

62 In the 1870s, the Chinese included almost 5,000 of Idaho's 17,804 population. Chinese miners shipped more than $5 million, out of a total of $13 million, worth of gold found in nearby Florence, Idaho.

CHAPTER 39

63   The 12x18 foot log cabin was about 200 sq. ft.

64   Also called a Jew's harp, it is a flexible metal tongue or reed attached to a frame about the size of a small fist. Placed in the performer's mouth, it is plucked with the finger to produce a note.

CHAPTER 41

65   These were actual people. August, Jr. ended up possessing this Subscription List and passed it down to his children. Total amount raised was $350.

66   The name remained Our Lady Help of Christians until 1972 when it was changed to St. Mary's. In 2017, because of a declining membership and only one available priest to serve them, the priest at that time combined three parishes: St. Mary's (Cottonwood), St. Anthony (Greencreek) and Assumption (Ferdinand).

67   World War I lasted from July 1914 until November 1918 and because of its repercussions, the Kopczynski's quit speaking German in their home after 1921.

EPILOGUE

68   August, Jr. and Lena were married on Monday, February 23, 1903.

61822396R00209

Made in the USA
Columbia, SC
27 June 2019